Praise for the Art Lover's Mystery Series by Hailey Lind

"Annie...is one-half Georgia O'Keeffe and one-half Gracie Allen. She can forge Old Masters for fabulous sums but chooses the straight and narrow, running a small finishing business called True/Faux Studios. She draws trouble like Warhol drew money."
—*The Virginian-Pilot* on *Feint of Art*

"A fun and fast-moving mystery novel that is sure to delight... loaded with interesting information about the art world and the shadowy world of art forgers and forgeries."
—*Spinetingler Magazine* on *Feint of Art*

"It has everything a successful caper should have, right down to the chase scene through the streets of San Francisco.... There's sexual tension, great characters, and disaster after disaster. Anyone who enjoyed *Foul Play* or *Moonlighting* will appreciate *Shooting Gallery*."
—*BookBitch.com*

"If you enjoy Janet Evanovich's Stephanie Plum books, Jonathan Gash's Lovejoy series, or Iain Pears's art history mysteries...then you will enjoy *Shooting Gallery*....The book is a fun romp through San Francisco's art scene with some romance and a couple murders and car chases thrown in for good measure."
—*Gumshoe Magazine*

"Lind deftly combines a smart and witty sleuth with entertaining characters who are all engaged in a fascinating new adventure. Sprinkled in are interesting snippets about works of art and the art world, both the beauty and its dirty underbelly."
—*Romantic Times* on *Brush with Death*

Arsenic
and
Old Paint

Arsenic and Old Paint

AN ART LOVER'S MYSTERY

Hailey Lind

2010 · PALO ALTO/MCKINLEYVILLE
PERSEVERANCE PRESS/JOHN DANIEL & COMPANY

A Perseverance Press Book
Published by John Daniel & Company
A division of Daniel & Daniel, Publishers, Inc.
Post Office Box 2790
McKinleyville, California 95519
www.danielpublishing.com/perseverance

Distributed by SCB Distributors (800) 729-6423

Book design by Eric Larson, Studio E Books, Santa Barbara,
www.studio-e-books.com
Cover image: Julie Goodson-Lawes

10 9 8 7 6 5 4 3 2 1

LIBRARY OF CONGRESS CATALOGING-IN-PUBLICATION DATA
Lind, Hailey.
 Arsenic and old paint : the art lover's mystery series / by Hailey Lind.
    p. cm.
 ISBN 978-1-56474-490-6 (pbk. : alk. paper)
1 Art thefts--Fiction. 2. Art forgers--Fiction. 3. Women detectives--Fiction.
4. San Francisco (Calif.)--Fiction. I. Title.
 PS3612.I5326A89 2010
 813'.6--dc22
                    2010006980

To Susan Jane Lawes,
whose imagination and love of beauty
are second to none.
Can't wait to read your book!

Acknowledgments

Many thanks to Shellee Leong and the good people of San Francisco's Cameron House, and to the spirit of Donaldina Cameron and all the denizens of Chinatown, past and present, from sixth-generation natives to the newly arrived. And to Jon Hee for his stories of tunnels and neighborhood history over *dim sum*.

From Julie: Thanks to the usual cast of wonderful characters who allow me to call them friend: Jace Johnson, Shay Demetrius, Suzanne Chan, Bee Enos, Pamela Groves, Jan Strout, Anna Cabrera, Mary Grae, Susan Baker, Chris Logan, Brian Casey, Kendall Moalem, and the entire Mira Vista Social Club. To all those incredibly supportive, talented writers who have taught me and laughed with me, especially my on-the-road roomie extraordinaire, Sophie Littlefield, and all the Pensfatales; the tavern gang (you know who you are—we miss you, Cornelia); and all my Sisters in Crime.

From Carolyn: Thank you to Janine Latus, Sandra Pryor, and Chris Casnelli for your unflagging friendship and support when it was needed most. To Scott Casper, Anita Fellman, Heather Jersild, Steve Lofgren, Buffy Masten, and Karin Wulf, who always see the joy in life. Thank you all for allowing me to be a part of your lives.

Finally, thanks from both of us to our wonderful, eternally supportive parents, Bob and Jane Lawes, for giving us the kind of childhood every soul should be lucky enough to experience. And lastly and most especially to Sergio Klor de Alva, the newest music sensation to emerge from Oaktown!

Author's Note

Theories abound as to whether there are tunnels under Chinatown. As in this book, it appears that there were sewer pipes and coal chutes that may have been used from time to time, but nothing like the system of tunnels found in other locales such as Portland, Oregon. Any tunnels under Nob Hill are pure conjecture for the sake of fiction. The Fleming-Union and the College Club were entirely fabricated by the author.

Arsenic
and
Old Paint

1

---

*To all my fans: It is I, the great international art forger,
Georges LeFleur. To all those who believe a man who
exalts the beauty of the Renaissance cannot become
part of the twenty-first century, I say, "Bah." I may be a
Luddite when it comes to egg yolk tempera, pure linseed
oil, and crushed-earth pigments, but here I am, with my
new blog, surfing these modern internets and sharing my
knowledge, free for the asking.*
          *—Georges LeFleur's blog, "Craquelure" (A web of fine
          lines indicating age, that results in greater beauty)*

"WHAT WAS *THAT*?"

"A ghost?" Samantha teased me.

"Naw, that ain't no ghost," my temporary assistant, Evangeline, said with surprising conviction, her stage whisper reverberating down the wood-paneled hall. "Sounded like a lady to me."

We picked up our pace down the stairs. Although the day outside was bright and cheerful, as befit San Francisco in the early fall, inside the Fleming Mansion it was dim and gloomy. Sunshine struggled to find its way past the floor-length, hunter green velvet curtains to cast a pattern of shadowy prison bars on the intricate Turkish wool runner. A bone-deep mustiness permeated the portrait-laden walls: the smell of old money.

I longed to tear down the curtains and fling open the leaded windows, allowing the sun and fresh bay breezes to air out the place, but we were already sort of trespassing. Two rules had been made crystal clear to me when I signed the contract for this job: what happened in the club stayed in the club, and double-X chromosomes who wandered beyond the service areas would be summarily fired. According to my birth certificate, that meant me.

Another sound split the tomblike silence.

A woman's scream.

The three of us gaped at each other for an instant before charging down the rest of the stairs to the second-floor landing, across the hallway, through an open bedroom door, and into an old-fashioned *en suite* bathroom.

Samantha, in the lead, stopped short. I bumped into her, and Evangeline—nearly six feet tall and built like an Olympic shot-putter—plowed into me, throwing me off-balance and causing me to clutch at Sam, who stumbled forward. Our Keystone Kops routine came to a halt as we took in the scene.

The man in the bathtub looked ill. The sword protruding from his bony white chest didn't help.

A curvy blonde with a cheap dye job knelt by the side of the claw-footed tub and sniffled, her blood-curdling screams having subsided to high-pitched whimpers. She wore a black-and-white French maid's outfit, complete with a stiff lace apron and cap, and her name, *Destiny*, was stitched in gold thread on her right shoulder.

Not so long ago I would have been screaming and whimpering right alongside her, but now I just felt woozy. In the past year and a half I had tripped over a few dead bodies. Apparently a person could get used to anything.

Chalk one up for personal growth.

What bothered me most at the moment was the way the sword's hilt swayed in the air...to and fro...to and fro...as if keeping time to a soundless beat. The movement started when the maid let go as we piled in. Which implied that she had been wielding the sword. Which, in turn, suggested that Destiny-the-maid had just stabbed Richie-the-rich man to death in his bathtub.

I heard Samantha repeating, *"Oh Lord oh Lord oh Lord"* in her Jamaican sing-song lilt as she hurried from the bathroom to the bedroom and snatched up the receiver of the old-fashioned black desk phone. Evangeline followed her, dropping with a *whoosh* onto a soft leather armchair next to the huge stone fireplace.

The flames from a gas jet hidden behind a fake log cast an incongruously cheerful glow across the dark bedroom. More heavy velvet curtains covered the arched floor-to-ceiling windows and shielded the ornate Victorian wallpaper and Oriental rugs from the sun's rays. Above the fireplace mantel, in lieu of the cheesy oil painting of an American Revolutionary naval battle so beloved of men's social clubs, was an empty set of brackets suitable for hanging a musket.

Or a sword.

I heard Samantha giving the 911 operator the street address, though it was probably not necessary. The Fleming Mansion is well known in the city. The forbidding historic brownstone holds pride of place at the summit of chic Nob Hill, and is home to the Fleming-Union, one of the most exclusive men's clubs in the country. The membership list is a closely guarded secret but is said to include past and present U.S. presidents, and the board regularly turns away mere corporate moguls, especially those who had committed the unpardonable sin of being born female. By and large, San Franciscans aren't big on gender or class deference; most of us refer to the Fleming-Union as the "F-U."

We four women were sorely out of place in such a masculine domain. I doubted the place had witnessed this much concentrated estrogen since the strippers from the last bachelor party decamped.

"Destiny, come away from there," I said gently, beckoning to the maid from my position in the bathroom doorway. Personal growth or not, I was *not* entering the Marbled Chamber of Horrors.

"What... What happened?" The maid seemed rooted in place, her gaze fixed on the corpse. "Who coulda done such a thing?"

I refrained from stating the obvious: she coulda. The flickering light from the ancient wall sconces gave an amber tint to Destiny's features, smoothing the crow's-feet at the corners of her eyes and making her appear younger than the forty-something she probably was. I scarcely knew her, but seldom loath to leap to conclusions, assumed any maid who plunged a sword into her wealthy employer's chest probably had an excellent reason.

I passed my flashlight beam over the scene. Even taking into account the fact that he was dead, the deceased looked unwell, more like an inmate at a tuberculosis sanitarium than an imminent threat. He appeared to be middle-aged, his blank dark eyes sunken into his skull and underlined by half circles. His body was frail, the ribs outlined beneath pale, almost translucent skin. A white towel was draped around the crown of his head, and a handful of dark hairs speckled his scrawny chest. He was unshaven, with tufts of black hair poking out from beneath the folds of the towel. One arm hung over the side of the tub near-ly grazing the floor, the fingernails broken and discolored. The other floated in the water as if playing with the blank letter-sized piece of paper that drifted about on the surface.

A single drop of blood oozed from the chest wound and slow-ly made its way down his ribs. Shouldn't there be more blood, I wondered, enough to tint the water? My stomach lurched.

"The police are on their way," Samantha called out, still hold-ing the phone to her ear, and I heard the faint wail of a siren.

"I'm not supposed to be here," the maid mumbled. She tore her eyes away from the body and looked around, as though sur-prised to find herself in the room. "None of us are supposed to be here!" She bolted for the door.

"Destiny, stop!" I shouted.

Evangeline, more comfortable with action than with words, grabbed the maid around the waist and lifted her clear off the floor. Destiny let out a string of vile curses and dug her French-tipped nails into Evangeline's forearm. Kicking and screaming, the maid reached back and tried to grab Evangeline's hair, but my assistant's signature buzz-cut was too short and spiky to grip.

"Need a hand here, Annie," Evangeline grunted.

I started toward them, but Destiny's flailing legs kept me at bay, so I picked up the wooden desk chair and approached the twosome like a lion tamer.

"Calm down, Destiny, it's okay," I soothed, though it was doubtful she heard me above her vitriolic shrieking. "Take a deep breath...."

Footsteps pounded up the stairs and a frightened-looking security guard stumbled into the bedroom and stopped short, mouth agape. I recognized him as the boyish blond who sat at the club's back door signing the staff in and out and guiding limited-edition Bentleys and DeLoreans into the club's coveted parking spots. He was clearly out of his comfort zone.

Close on his heels were two San Francisco police officers.

The cops pulled their guns and assumed the shooting stance. "Put her down!" one cop yelled at Evangeline. "Put her down *now. Don't move! Nobody move!*"

Nobody moved except Destiny, who added spitting to her repertoire of wailing and kicking.

"*You!*" One cop focused on Evangeline. "Let her go. *Now!*"

Evangeline promptly released Destiny, who fell to the floor on her butt before bounding to her feet and bolting for the door. Unsure who the evil-doers were, one cop kept his eye and gun on the rest of us while the other launched himself after Destiny, tackling her in the doorway.

More uniformed police thundered up the stairs and poured into the room, eyes wary, radios crackling. The tension eased when they spied the first responders, and then the interminable discussing and speculating began.

All talk halted when a woman materialized at the top of the stairs. The cops fell back, making way as if she were Moses and they the Red Sea.

Tall, more striking than pretty, she wore a dark gray tailored suit and royal blue silk blouse, and projected an imperious air. The type of woman who never had to ask twice.

Inspector Annette Crawford.

Of all the cops in all the towns...

"Are you the *only* homicide detective in San Francisco?" I asked as she approached.

"Are you the *only* artist and faux finisher who sniffs out murder scenes? Oh, that's right, you *are*," the inspector replied, her sherry-colored eyes giving me the once-over. "I happened to be on duty. Besides, whoever called 911 asked for me by name."

"That would be me," Samantha said, holding up her hand. "I thought it might reduce the need for lengthy explanations. Hello, Inspector."

Inspector Crawford and I had met last year, when a museum custodian had been murdered to hide the knowledge of a stolen, and forged, Caravaggio masterpiece. Since then, our paths had crossed at crime scenes more often than either of us would have liked. I admired the intelligent, acerbic inspector, and had once entertained the notion that we might become friends, but circumstances had made friendship difficult. Especially the part where I kept ending up on the wrong side of the law.

On the other hand, I no longer hyperventilated in the presence of what my felonious grandfather, the internationally acclaimed art forger Georges LeFleur, called "the constabulary."

Score two for personal growth.

After scoping out the scene and issuing orders, Annette led the way down the cop-clogged hallway to a small sitting room, whose flocked burgundy wallpaper and gold-leaf trim gave it the appearance of a down-at-heels bordello. Plopping onto a tufted velvet settee that looked more comfortable than it turned out to be, I watched Annette settle gracefully into a blue brocade armchair, her notepad and pen at the ready. What would it be like, I wondered, to be able to literally poke at a corpse one minute and then appear ready to sit down to tea with the queen, the next?

"I hear I missed a good time," the inspector said. "The men said something about breaking up a catfight?"

"That makes it sound like we were mud-wrestling."

"So what *did* happen?"

"We were trying to keep Destiny from leaving. She wasn't cooperating."

"Okay, we'll come back to that. Let's take it from the top, shall we?" The inspector's eyes shifted to an ornate hunting scene in oils hanging on the wall behind me. "*Please* tell me there isn't a forged painting here somewhere."

"Not that I know of. I'm working, actually. Upstairs, with Sam and Evangeline."

"Doing what?"

"Stripping wallpaper in one of the attic rooms, where—"

"You're in the wallpaper business now?"

"Not normally. The club wanted to convert the attic rooms into overflow guest chambers, but there was a roof leak, which damaged the wall coverings. See? The water came all the way down into this room, as well." I gestured to the corner where ugly rust and black stains marred the old yellow-and-brown wallpaper, which was pulling away from the wall in some places. "The contractor who repaired the roof is a history buff, and recognized the wallpaper as an original William Morris print dating from the nineteenth century, when the Fleming Mansion was built."

The contractor, Norm Berger, was an incongruous mixture of good ol' boy and amateur local historian. We'd worked on a few jobs together, and had become semi- sort-of friends. Or at least as good a friend as I could be with a man whose favorite T-shirt bore the slogan WILL FART FOR FOOD.

"The board chairman, Geoffrey McAdams, hired me to re-create the look of the ruined Victorian wallpaper, using paint. Milk paints are preferable to wallpaper because they allow the walls to 'breathe' so that the plaster doesn't develop mold, which means—"

"That's fine," she said, waving off my treatise on plaster and paint. I adore talking about restoration and the artistic process; wind me up and it can be hard to shut me down. Annette knew me well.

"Where's your assistant, Mary Grae? Upstairs?"

"Thailand."

Annette raised one eyebrow.

"She has a friend who opened a bar in Bangkok, and...it's a really long story involving a punk rock band, a beer bottle collection, and a gangrenous thumb. You sure you want to hear it?"

"Never mind. Mary's out of town, got it. Sam's your new assistant?"

"Evangeline Simpson's giving me a hand until Mary returns. Sam's here today because of the wallpaper." I lifted a purple-patterned paper curl caught in the bib of my scruffy overalls: Exhibit A. "Sam and her husband renovated three Victorians, so she knows a lot about removing old wallpaper."

"Given the club's reputation, I'm surprised they allow women to work here in any capacity other than housekeeping."

"Most of the women *do* have to wear those French maid outfits," I conceded. As far as I was concerned, that sort of thing belonged behind closed doors, between consenting adults. "I prefer my overalls."

"Tell me something I don't know. Such as how you got this gig."

"The contractor gave them my name, and Frank DeBenton, who installed the security system, vouched for me."

"How *is* Frank?"

"Technically, he's not talking to me, but since he vouched for me I guess there's still hope."

"Where are all the club members, anyway?" Annette asked.

"Other than you three, a few housekeepers, and the parking lot guard, this place is deserted."

"Most of the staff is on vacation while the members are on a retreat in Sonoma County. You know, like the Bohemian Club?" The Bohemian Club is a super-secret fraternal society whose elite membership engages in an annual male bonding retreat that, rumor suggests, involves pagan rituals, cavorting nude in the forest, and urinating on centuries-old redwood trees. I didn't get it, but I wasn't really the target audience. "The board asked me to finish the job while they were gone."

"Don't want your arty self polluting their rarified atmosphere?"

"Something like that."

A cell phone trilled, and Annette answered, murmuring softly. It occurred to me that the F-U boys would have a collective aneurysm when they returned from their fresh air frolic to learn that not only had one of their own been murdered in the mansion, but also an African American woman was running the investigation. The thought made me smile.

Annette snapped the phone shut, dropped it in her jacket pocket, and resumed the interrogation. "Continue."

"We were working upstairs, but when I plugged in a hairdryer to dry some plaster, a fuse blew. This place not only has the original wallpaper, it must also have some of the original wiring. We were on our way downstairs to look for the electrical panel."

"All three of you?"

"Sam's better at electrical stuff than I am, and Evangeline refused to be left alone. This place creeps her out, and I can't say I blame her. Even in the middle of the day it's full of shadows. Feels like bad juju."

"And by juju you mean...?"

"Negative energy."

"Have you been hanging out in Berkeley again?"

I nodded. "I'm taking a yoga class."

"How's it going?"

"I pulled a groin muscle, but I'm learning to breathe."

Annette smiled and nodded. "Go on."

"The three of us were coming down the staircase when we

heard a woman screaming. We found Destiny in the bathroom with the, um, body."

"Do you recognize the victim?"

"Never saw him before."

"How well do you know Destiny?"

"I've seen her around, but we haven't had any real inter-action. She's one of the few housekeepers working during the retreat."

"Describe what you saw when you entered the bathroom."

"The man was in the tub, just as he is now, with the sword...." Something about the gruesome tableau nagged at me, like an itch in the brain that I couldn't scratch.

"Where was Destiny?"

"Kneeling over him. She was...sort of...touching the sword."

"What do you mean, 'sort of touching'?"

"She was holding it."

"Stabbing him?"

"No, the sword was in his chest and—" I took a deep breath. Murder made me queasy; I hadn't outgrown that "—she had both hands on the hilt."

Annette scribbled furiously, and I hastened to add, "Maybe she was trying to pull it out."

"Mm-hmm."

"No, really. She seemed confused, asked me what happened, who would do such a thing. It could be, she discovered the body and grabbed the sword as a reflex. You know, trying to help him."

"Could be."

"We don't know—"

Annette reached into her jacket pocket, took out a well-worn brown leather case and flipped it open, revealing a shiny gold badge. "Oh look, I *am* still a detective. I thought for a moment we had switched roles."

Chastened, I held my tongue. Despite our earlier tussle, something about Destiny tugged at my heart. I couldn't imag-ine her as a cold-blooded murderer, capable of running a man through the chest with a sword.

Still, the inspector was right: I wasn't a detective, and I didn't know anything about Destiny. Maybe her usual mild manner and sweet face masked a homicidal soul. Maybe she was working through some childhood issues by stabbing a man who reminded her of her father/grandfather/pervy uncle. Maybe she'd changed one too many sets of five-hundred-thread-count Egyptian-cotton sheets and decided to off the first rich snob she encountered. I'd done a brief stint as a summer housekeeper at the Olive You Motel in my hometown of Asco, and by the time my first coffee break rolled around I was prepared to wield the toilet bowl brush to inflict grievous bodily harm upon the first rude guest to cross my path.

"What did you do then?"

"Sam called 911. That's when Destiny freaked out and Evangeline grabbed her."

"And you threatened her with a chair?"

"I was just trying to get her to calm down, and help Evangeline."

"Did Destiny say anything?"

"She said she wasn't supposed to be here. That none of us were supposed to be here."

"Did she indicate what she meant by that?"

"When I was hired the board told me in no uncertain terms to stay out of the public areas and to use the rear servants' stairs, never the main stairs."

"Why?"

"I'm the hired help. And I don't have a penis."

On that note a middle-aged officer entered the room and mumbled something in Annette's ear. As he turned to leave I forced myself to meet his eyes and smile like an innocent person.

When I was a mere stripling, my grandfather Georges had not only trained me in the techniques of art forgery, but had also implanted a deep and abiding distrust of officialdom in its many guises. I was starting to run out of patience with this trait—I was thirty-two years old, for crying out loud, surely the shelf life of Georges's teachings had expired—and reminded myself that I was entirely, one-hundred-percent blameless. This time.

"Is that it?" As Annette cocked her head, her pounded copper earrings flashed in the light, accentuating the strong planes of her otherwise unadorned face. "Any other details, no matter how insignificant? Did you see anyone, hear anything else?"

I shook my head. Annette wrote another note to herself in her notebook.

"Annette, what will happen to Destiny? Are you going to arrest her?"

"Let's see…. She was found standing over the victim, holding the alleged murder weapon with both hands, and tried to flee the scene. What do you think?"

"But you don't know that she—"

"Do I need to bring out my badge again?" Annette looked up from her notes, and her tone softened. "I'm not going to railroad an innocent woman, Annie."

"Do me a favor?" I dug a business card out of my wallet. "Give her this?"

"I doubt she requires the services of a faux finisher," Annette said, and glanced at the card. "A defense attorney?"

"Sounds like she needs a lawyer."

Annette stuck the card in her notepad. "Anything else?"

I shook my head.

"All right. Should you think of something, get in touch." The inspector rose and handed me her business card. "In case you've forgotten the number."

"Thanks."

"Believe it or not, it's good to see you again, Annie. I want to speak with your friends for a few minutes, then you'll be free to go."

"Annette, I hope this doesn't sound heartless, considering the circumstances, but I really need to get back to work. The attic's one floor up, you won't even know I'm here."

When I had mentioned this project to my Uncle Anton, an art-forger-turned-art-restorer whose decades of hands-on experience made him a font of useful information about the chemistry of paint and dyes, he'd subjected me to a lengthy lecture on the dangers of "killer wallpaper." I had delayed stripping the paper until I tested for nasty toxins like lead, arsenic, and mercury in the original dyes to be sure I wasn't about to accidentally melt my brain or those of my friends. Now the clock was ticking on the club members' return, and I prided myself on finishing jobs on time, as scheduled.

"Sorry, no. You'll have to wait until we've finished processing the crime scene. I'll have an officer go upstairs with you while you retrieve your things, and escort you out."

There was no point in arguing. Inspector Crawford Hath Spoken.

"When do you think I'll be able to get back to work?"

"I'll keep you posted," she said over her shoulder as she headed for the door.

The unscratchable itch suddenly presented itself. "Annette, wait."

She paused, one hand on the doorknob.

"It sounds silly, but... You're going to think I'm nuts."

She lifted a single eyebrow again. Apparently that ship had sailed long ago.

"The murder scene reminded me of a painting."

"A painting."

"David's *Death of Marat*."

2

*Betrayal can be beautiful: it is the source of exquisite
pain, and therefore a fountain for great art. Always
remember: artists must suffer for their art...but a lovely
bottle of wine makes the suffering much easier to bear.*
— *Georges LeFleur, "Craquelure"*

"ISN'T *DAVID* A STATUE by Michelangelo?"

"No—actually yes—but this has nothing to do with Michelangelo," I said. "Jacques Louis David was a painter who supported the French Revolution. *The Death of Marat* is one of his best-known paintings."

"Who was Marat?"

"One of the most radical of the French revolutionaries, which if you think about it is saying a lot. He was assassinated in his bathtub."

"Stabbed?"

I nodded. "By a woman, something Corday. Charlene...no, Charlotte, I think."

I couldn't remember what I ate for lunch or the names of influential clients I had met three times, but when it came to art-related trivia, I was a rock star.

"How did she manage to corner him in a bathtub?"

"Marat suffered from a skin disease that was relieved by cold water. He spent so many hours soaking in the bathtub that he habitually worked there. Corday was a moderate revolutionary who didn't like Marat's penchant for guillotining political opponents; she got in by claiming to have information about an uprising, but instead she stabbed him in the heart. In David's painting, Marat's head is wrapped in a white cloth, his arm is drooping to the floor, and in his hand is a piece of paper—a petition from his assassin, Corday."

"Talk about your bad juju," Annette said. "What else can you tell me about this painting?"

"David painted two other revolutionary martyrs, but only *The Death of Marat* survived the counter-revolution. I imagine it's in one of France's state collections, but I'd have to look it up."

"And you're saying the murder scene was staged to look like this painting?"

"It sure looks like it."

"If that's true, we may be dealing with a lunatic."

"Or someone sending a message."

"About what? The French Revolution?"

I shrugged. "You asked if I noticed anything unusual. You have to admit this fits the bill."

"Write down the name and artist. I'll compare it to the crime scene photos." She handed me her pad and pen, then gave me a searching look. "How well known is this painting? Would a normal person have heard of it?"

Annette considered my endless store of Fun Facts about Fine Art to be "eccentric" because she was too polite to call it "freakish." I suspected what bothered her most was the contrast between my expertise in art and forgery and my dearth of common sense in other areas: cooking, balancing my checkbook, staying out of jail....

"It's well known in France, both because of its history and because of its beauty. The poet Baudelaire praised the painting's visual elegance."

"What about Americans?"

"Most wouldn't recognize it unless they'd studied art or French history," I conceded.

"That's what I thought."

———

Evangeline turned down my offer of a ride in the cramped cab of my two-seater truck, declaring her intention of picking up some takeout from her favorite Pakistani restaurant and holing up in the apartment she was subletting from my vacationing assistant, Mary. It wasn't an apartment in the strictest sense, just the dining room of an old Victorian in the Mission District that was separated from the rest of the flat by a blanket slung over a clothesline. But to Evangeline it was home.

She also muttered something about looking for another job. "No offense, Annie," she honked in her upstate New York accent before heading for the bus stop. "But you're kinda scary. I never did see no dead bodies where I come from."

Given all we had been through in the past year I didn't blame her. Sometimes I thought *I* wouldn't hang out with me if I had other options. I needed an assistant, though, because for the next few weeks I had a full painting schedule in addition to running my new Internet art assessment business.

Not to mention coping with my ex-felon of a business partner who, despite the terms of his parole, had taken an unauthorized leave of absence.

Samantha and I climbed into my little green Toyota truck and headed across town towards our studio building in China Basin. Sam spent her days creating one-of-a-kind jewelry, while I ran a mural and faux-finishing business, True/Faux Studios. My real love was portraiture, but faux finishing was much more lucrative. The days of artists becoming celebrated revolutionaries while making a living painting portraits were long past.

I caught a faint whiff of patchouli oil and looked over at my calm, steady friend. With her long, thick locks, her penchant for wearing bright African-print fabrics, and the slight Caribbean lilt that was intensified under the influence of stress or too many mojitos, Samantha Jagger scored about a twenty on the Cool-o-Meter scale of one-to-ten. I looked at my paint-splattered overalls and worn athletic shoes. I cleaned up okay, given sufficient time and motivation, but even on my best days the Cool-o-Meter hovered around four and a half.

Neither of us was in a chatty mood, but I needed a distraction from the ominous sounds emanating from beneath the hood.

"Talk to me so I don't have to listen to the engine's death wail."

Sam was game. "How's your love life?"

"Nonexistent."

"C'mon, I've been married for twenty-one years. I have to live vicariously. Tell me the good stuff."

"I'm afraid there's not much to tell these days."

Not long ago I had broken up with Josh, a sweet, decent carpenter because I decided he was a little too sweet, and a lot too decent, for the likes of me. Sam was rooting for me to hook up with our studio building's straight-arrow landlord, Frank DeBenton, but he had treated me with icy aloofness since I announced my intentions to set up shop with an art thief. The criminal in question, Michael, was sex-on-wheels but bad news, all of which was a moot point at the moment. He had been AWOL for the last week.

My mother advised me to find a nice, steady computer engineer with health insurance and a 401(k) plan. For the moment I was doing a fairly good job sublimating with chocolate.

"Frank's being exceedingly polite to me," I said.

"He's not thrilled about your new online business. Or should I say, your new business partner. What's his full name, Michael X. Something?"

"Michael X. Johnson is his current moniker."

"Meaning?"

"It's the name he uses on the paperwork. I've given up trying to discover his real one."

"Was forming a business partnership with a man whose real name you don't know such a good idea, d'ya think?"

"There were extenuating circumstances."

"Such as?"

"Poverty. Besides, Doug—Michael's parole officer—believes that thieves like Michael can sincerely repent their lives of crime and be rehabilitated."

Sam laughed. "Let me guess: Doug's a Buddhist from Berkeley."

She wasn't far from the mark. I, on the other hand, was a lapsed Presbyterian from a small Sacramento Valley town—by way of Paris—who believed that felons such as Michael could sincerely rue getting caught and develop a healthy respect for the authorities.

Last spring I had come to the realization that I would never attain economic stability—much less comfort, still less retirement—through my art studio alone. So when the allegedly reformed art thief I knew as Michael X. Johnson proposed we join forces to offer online assessments of art and antiquities, it seemed like a relatively straightforward cash cow.

Besides, the FBI's Art Squad was in on the whole thing. With their approval, Michael and I set up a website offering online assessments, while sending out a few rumors that we might be morally flexible when it came to assessing less-than-legitimate art. Despite the Hollywood archetype, most thieves are neither clever nor suave—Michael being the exception that proved the rule—and every so often a crook would contact our website looking for an online assessment of a stolen work of art. We forwarded the information to our "handler" at the Art Squad, and collected a hefty reward if the FBI arrested the perp.

Last week, using information from our site, the police tracked down two Riker's Island corrections officers who had swiped a Salvador Dalí drawing from the prison lobby and replaced it with a twelve-dollar poster. It had taken the prison authorities eight months to notice their Dalí was missing, and the thieves might have gotten away with it had they not quarreled over the value of the purloined piece and decided to seek an outside opinion.

The naiveté of the average art criminal had paid the last few months' rent with a few dollars to spare, and I had begun to dream about cutting back on my faux finishing to concentrate on portraiture. First things first, though: I was shopping for a new truck. I planned to call it the Thief Mobile.

I pulled into a parking spot right in front of Frank DeBenton's office, next to one of his armored cars. In addition to owning the building, our landlord Frank ran his own secure transport business specializing in—ironically enough—valuable art and antiquities.

My gaze lingered for a moment on the sight of his dark, well-coiffed head bent, as usual, over the papers on his desk. I missed him. A couple of months ago, it looked as though our growing mutual attraction might be able to overcome our differences in temperament. But shortly afterward, Frank threw a memorable hissy fit in which he vowed to disown me as a friend, a tenant, an employee, and a romantic interest if I "took up" with the likes of Michael X. Johnson. The FBI must have gotten to him, because he finally agreed to rent the X-man and me a small office space right next to my faux-finishing studio. But since then Frank had treated us both with exquisite politeness, a sure indication that he was pissed.

Sam caught my eye and smiled knowingly as I wrenched my

gaze away from the man. We clomped our way up the exterior wooden stairs and down the second-floor hallway, then hugged good-bye and retreated to our respective studios, seeking the solace of art. It had been one hell of a Monday morning.

I paused to straighten the wooden sign I had painted recently:

BACCHUS ART APPRAISALS
ONLINE ART & ANTIQUITIES ASSESSMENTS
"WHAT'S IN YOUR GRANDMOTHER'S ATTIC?"
WWW.ARTRETRIEVAL.COM

Easing open the door, I fostered a tiny spark of hope that Michael X. Johnson—or whatever his real name was—would be sitting behind the gleaming antique mahogany partner's desk he had insisted on buying when we set up shop. I tried to visualize him with a bag of Peet's French Roast coffee beans in one hand, a recovered art masterpiece in the other, and a plausible explanation for his recent absence on his sexy lips.

The office was empty.

I hadn't been able to bring myself to admit to Sam, or to anyone, that the X-man had skipped out on me. Again. But it was time to face facts: Going into business with a known art thief and convicted felon had been a mistake—especially for an ex-forger like me who had aspirations to legitimacy. A wise woman would have known this from the start, but I've always been a little slow on the uptake—especially when felonious tendencies are masked by a pair of sparkling green eyes and a deep, smoky drawl.

Still, sooner or later someone official was going to figure out that the X-man had disappeared. I would be up to my ears in FBI harassment if I didn't inform on him.

Tossing my satchel onto a silk-upholstered hassock—another new item—I changed out of my grimy overalls into a red-and-black patterned skirt, simple black tank top, and black crocheted sweater. I exchanged my worn athletic shoes for a pair of low-heeled leather sandals, smoothed my curly brown hair, and checked out the overall effect in the full-length mirror inside the door of the armoire that held several changes of clothes. Since starting the desk job, I had been dressing less in paint-spattered clothing and more in acceptable business-wear such as skirts and blouses. People—male people, especially—had noticed. It seemed my mother was right: having the appropriate wardrobe was more important than frivolous things like, say, knowledge and talent.

I sank into a plush leather desk chair, powered up the computer, and logged on to an art search site. While it loaded I drummed my fingers on my new desk, wondering how much I could get for it down in the Jackson Square antiques district. While I was at it, I could hock the leather chairs and silk hassock my absent partner had insisted on purchasing before his inconvenient disappearance.

This was the crux of the last argument I had with Michael: I insisted he prove he had bought the furniture in some sort of above-board retail relationship. Feigning hurt, he informed me he had used the company credit card.

What company credit card? I shrilled. *We don't have any money, how can we have credit?*

And you call yourself an American, he said. *Some capitalist you are.*

Michael, we're going to go bankrupt before we get this business off the ground if you keep spending like this.

You're caffeine-deprived again, aren't you? he said, targeting my weakness like a heat-seeking missile. *I'll just make a quick run to Peet's. Back in a few.*

That was a week ago. He never returned, leaving me vaguely insulted, overworked, and under-caffeinated to boot.

Like now. I needed a fix. Not just any coffee would do, either. It had to be Peet's.

I taped a note to the door telling anyone who might stop by that I was next door, and went to my studio, where I found a large man in the little kitchen area. My heart soared. It wasn't Michael-the-thief, but he would do in a pinch.

"Annie!" boomed my Bosnian-born friend, Pete Ibrahimbegovics. "Cuppa Joe?"

Pete ran the stained glass warehouse across the parking lot from the DeBenton Building. We'd been friends for years, and among his many charms was that he was the only one in our circle who could coax something approximating espresso from my cranky garage-sale cappuccino machine. This talent had earned Pete a lifetime pass to the studio and free access to my stash of Peet's coffee beans.

"Love one, thanks. How'd you know?"

"Oho, I know you by now," he chuckled. "You are joking me with this. Annie, I must speak with you."

"What's up?"

"I come today because I have a very important question. Please, sit and I will attend you and you can answer my question."

Uh-oh. The last time Pete had a Very Important Question to ask I wound up drinking too much *loza* and spent the night trapped in a crypt. I had already encountered a dead body today. A woman could only take so much.

Pete balanced two cups of coffee plus a hand-painted ceramic bowl of sugar and pitcher of cream on a vintage decoupaged tray and joined me on the purple velvet couch. He set the tray on the antique steamer trunk that doubles as a coffee table, and fanned out an abundance of napkins, spoons, and small plates.

"We both take our coffee black," I said. "You know that, right?"

"Coffee is to you the elixir of love, yes? And love must be celebrated."

What could I say to that? I took the cup he held out and waited. He took a deep breath, blew it out, and turned to face me. At six foot four, two-hundred-plus pounds, Pete made an incongruous little boy.

"Evangeline."

"What about her?"

"Do you think Evangeline, she likes me?"

"Evangeline?"

"She is so lovely," he said, a dreamy note in his voice. "She is so... What is the English word..."

Robust? Hearty? Strapping?

"...delicate."

I didn't see that coming. Evangeline was about as delicate as a runaway truck.

"So you like her? Have you asked her out?"

"No, no. This I cannot."

"Why not? She won't bite." At least, I hoped not.

"I can't just *talk* to her." He blushed and fussed with the napkins.

"Sure you can. Pete, you're a good-looking man. Very handsome. Even better, you're kind and sweet, and you have a good job and a good heart. You've got a lot to offer."

He blushed some more and started to rearrange the couch pillows. "I—"

The studio door banged open and in strode my assistant Mary, a pink plastic bag clutched in each hand and a worn purple knapsack on her back. "Heya!"

Mary was dressed, as usual, in some sort of gauzy, multi-layered concoction in different shades of black. Her chipped nail polish, her boots, her eyeliner—all black. The only exceptions to the mourning look were her bright blue eyes, pale skin, and long blond hair.

"Mary! How was Thailand?"

"Awesome; I've got stories. But I'm out of money. Hope you have some work for me."

"As a matter of fact I do," I said, watching as she dropped the bags, shrugged off the knapsack, and sprawled on the floor. "I'm glad you're back."

"Me, too," she said, riffling through her things. "Now where is that... Aha!" She held up an airplane-sized bottle of tequila. "I knew that sucker was in there somewhere. I brought presents for you guys."

She handed me a pair of small bronze birds on round bases engraved with stamps.

"They're called opium weights."

"Opium weights?" I asked. "What line of work do you think I'm in?"

"I don't think they were really used for opium. They're in all the curio shops. And this is for you," she said, handing Pete an intricately painted mask. "I thought of you when I saw it."

Pete looked delighted. "I am touched. She is beautiful, this mask. I will wear it near my heart, always."

"I was thinking you could hang it on your wall, but whatever."

"You came straight from the airport?" I asked.

"It's a work day, right? It's not, like, still the weekend is it? I kind of lost track of the days. Everything got all jumbled when we crossed the International Date Line and I never got it straightened out. Kind of like going backwards in time, except not."

Pete nodded gravely. Mary took a swig of tequila, jumped up, and donned a painting apron. "Hey, did you know Chinese vampires hop?"

I had long ago given up trying to follow Mary's thought process.

"The Chinese, they have vampires?" asked Pete.

"Sure," said Mary.

"Who hop?" I said.

"That is their name?" Pete asked. "Who Hop?"

I tried not to laugh.

"Every culture's got vampires," Mary said. "It's, like, universal. Thing is, though, they're all way different. Like, a lot of places? They only have female vampires, who get that way when they die in childbirth, which is kind of like blaming the victim if you ask me. The Chinese vampires, though, are the coolest, 'cause they hop instead of walking like normal, and hold their arms out stiff in front of them, like this. Like a mummy. How awesome is that?"

"Sure you don't want to rest a bit after your trip?" I asked, trying to erase the visual of a Chinese vampire hopping toward me, arms outstretched like a zombie.

"Slept on the plane. And I so totally need to make money 'cause I sort of misjudged things by a credit card payment or, ya know, several. Tricia says hi, by the way."

Tricia was the friend who was opening the bar in Bangkok, and who somehow wound up with a gangrenous thumb. I figured it was best not to ask.

Pete stood. "We will speak again, Annie, yes?"

"Call me later. We'll figure something out."

"Figure out what?" Mary asked.

"Nothing," Pete and I said in unison.

I put Mary to work creating sample boards for a faux-finish job scheduled for next week. In theory sample boards demonstrated to clients what the faux finish would look like so that they could change their mind *before* we started painting the walls. This didn't always succeed. My wealthy clients tended to be rather high-strung, and many's the time I'd been stuck re-painting rooms multiple times until we got it "just right." But at least when they'd signed off on the boards, I got paid for each new round of faux finishes.

Mary and I were mixing glazes in subtle shades of putty and beige, this year's exciting color palette, when the door opened again and a stranger stuck his head in.

"G'day. I'm looking for Michael Johnson?"

"I'm his partner, Annie Kincaid. Is there something I can help you with?"

"D'you suppose we could speak in private?"

"Of course. Why don't we go next door?" I said.

The man was short, just a little taller than I, with a thick prizefighter's physique. His face sported two prominent scars, one running from beneath his left ear to the side of his neck, the other slashing down his right cheek. The scars were probably the result of a simple accident—I'd narrowly escaped similar injuries when I caught my head in a storm drain at the age of seven; long story—but they lent the man a sinister air. This was mitigated by a broad smile and his clothes: he wore khaki shorts with a multitude of pockets, a black T-shirt with a slogan for something called the ALL BLACKS, and scuffed tan hiking boots. Except for his modern clothing, mocha skin, and jet-black hair, he might have stepped out of one of Pieter Bruegel the Elder's rollicking portrayals of feasting Flemish peasants.

"Shout if you need anything, Annie," Mary said, eyes nar-rowed. "You know how thin the walls are in this place."

"Thank you, Mary."

I led the way next door to the Bacchus Art Assessments office.

"So you are the famous Annie Kincaid," he said with a broad accent as he sank into a leather chair.

"Famous?"

"Within certain circles."

That gave me pause. My grandfather Georges is a notorious and entirely unrepentant art forger, currently on the lam in Mo-rocco. I was once implicated in a European art scam myself. And though I had worked hard over the last several years to build up a legitimate decorative painting business in San Francisco, my current—though absent—business partner was a convicted art thief.

It was hard to know which "circles" the stranger was referring to. And more to the point, whether or not I was supposed to
own up to my membership in any of those rarified cliques.

"What can I help you with?" I evaded.

"I need your help finding a painting."

"We deal with art assessments here. We're not really investigators, per se."

"No worries. I am." Reaching into his pocket, he handed me
a cream-colored business card:

JARRAH PRESTON

SENIOR INVESTIGATOR

AUGUSTA CONFEDERATED RISK

LONDON—PARIS—MOSCOW

Preston's white teeth flashed brilliantly against his dark face.
"I'm a glorified insurance agent, but not to panic—I don't sell
policies. As it happens, Augusta Confederated has a painting in
custody that we have reason to believe is not the one we originally insured. I hear that when it comes to art, you have, shall we
say, a special expertise."

"I'd be happy to assess your painting, but I'm not qualified
to track down a missing one. Why not go to the police? Or, presuming it's worth more than a hundred thousand dollars, or older than one hundred years, you could turn it over to FBI's Art
Squad. I could give you a name."

"For the moment, I'd like to take a, shall we say, less for-
mal approach." He flashed another smile. "You may have noticed
from my accent that I'm not from around here."

"Australia?" I guessed.

"New Zealand. A Kiwi through and through. Maori on my
mum's side."

I tried to think of something relevant to New Zealand besides
sheep and the *Lord of the Rings* movies, but only one thing came
to mind. "I hear you have a fence made of toothbrushes in New
Zealand."

"Just outside of Te Pahu," he nodded. "In my estimation,
though, it doesn't come close to the interest of the Cardrona Bra
Fence."

"A fence made of bras?"

"A bunch of bras hung on a fence, more like. Officials declared it a danger to public decency, took about a hundred bras down, and a thousand more took their place. That's what made it art."

I smiled at the thought.

"But I'm not here to talk about bras," Preston said.

"That's a relief. I spent all day yesterday talking about girdles with a client."

Preston chuckled. "Point is, I'm a stranger in your beautiful city. I don't know the local smuggling routes, and I don't have contacts among the city's black market fences. I understand you and your partner do."

"What gave you that idea?"

"I'm not the law, Ms. Kincaid. I'm not concerned with your past, or Michael X. Johnson's for that matter. Quite the contrary. I'm in need of information of a highly specialized nature. I've admired your work—and your partner's—for some time."

Our eyes met, and I realized he was serious. He liked me *because* of my shady past. It was a novel sensation.

Preston's wide mouth twisted into an odd but pleasant grin, and he set a battered leather briefcase on the desk between us. Unlocking it, he extracted several bags of honey-roasted peanuts from Qantas Airlines and handed me one.

"D'ya mind? I haven't had lunch." He pushed a thick file folder toward me. "In here are photographs of a painting stolen seven years ago. Can you tell whether or not it's genuine?"

Whoever he was, Jarrah Preston had piqued my curiosity, and my appetite. I munched as I leaned forward and started flipping through the file. I stopped chewing when I realized what I was looking at.

It was an exquisite Gauguin, but not one I had ever seen. Couched in tropical greenery and lush flowers, a couple embraced, their erotic intent made clear by their positions. Many great artists had produced erotica, but I had never heard of Gauguin doing so. His nudes of thirteen-year-old girls were suggestive, often distasteful to modern sensibilities, but they were not explicit. Not like this.

I felt my cheeks redden at the overt sexuality of the painting. I was no innocent, but it was disconcerting to have a strange man watch me as I studied erotica. Forcing myself to ignore the content, I focused on the artist's technique.

Paul Gauguin's Post-impressionist style is primitive in its simplicity, making the artist's work easy to duplicate—on the surface. But the mark of a true Gauguin is his use of hue and tone. The French banker–turned–island-hopping bohemian played with combinations of complementary colors, overlapping and combining them in ways that fool the eye and render the pigments more vivid than they really are. Particular shades of green and orange placed next to each other, for instance, create the illusion of a shimmer.

Gauguin's exceptional understanding of color means that his works do not reproduce well in photographs. They have to be seen in person to be appreciated. The same is true of van Gogh and, indeed, most of the Impressionists as well, whose art was all about the interplay of light and pigment, color and texture.

"It's not an obvious forgery," I said, clearing my throat. "As far as I can tell from the photo, the colors and brushwork are consistent with Gauguin's work. But I can't determine if it's genuine or a good fake without seeing the actual painting. You say you have it in custody?"

"It showed up for sale at Mayfield's Auction House last week. I'd like you to swing by there and take a look. But I'm pretty sure it's a fake."

"Why is that?"

"When it was x-rayed, a secret message appeared."

3

Dear Georges: Should a true artist paint what he or she sees, warts and all?

—Clear-eyed in Belgrade

Dear Clear-eyed: Caravaggio painted fruit and leaves as he saw them, blemishes and all. Years later, Cézanne did the same, including tiny areas of rot in his exquisite bowls of fruit. Bien sûr, in the hands of a true master, there is no such thing as ugliness, only beauty re-envisioned. Do not the faults make the picture more beautiful?
—Georges LeFleur, "Craquelure"

JARRAH HANDED ME an X ray.

A sentence leaped out of the black-and-white image: *Nature morte est un plat qui se mange froid.*

The artist had probably written the message in lead white before methodically covering it up with layers of paint. Invisible to the naked eye, the sentence was revealed when the lead in the pigment fluoresced under the X rays.

The phrase looked as though it had been drawn by an artist's paintbrush, I thought, probably a number nine or ten filbert, and the grammar was perfect. But the handwriting was not the upright, looping script drilled into every French schoolchild by stern-faced *professeurs des écoles.*

" 'Dead nature is a plate that one eats cold,' " Preston translated literally. "Any idea what that refers to?"

I shrugged and shook my head. "In French—in all the Romance languages—'dead nature' is the term for what is referred to as a 'still life' composition in English and the Germanic languages."

"I didn't know that."

"It's a rare example of the northern Europeans having a

41

sunnier outlook than their Mediterranean counterparts. I don't understand its use in this context, but maybe it was Gauguin's idea of a joke? Or maybe he used an old canvas that had been written on. In any event, by itself the sentence doesn't suggest forgery."

"Except for one thing: the painting was tested before Augusta Confederated insured it. The message wasn't there."

"Could it have been missed?"

In point of fact, dealers, owners, even paid assessment "experts" might all have reason to conspire in keeping a fake painting on the market. For these folks, a fake is as good as an original if it could turn a profit. Only insurance companies—which pay out millions of dollars when an insured painting is stolen—stand to lose, and lose big, by being duped into insuring a fake. One way to make money fast is to insure a painting for millions and arrange to have it "stolen." Lie to the insurance investigator, cash the check, and *voilà*—instant millionaire.

Insurance companies are of course aware of the con and go to great lengths to avoid falling for it. It seemed unlikely that Augusta Confederated would skimp on the authentication before insuring a Gauguin, but it was possible.

"I'm double-checking with the lab, but it's a reputable group and I can't imagine their technicians would have missed something so easily revealed by a simple X ray."

"True enough."

"Which leads me to the next question: if the Gauguin was genuine when we had it assessed, did its owner, Victor Yeltsin, sell the original and subsequently replace it with a forgery?"

"You suspect fraud?"

He nodded. "Yeltsin reported the painting as stolen, and filed an insurance claim to the tune of nearly ten million dollars."

"That's a big pay-out."

"It's a Gauguin."

"Maybe the original really *was* stolen, and someone knew the painting was missing and painted a copy to 'show up' at auction, see if they can slip it past the authorities. That happens."

"That's why I'm investigating before making specific accusations."

"I'm still unclear how I can help other than to confirm what you already suspect: that the painting in your possession is probably a fake."

"I spoke with your business partner, Michael Johnson. According to him, you're the 'girl-wonder of the art forgery world.' And your Uncle Anton seconded that view."

"You spoke with Michael? When?"

"I called him last week. He said he was headed out of town, but thought he'd be back today."

"Really?"

Preston gave me an odd look. It dawned on me I should at least pretend to know more about my business partner's whereabouts than a potential client.

"I wasn't aware that his cell phone had service...where he is," I improvised. I had been calling Michael's number for a week, with no response. "And you say you spoke to Anton?"

"He assured me you were the woman for the job."

Anton Woznikowicz wasn't my real uncle—for that matter, I wasn't entirely sure "Anton" was his real name, either. There's a lot of this sort of thing in my life. Still, I had known him since I was a teenager learning the fine art of forgery from my grandfather in Paris. I still remembered one long, rainy weekend when Anton taught me the basics of traditional tempera, using egg yolks as a medium; afterwards he made us delicious egg-white omelets. Painting and cooking, he insisted, were two sides of the same coin. It worries me that the closest I come to producing an edible meal is dialing my local Thai food delivery service.

I sat back, munched on a peanut, and thought. Jarrah Preston might be a fancy-pants international insurance investigator, but he had a thing or ten to learn if he was willing to take the word of a once-and-future scoundrel like Michael. And "Uncle" Anton's reliability was just as suspect, albeit for different reasons. Why would both of them have recommended me for this job?

I glanced up to find Jarrah's near-black eyes studying me. The inspection went on so long I glanced down to be sure I hadn't dribbled peanuts down my chest. There was a high-energy intensity to him that made me nervous. A slow smile spread across his face.

"Mr. Preston, I'd like to help but I don't want to give you any false hope. I exchange e-mails with people about the treasures—and I use that term loosely—they find in their grandmother's attic. If I suspect something is stolen, I report it to the FBI and let them do the investigating."

"Call me Jarrah," he said with a confident half smile. "As I said, I don't know this town like you do. I'd like you to sniff around, ask a few questions, that's all. I'm not expecting miracles."

I shook my head.

"And whether or not you actually locate the original, my company's willing to pay an obscene amount of money for your time and expertise."

I stopped shaking my head.

"Do I detect a change of heart?"

"You had me at 'obscene.'"

I pulled a notepad out of the desk drawer and jotted down a to-do list, beginning with *1. Find painting.* I figured I'd elaborate from there.

"Okay, let's start at the beginning," I said. "Mayfield's Auction House notified you that it had acquired a Gauguin that was listed on the Art Loss Register?"

The international Art Loss Register helps art dealers, museums, and honest citizens avoid being scammed by forgers, thieves, and those who traffic in stolen goods. Most insurance companies require such a listing before they pay a claim.

"Yes. The auction house ran the required search, and found that it matched the description of the missing painting."

"And the painting has its provenance papers?"

He nodded.

"One thing I still don't understand," I said. "You're an investigator. Why hire me?"

"As I said, you have a unique background—"

"I don't buy it, Jarrah," I interrupted. Once I had recovered from the uncommon thrill of not having my past held against me, I realized that Jarrah Preston's stated reason for hiring me wasn't plausible. I painted forgeries—at least I *used* to—I didn't hunt them down. "A licensed PI or a retired SFPD inspector would be far more familiar with the local black market than I am. Why me?"

Jarrah smiled. "Well done."

I eyed him for a moment, trying to decide if that crooked smile was endearing or menacing. One thing for sure, it was patronizing. "Well done?"

"You're not easily fooled."

"Just wait. You don't know me very well."

"Well enough. You have something else going for you. Victor Yeltsin happens to be a member of the Fleming-Union."

Uh-oh.

"I understand you have access to the mansion."

"Limited access. Very limited."

"You could poke around a little.... Perhaps you could blend in with the housekeeping staff."

I flashed on a visual of myself in a French maid's costume. Not happening.

"How did you know I was working there?"

"Johnson mentioned it. Lucky coincidence, eh?"

"Very lucky. Very coincidental." I watched him closely. "You wouldn't happen to know anything about David's painting called *Death of Marat*?"

"Remind me?"

"French revolutionary, Neo-classical..."

"Oh, right. Dead bloke in a tub?"

"I thought you were in the business of insuring art. Doesn't that require a certain amount of art knowledge?"

"I study up on what I'm after. Ask me anything you want to know about Gauguin, and I'll wager I know it."

"It just so happens that there's a police investigation at the Fleming Mansion at the moment. I don't suppose the missing Gauguin would have anything to do with that?"

"What kind of investigation?"

"Someone was...murdered."

"Bloody hell!" Jarrah looked genuinely shocked. "Who was it?"

"I don't know who he was, but the scene was pretty gruesome."

He shook his head and blew out a breath. "I'm looking for information on a painting nicked years ago from Yeltsin's home. I don't see how it could be connected to a recent murder at the Fleming-Union."

Silence reigned while I pretended to study the photos. I'd spent more than thirty years on this planet without giving a second thought to the Fleming-Union; all of a sudden I'm offered two jobs there? Coincidences tend not to bode well in my life.

Still, I needed a new vehicle, and I was bone-tired of worrying about making the rent every month. Preston was offering the kind of financial boon I had been hoping for when I decided to go into this business with Michael. So why was I so worried?

Because I wasn't an idiot.

If there was one thing I had learned over the last couple of years, it was to be cautious when, for instance, a smiling half Maori shows up out of the blue with an inflated check and no personal references. I would go along with him for the moment, but before involving myself in anything too dangerous or stupid I would have to check him out.

Jarrah picked up the X ray. "There's an old saying, 'Revenge is a dish best served cold.' D'ya suppose that's what this message means?"

"Hard to tell. Forgers are an odd group. Many have an axe to grind with the art establishment. It might be a phrase the artist paints under all his fakes, like a signature. I'll have my guy run a check on known forgers, see if it rings any bells."

"My guy" is Pedro Schumacher, a dear friend who knows how to use Google's advanced search function, but I saw no reason for my deep-pocketed client to know this.

Jarrah patted the stack of papers. "You'll find most of what you need here: a copy of the original police report, profiles of the individuals I've interviewed, and information on the painting's last owner, Victor Yeltsin."

"Who brought the Gauguin to Mayfield's Auction House for sale in the first place?"

"A man named Elijah Odibajian."

I dropped a peanut.

"As in Balthazar and Elijah Odibajian, the Brothers Grimm of Bay Area real estate? *Those* Odibajians?"

"Elijah seems to have disappeared, up the *boohai*, as we Kiwis say. I'm off to run him to ground." Jarrah sat back, his black eyes twinkling. "Big brother Balthazar insists he knows nothing, but

I'd like you to talk with him. As it happens, Balthazar's a member of the Fleming-Union, as well."

"How handy."

"He's a bit of a dag, I'll warn you."

"Translation?"

"Rather difficult. A hard case." He smiled that strange smile again. "But I have a feeling you'll have a way with him. As the saying goes, *Ka timu te tai, ka pao te torea, ka ina te harakeke a Hine-kakai.*"

"Oh sure, I say that all the time."

"It means, 'The oyster catcher swims when the tide is ebbing and the flax of Hine-kakai burns.'"

I had no idea what Jarrah Preston was talking about, and wondered what I was getting myself into. But as my grandfather was fond of saying, *The road to wealth is strewn not with rocks but with boulders, Annie. Bring your hiking boots.*

———

Preston left me with the case file, a fat retainer, and an uneasy feeling that there was more to this case than he was letting on. I glanced down at the computer screen.

Google had obligingly answered my earlier query, and produced a full-color illustration of David's magnificent painting of a dead bloke in a tub. *The Death of Marat* was housed in the Musées Royaux des Beaux-Arts in Brussels, I read, and there had been no reported thefts or scandals associated with it. Studying the painting—the position of the body, the letter in Marat's hand—I was more convinced than ever that the poor schmuck at the Fleming-Union had been arranged to mimic the painting.

But why?

The more I thought about it, the surer I was that Destiny couldn't be the killer. Among other things, it was hard to imagine her having the requisite knowledge. She seemed more like an ex-stripper than an art history major.

I reminded myself that this wasn't my problem. Annette Crawford and the SFPD were on the case, I was in no way implicated, and despite the staged reconstruction of a famous painting, it didn't even have anything to do with stolen or forged art.

Unless of course Jarrah Preston was lying through his Kiwi teeth.

I dialed my guy, Pedro Schumacher.

"You need somebody to post bail again?" Pedro answered without preamble.

"No, I—"

"Then don't bother us. I finally got my woman to take a long lunch, and we're napping."

"Oh, I'm sorry! Did I wake you?"

"No, we're *napping.*"

"*Oh*. Then why did you answer the phone?"

"I'm just giving you a hard time. I knew it was you." I heard a woman laughing in the background. "We high-tech folks have this little gadget, Caller ID, that tells us who's calling. I think it'll catch on one day."

A self-employed computer geek with a genius IQ, Pedro spent his days rescuing his corporate clients from multi-million-dollar software snafus and his nights reveling in hardboiled detective fiction. We had been friends for years, and his longtime girlfriend Elena Briones happened to be an attorney who had helped me out on more than one occasion. I had the sneaking suspicion my antics kept them entertained.

"Funny. I have a couple of things for you to look up," I said. "And I'm getting paid this time, so keep track of your hours and eventually I'll pay you a tiny fraction of what your skills are worth."

"Hearing your lovely voice is payment enough, *mi amor.*"

"You're such a charmer, Pedro."

"It's a Latin thing. Whaddaya need?"

"A background check on an insurance investigator named Jarrah Preston, employed by Augusta Confederated Insurance." I spelled the name. "He's from New Zealand. I'd also like you to search for any cases of forged paintings that involve hidden messages."

"Like how many animals can you find hidden in the drawing of Old MacDonald's Farm? Man, I loved those. Remember *High-lights* magazine?"

"I liked those, too. But that's not what I mean."

"How else would you hide a message?"

"By painting over it. The lead in certain types of pigment fluoresces under X rays. Look for a French phrase that translates into 'Dead nature is a dish best served cold.'"

" 'Dead nature'? Twisted."

"You speak Spanish, Pedro. It means 'still life.' "

"Dead nature's more interesting."

"One more thing: I need information on a Victor Yeltsin, and Balthazar and Elijah Odibajian."

"As in the Odibajian brothers? The Brothers Grimm of Bay Area real estate?"

"I read that article, too." This was an exaggeration. I had read the headline but hadn't gotten around to the article, which at the moment resided in a two-foot-tall stack of "to be read" newspapers slowly yellowing in a corner of my bedroom. "Would you look them up, please?"

"Don't need to. I can tell you all you need to know right now: those boys are bad news. I don't know much about Elijah, but Balthazar is a major player whose opponents have a habit of abruptly moving out of state or disappearing altogether. More what you'd expect in Jersey than in kinder, gentler San Francisco. Steer clear of that guy."

"I just want to ask a few questions."

"What about?"

"Elijah, the younger brother, brought a stolen painting to Mayfield's Auction House for sale."

"He stole a painting?"

"Hard to say. He had it in his possession. Actually, he had a *copy* in his possession."

"He stole a fake?"

"Another good question. All I know for sure it that he was trying to sell a fake."

"Rewind. I'm confused."

"A painting was stolen seven years ago, and the insurance company paid the claim. Recently a copy of that painting turned up for sale at Mayfield's Auction House via Elijah Odibajian. The insurance guy wants me to help him figure out if the painting was original when it was stolen, and where the original might be."

"Insurance fraud."

"Exactly. The owner of a genuine painting has it insured, then copied, then sells the original, has the copy stolen, and claims the insurance money on the supposed loss."

"Why even bother with a copy? Why not just have the original 'stolen' and leave it at that?"

"It's much more convincing if the insurance folks, or the cops, have a trail to follow."

"The insurance guy is Jarrah Preston, the fellow you want me to check out?"

"Just in case he's not who he says he is."

"Gotcha. I still say, keep away from the Odibajians, Annie. Insurance fraud isn't the kind of thing they're likely to bother with, frankly—the payoff's too low and the downside's too great. Their real estate holdings alone are worth close to half a billion, and that's only what they admit to the IRS."

"Elijah probably had no idea the painting was a fake when he put it up for sale. Just see what you can find out about them for me, will you?"

"You know who you remind me of?"

"Salma Hayek?" Hope springs eternal.

"A stubborn *burro* on my grandmother's ranch."

"I prefer to think of myself as dedicated."

"I'll just bet, my little *burrita*."

"This is me ignoring you. Could I talk to Elena for a second?"

"Don't tell me you really *do* need to be bailed out...?"

"No, oh ye of little faith. But I know someone who does."

Pedro's girlfriend came on the line. Elena had recently left the Oakland Public Defender's office to set up her own criminal defense practice. Smart, aggressive, and savvy, her dedication to progressive causes made me feel I should be out protesting global warming, or raising money for AIDS orphans, or scaling a fence at a nuclear silo. I put in my time on peace marches and volunteer work, but Elena seemed disappointed that I had never been arrested for anything political.

I told her about Destiny and the murder at the F-U, and explained that I wasn't sure if the maid had been charged with anything. Elena assured me not to worry, she would take it from here. The steely note in her voice made me feel a little sorry for Inspector Crawford.

Next I tried my Uncle Anton's number. No answer. A Luddite of the highest order, the old forger didn't even have an answering machine.

The pictures I saw of the fake Gauguin were good enough to prove one thing: it was the work of a gifted forger. Anton loved the Post-impressionists, and would have especially enjoyed mixing his own authentic period paints and then mimicking the layering to recreate a true Gauguin. But if he had painted the Gauguin forgery, why would he have spoken with Jarrah Preston, much less given him my name?

Maybe Anton had nothing to do with anything. Could the forged Gauguin have something to do with Michael's recent absence? I had no reason to think so...but coincidences make me nervous.

My hand still lingered on the receiver when there was another knock on the door. I looked up to see my landlord, Frank DeBenton, looking elegant as always in gray slacks and jacket, a striped tie, and a tailored cream shirt. My mind leapt to a memory of Frank a few months ago: tipsy, tie loosened, hair tousled, mouth coming down on mine.... I reached for a Hershey's Kiss from the blue ceramic bowl on my desk.

"Frank."

"Annie." He glanced around the office. "Nice furniture."

"I don't suppose you'd like to buy it?"

He raised his eyebrows in silent question.

"Never mind. Did you get my rent check?"

"Yes, thank you."

"Have a seat. Would you like a Kiss?"

"Beg pardon?"

"Hershey's Kiss?"

"No, thank you."

Silence. Usually if Frank was quiet long enough I would start babbling, say something stupid, and either incriminate myself or agree to something I shouldn't. I used to think it was just his way, but having learned recently that Frank was a former Special Ops agent, I now concluded it was an interrogation technique that, unfortunately, worked like a charm on mere mortals like me. I swore I would no longer buckle under the pressure. From this day forth, Frank's sneaky tactics of silence were useless on me.

I stared at the beams in the ceiling. I stared at the desk blotter. I stared at my paint-stained nails.

I cracked.

"Something I can do for you?"

"I need a favor."

Well. *That* was unexpected. "Shoot."

"It's about the College Club."

The College Club isn't nearly as exclusive as the F-U, though it does rank high on the city's list of Privileged People's Lairs. But it admits women, which no doubt brings it down a rung or two on the ladder of social snobbery.

"You want to join? I'd be delighted to write you a letter of recommendation."

"Cute. I'm already a member."

"You're not here to sell me some magazine subscriptions, are you?"

"Annie—"

"I'm not buying any cookies, either. Unless you have Thin Mints."

Frank grinned despite himself, and our gazes locked. It was the first real connection we'd had since the beginning of the Ice Age, and I had a sudden sensual memory of his lips on mine.

Zing.

"I need you to find Hermes."

"The French fashion designer? I think he's dead."

"No, the Greek god, also known as Mercury to the Romans."

"Have you checked Mount Olympus?"

"*Resting Hermes* is a life-sized bronze statue from the 1915 Pan-Pacific Exposition. It stands outside the College Club, near the sidewalk. At least it used to. Somebody absconded with it."

"A bronze that size would weigh hundreds of pounds."

"More than three hundred pounds, so they say."

"Why would someone steal it? For that matter, *how* would someone steal it?"

"That's what I'd like you to find out."

"*Me?* Call the cops." What was it with men and their missing art these days?

"I did. They're swamped; it's been a week, and the police haven't had much time to spare to search for a statue. I put out a few feelers, but nothing's turned up."

"And you think I can find something you and the cops can't? Have you learned nothing about me, lo, these many moons?"

Frank's eyes swept over me. "Quite a few things, actually."

It was my turn to squirm. I glanced over at the Hershey's Kisses, but told myself "no."

Frank continued, "I hoped you would be willing to...talk to some people."

"People?"

"You know who I mean. *People.*"

"People who need people? The luckiest people?"

"People who deal in this sort of thing."

"You think I know the people who stole your *Hermes*?"

Frank tugged at his shirt collar. "I wouldn't ask if there was any other way."

"Gee, thanks."

"The sculpture is important to the club, Annie. It's important to *me*."

It was on the tip of my tongue to deny, for the second time in twenty minutes, any contact with the art underworld. Regardless of how hard and long I had worked to be an honest artist and faux finisher, my reputation as a teenaged forger—combined with that of my scalawag of a grandfather—always preceded me. To be fair, going into business with Michael-the-ex-con had not exactly burnished the luster of my good name. Still, it seemed past time for the art world to forgive and forget. What was a fake Old Master drawing or forty among friends and colleagues?

But it was undeniably flattering to have Frank come to me for a favor. Maybe I should make the most of it. Besides, I rather liked the image of *Annie Kincaid, Ace Investigator—Annie's my Name, Art's my Game.*

Too bad I hadn't the slightest idea how to find a missing *Hermes*, much less a lost Gauguin. Half the time I couldn't find my keys in my backpack with a flashlight and a metal detector.

"The club will pay you for your time, of course," Frank continued.

"Frank, I'd love to make some extra money, but I can't imagine I'll be able to help."

"All I'm asking is that you look into it. If you don't find anything, then we'll just have to presume it's gone for good."

This no-results-necessary thing was new to me, and darned attractive. I tried to imagine telling my painting clients, "Gee, I tried but the mural didn't quite work out. Such a shame. Now, where's my money?"

"Won't you at least ask around? I would consider it a personal favor." Ever the gentleman, Frank did not point out the many times he'd done me a favor. He didn't need to.

I blew out a breath.

"I take it that's a yes?"

"All right. But remember—I can't guarantee results."

"Understood." He reached into his inside jacket pocket, brought out an envelope, and slid it across the desk. "Here's a copy of the police report and two hundred dollars. The cash is for expenses. If you need more, let me know. Just keep track so I can get reimbursed by the club. Your fee is, of course, separate. What is the going rate for your services?"

I debated quoting Jarrah Preston's offer, but Frank was, after all, a friend.

"Why don't I charge my hourly rate for faux finishing? Double for overtime. Triple if goons or guns are involved."

"Back off if anything dangerous comes up, Annie. No sculpture is worth your getting hurt."

"Those clubby types *are* a little scary," I mused.

"I'm a club member."

"You'd scare me, too, if I didn't know what a marshmallow you are under your silk Armani. Oh, by the way, would you happen to know an insurance investigator named Jarrah Preston?"

Frank's dark eyes stared at me for a long moment. "How do you know him?"

"He offered me a lot of money to track down a painting."

"Why?"

"Why what?"

"Why isn't he tracking down the painting himself?"

"He doesn't have the, um, connections that I do."

"Would these be illegal connections?"

"These would be the same sort of connections you just asked me to exploit, if I'm not mistaken."

A slight inclination of the head: I won that round.

"He also asked me to speak with Balthazar Odibajian."

"Don't."

"Don't what?"

"Don't mess with Odibajian. He's not a man to trifle with."

"But if I were, hypothetically, to wish to speak with him, how would I go about it?"

Frank sat back in his seat. I couldn't tell if his eyes were sweeping over me as a man who appreciates a woman, or as a concerned citizen who thought I was nuts. Pedro's *burrita* comment had stung.

His gaze paused for a fraction of a second on my lips. *Aha!*

"Odibajian's tougher to get to than the president," he said. "He won't talk to you. But he'll know you tried to get to him, so you'll be on his radar. Trust me on this one, Annie: you don't want to be on that man's radar."

"You know, the more people warn me away from him, the more I want to talk to him."

"Pardon me for pointing it out, but isn't that the same character trait that almost got you killed a couple of months ago?"

"But I saved—"

"And the time before, when you spent Thanksgiving in jail after an encounter with homicidal drug runners?"

"There was a good explanation—"

"There always is."

This was the crux of the problem between Frank and me. Our interactions almost always led us to this point: Frank accusing, me defending. It did not bode well for the romantic relationship we had been dancing around. For several seconds, silence reigned.

"So, what do you think about the Giants' pitching lineup?" I asked.

"I beg your pardon?"

"I'm changing the subject."

"And you think I'm a baseball fan?"

"Actually, I had you pegged for tennis. Or polo. Something expensive and exclusive. But even *I've* heard of Barry Bonds."

Frank chuckled. "I play squash, actually, which is why I'm a member of the College Club. Okay, Annie. Since I know you'll do what you want to anyway, here's some advice: don't bother going to Odibajian's home or office. He's fortified against attack there. But he's a member of the Fleming-Union. Aren't you working there?"

"Sort of."

"If I were suicidal and pigheaded like you, I would find out when Odibajian eats lunch and surprise him before he gets inside the dining room. It's members-only—and by members, I mean men. Women are allowed in only by invitation, and even then they have to go in the back door."

"That place is so bizarre. You're not a member, are you?"

"Do you think I would spend my days dealing with unruly tenants such as yourself if I had that kind of money?"

"And here I was thinking your opposition might be a social protest."

"It does boggle the mind that some men use their wealth to hide from women," he said with a crooked smile. "I'd rather use my money to capture their attention."

Our eyes held. I thought about kissing him again.

My hand inched toward the bowl of chocolates.

"Don't I get a Kiss?" said a deep voice from the doorway.

4

I believe that a great deal of art, as life, is accidental. Alors! The route that an artist takes to expressing his creativity is a labyrinthine affair, full of twists and turns, full of joy yet always ending in sweet loss.
—*Georges LeFleur, "Craquelure"*

FRANK ROSE AS my misplaced business partner, Michael X. Johnson, sauntered into the room.

"Frank."

"Michael."

The air crackled with tension as the two alpha males bristled and tried to stare each other down. The contest went on so long I cleared my throat.

"Uh, guys?" I interrupted. "This is entertaining as all get-out, but I've got work to do."

"As do I," Frank said. "Let me know what you find out, Annie. Michael."

"Frank."

The door shut quietly.

"Call me crazy, but I feel as though I interrupted something," Michael said, taking the seat Frank had just vacated and cupping his hands over his heart. "A declaration of undying love? A marriage proposal, perhaps?"

"Where the *hell* have you *been*?" I turned on him.

"You missed me." He looked pleased.

"I was on the verge of informing the FBI that you had violated your parole."

Now he looked hurt. Sighing dramatically, he laced his fingers behind his dark head, crossed his ankles on the desk, and fixed his green gaze upon me, concern sketched on his even features. "I don't remember you being such a drag before. I think this business is bringing out the worst in you."

"*Where have you been?* It's like Remington Steele in reverse around here. I've been pretending to have a partner who doesn't exist or...the other way around. Whatever. Not only did you leave without a word, but you seem to have forgotten that you're supposed to be responsible for half the work load—"

"Hey, I've been working. I arranged the insurance gig with... whatshisname?...the guy with the accent. That should be a real money-maker."

"About that 'insurance gig'...when we established this business you assured me it wouldn't involve anything more than answering a few e-mails."

"I may have exaggerated a tad."

"I have another business, you know, which requires at least half my time and attention. Among other things, I have to get started on some sketches for a seascape in a house out in the Avenues, near the Legion of Honor."

"I thought you were cutting back on your painting-for-hire."

"There was a backlog."

"Must be nice to be so popular. I envy you."

I ignored him. "Which reminds me, a nightclub on Broadway wants me to faux-finish a metal stair-railing...." I jotted a note to myself on the back of a flier for an art supply store. I should stop by and give them a quote.

"A railing?"

"They want it to look rusty."

"I'll sell them the one from my mother's porch. That'll save you time."

"They don't want it to *be* rusty, just to *look* rusty."

"Well, there's no accounting for taste," he shrugged.

"Wait a minute—are you admitting you have a mother?"

"Everybody has a mother, Annie."

I remained skeptical. Anyone as effortlessly gorgeous as he was must have emerged, Venus-like, from the sea on a scallop shell. Tall and slender but well-muscled, Michael was a manly man in his mid-to-late thirties—I'd given up trying to discover his age—with glossy dark brown hair and the deep green eyes of a Norse god. At times I feared I had agreed to our partnership purely out of an aesthetic appreciation for his abundance of masculine pulchritude. It was like having a walking, talking work of art hanging around the office.

Fortunately, I'm philosophically opposed to fraternizing with co-workers. Unfortunately, I had coped by upping my chocolate intake to imported seventy-percent-cocoa chocolate bars, and had gained three pounds.

"You're wasting your time faux-finishing banisters," Michael said, looking pained. "Yet you're complaining because I got us a real job?"

"This may come as a surprise to you, *partner*, but we're not private eyes."

"How hard could it be?"

"I have a feeling it's a learned skill set. People go to school to become investigators. I think you're even supposed to be licensed."

"That's only if you carry a gun."

"Really?" I made a mental note to check on that. "Still, we have no investigative skills or training."

"Ah, but we understand the criminal mind."

"I hate to disappoint you, but I don't know the first thing about tracking down stolen goods."

"It just so happens I know a little. And don't act so naive— surely your dear old grandpapa mentioned it from time to time. Speaking of whom, have you checked out his new blog?"

I adored my grandfather, but whenever I thought about him my stomach clenched with worry and irritation. First Georges had published a memoir that not only outed the plentiful fakes and misattributed paintings hanging on the walls of museums from Antwerp to Zaire, but also functioned as a "how-to" manual for aspiring art forgers everywhere. Then he publicized his book with an international campaign whose antics rivaled those of Napoleon's march across Europe. Interpol gnashed its teeth, but Georges was so well connected to the art world's underground that he was able to remain one step ahead of the law. Lately, he had decided it was time to embrace technology and had started his own blog, the better to answer questions from his legion of adoring fans and to wage his ongoing war against the art establishment. My blood pressure had increased in direct proportion to the death threats against the flamboyant old man. I was hoping the yoga would help.

"Where's your curiosity? Your sense of adventure?" Michael asked, interrupting my thoughts.

"On parole. Like you, if I'm not mistaken." Curiosity and a sense of adventure had landed me in plenty of trouble in my life, which was why respectable people such as Inspector Annette Crawford—and even Frank—hesitated to associate with me.

I glanced at the clock. It was too late in the day to start a new painting project, and the Thief Mobile was calling my name. If the College Club was willing to pay, results or no, who was I to refuse the gig? Besides, given my strange luck I might manage to stumble onto some sort of clue, and I wouldn't mind getting back in Frank's good graces. I put the computer into sleep mode, picked up a few bills and invoices I needed to mail, and grabbed my satchel.

"Okay, fine. You're so dead-set on playing Sherlock Holmes, let's go find us a *Hermes*."

"Excuse me?"

"I'll explain on the way. Right after you tell me where you've been for the last six days."

———

As we drove across town Michael talked a blue streak but managed to tell me precisely nothing about his whereabouts the last week. I replied in kind, telling him precisely nothing about the identity of our client for the missing *Resting Hermes*. I imagined Michael would balk at working for his arch-enemy. A tense silence then descended, broken only when Michael started to hum the *Marseillaise* to "remind me of my roots."

His ploy worked, to a point. I recalled vividly that hanging out with criminals such as Michael and my grandfather Georges had almost always gotten me into trouble with the law.

Nob Hill is about as Old Money as San Francisco neighborhoods get, which is to say it dates from the Gold Rush era. Jutting hundreds of feet above the rowdy Barbary Coast waterfront, Nob Hill became a retreat for the city's elite, who led upper-crust lives on what Robert Louis Stevenson called "the hill of palaces." The City's Big Four—Leland Stanford, Charles Crocker, Mark Hopkins, and Collis Huntington, who made their fortunes in gold, silver, and railroads—took advantage of Nob Hill's central location and spectacular views to build homes as grand as their images of themselves. The steep grade proved so hard on horses and pedestrians alike that in 1878 the residents had their own cable car line installed. Today that same cable car rumbled past,

packed with excited tourists clutching cameras and plastic shopping bags filled with trinkets, loaves of sourdough bread, and
Ghirardelli chocolate.

My truck emitted an alarming groan as I pulled into a rare
metered spot on Powell, not far from where the red brick College
Club clung to the side of Nob Hill.

On the corner, a large soapstone pedestal sat empty save for
a metal rod sticking straight up from its core. Yellow police tape
warned pedestrians to keep their distance lest one, in a feat of
acrobatic clumsiness, trip and impale himself. The City's ever-
vigilant Visitors Bureau would not be amused.

"Gouge marks." Michael pointed to parallel grooves marring
the surface of the pedestal. He jotted notes on a steno pad, muttered and scratched his head, to all appearances channeling television's classic Columbo. I watched to see whether he was going
to whip out a nasty stogie and start squinting. "Looks like the
thieves used a crowbar."

Impatient with his newly formed PI persona, I sent Michael
into the College Club to ask for the representatives listed on
the police report. A few moments later the club's tall front door
creaked open and two men in expensive suits emerged. A tanned
fifty-something, who looked as though he took full advantage of
the club's vaunted athletic facilities, shook our hands vigorously
and introduced himself as Duke. The withered, elderly man at
his side announced his name was Brown, making me wonder
if a prerequisite for membership in the College Club was being
named for a stuffy private school.

"The club bought *Resting Hermes* from the Italian government after the 1915 Panama-Pacific Exposition," Brown piped in
a querulous voice. "For years he sat in the rotunda, until our former president suggested we share him with the neighborhood. I
told him it was a bad idea, but would he listen?"

He glared at us, and I surmised that the club president had
not, in fact, listened.

"The Pan-Pacific Exposition was held only a few years after
the earthquake and fire," the sportier Duke explained. "*Hermes*
represented San Francisco rising from the ashes, and assuming
its rightful place among the world's greatest cities. *Hermes* said to
the world, 'We'll be back! Better and stronger than ever...'"

Duke's voice trailed off and he gazed in the direction of

Chinatown and the Ferry building. Brown, too, had a faraway look in his rheumy eyes. They were a little over the top, but then again every artist should be lucky enough to create for such an appreciative audience.

"Do you have any clues as to the identity of the thieves?" I asked. "A disgruntled employee? Anyone been laid off recently?"

Brown shook his glossy gray head. "Most of the help have been with us for years."

"Does the College Club have any enemies? A rivalry with the Fleming-Union, perhaps?"

The three men stared at me as though I were one sandwich short of a picnic. The suggestion sounded far-fetched even to my own ears, but the frat-boy nature of these clubs made me ask.

Duke shook his head.

"Has anyone shown any undue interest in the statue?" I persisted.

"*Hermes* was taken once before, in 1974, but it was merely a schoolboy prank. He was found in a student's apartment, holding a cigarette and wearing a fur coat."

"And last month someone painted pink polish on his toenails," Brown added. "Cretins!"

Michael coughed to cover a throaty chuckle.

"I hope nothing untoward has happened to him," Brown said.

"Don't worry," I replied. "Bronze is sturdy stuff. There might be a few scratches, or a nick in the patina. But those are easy to fix. I'm sure he'll be fine. So, have you canvassed the neighborhood for witnesses?"

"Don't worry about a thing, gentlemen," Michael interrupted in a crisp tone. "We'll take it from here. Leave it to the professionals, I always say."

"It's a relief to know you're on the case," Duke said.

"It's the least we can do for the venerable College Club." Michael touched his forehead in a salute.

I waited until Duke and Brown made their way back up the stairs and into the club before turning to Michael.

"If we go home now, we can still charge for the full hour, right?" I was still trying to work the kinks out of this consulting game.

"We haven't done any actual investigating, Annie."

"That's because we're not investigators. I said I'd look into *Hermes'* whereabouts, but there's no evidence, nothing to go on. I did the best I could."

"This was your best?"

"Listen, apparently we get paid whether we produce results or not."

Michael gave me a disgusted glance. It was unsettling to have a career criminal look at you as though you had the ethics of a bedbug.

"Couldn't you just make some calls or something and track it down?" I asked.

"Track it down, how, exactly?"

"You probably know some people...."

"You think I know the people who stole the sculpture?"

"I thought you might run in the same circles. Use the same fence, maybe?"

The world-class thief's jaw tightened in anger and his eyes swept over the buildings in front of us, avoiding mine. Nothing like implying that swiping something off the street was in the same league as stealing something from a wealthy, well-defended adversary. It didn't escape my notice that I was making the same sort of assumptions about Michael that Frank had about me.

I squirmed.

"I apologize. I forgot you're no longer a crook. And even if you were, you wouldn't be snatching sculptures off public streets."

"Damned right."

"Okay," I said with a martyred sigh. "What do you want to do?"

"Think about it, Annie. The sculpture weighs hundreds of pounds. It would take at least two men and some heavy equipment to move it. This street isn't exactly off the beaten path. *Someone* had to have seen something." Good humor restored, his eyes sparkled in the muted light, reminding me of an Antonello da Messina portrait in London's National Gallery that I had admired for two entire days. It almost made me forget my irritation with him.

"Let's start knocking on doors." Michael grasped my elbow, intent on steering me across the street.

This from the man who still hadn't accounted for his where-abouts for the last six days.

"I've got a better idea. *You* start knocking on doors," I said, getting back in touch with my annoyance and yanking my arm away. "You can make up for your unexcused absence. I need coffee. I'll catch up with you."

I puffed up the steep grade of California Street until I reached the very top of Nob Hill, where the Fleming Mansion sat, silent, somber, and foreboding. Ornate bronze filigree gates, greenish with the patina of a century of urban life, guarded the lush grounds; discreet plaques studded the walls, reminding passersby that the building was PRIVATE. MEMBERS ONLY. These Fleming-U boys could out-snob poor Duke and Brown with their silver spoons tied behind their backs.

Several cop cars crowded the mansion's rear parking lot, and the press had arrived and set up their vans nearby, cameras trained on the building's back door. The beleaguered blond guard/parking attendant was back at his post, but still looked ashen. I noted several expensive cars parked in amongst the police units, including a dusty red Aston Martin convertible that I recognized as belonging to Geoffrey McAdams, chairman of the board and the man who had hired me. Next to it sat a mud-splattered black Mercedes sedan proudly proclaiming itself to be a V-12 Biturbo. The police must have tracked down a few of the F-U boys and called them back from their bohemian frolic in the woods.

In contrast to the flurry of activity in the rear, the front door of the building was quiet. As I walked by I noticed that there was a blue U.S. Postal Service mailbox right up on the porch.

Typical. The powers that be had removed all mailboxes within a two-mile radius of my apartment in Oakland, but here the F-U boys had their own right up on the porch. Mounting the broad stone steps, I extracted my bills from my backpack, dropped them in the mailbox, and stole a quick peek through a front window into a messy office with a Diet Coke can perched on a stack of files. Disappointingly normal.

"They won't let you in this way," a voice came from behind me.

I started, stifled a squeak, and turned around to see a tall man at the bottom of the stairs. He had wavy reddish-brown hair and wore heavy, horn-rim glasses, like Mr. Science.

"Women have to go round the back," he said with a sheepish smile. His accent was pure California, but his demeanor and sentence structure made him seem as though he had walked off the set of a British comedy featuring an affable Lord of the Manor. "And I'm afraid even then you'll need to be invited in by a member. Beastly tradition, that. And in any case, there seems to be something untoward going on. Didn't you see all of the police vehicles?"

"Um, yes I did."

"I saw it all from my balcony, right up there," he said, pointing to a very tall, sixties-style building a block northwest of the Fleming-Union. "The police started arriving a couple of hours ago. I was going to go see if I could be of service when I noticed you trying to get in through the front door. I wanted to save you any embarrassment. Women can't use this entrance, except during special events, and even then only with club escorts."

"I wasn't actually going in," I said, returning his smile and trying to calm my still-pounding heart. "Just mailing a letter and couldn't resist a peek. Are you a member here?"

"They had to let me in, didn't they?"

"Did they?"

"I'm Wesley Fleming the Third."

"As in the Fleming Mansion?"

"Indeed. My great-grandfather built this place. And you are...?"

"Annie Kincaid," I said, extending my hand. His was cold and clammy as we shook. Still, his puppy-dog eyes were so open and eager it was hard not to like him. It dawned on me that I could ask him a few questions about the F-U members Victor Yeltsin and Balthazar Odibajian, thereby killing two birds with one stone. Could I double-bill for my time? "Listen, Wesley, could I ask you a few questions about this place? I'm doing a kind of research project about this area...."

"You're a student?"

"Um..."

"I love students."

"Sure am." A student of life, I always say.

"What do you study?"

"Ar—, uh... architecture," I stammered.

"I *love* architecture!" He checked his wristwatch. "Sure, I have a few minutes."

"I saw a sign for Peet's over at the cathedral. Could I buy you a cup of coffee?"

"Love it."

We both turned and started down the stairs. Wesley moved as though all his parts weren't exactly held together, reminding me of an old marionette I had as a child, whose lone surviving string barely kept all its parts connected, much less in alignment.

"After the 1906 earthquake and fire destroyed nearly all the mansions on Nob Hill, Arabella Huntington donated the land her house had sat on to the City of San Francisco to be used as a public park," Wesley said, taking on the role of tour guide. "My grandfather's home was the only one to withstand the flames. Good, solid stone. The Fairmont Hotel was under construction at the time and though it was gutted, the walls remained intact. Julia Morgan later redid the interior."

We walked past the park's central fountain.

"That's a replica of Rome's *Fontana delle Tartarughe,* by Taddeo Landini," explained Wesley. "Grace Church was destroyed in the fire as well, and the cathedral was built in the style of Notre Dame to take its place. The front doors are bronze casts of the Ghiberti doors made for the Baptistery in Florence, depicting scenes from the Old Testament. Michelangelo had called the original Ghiberti doors the *porta del paradiso,* the gates of heaven. Shouldn't you be taking notes?"

"It's all up here," I said, tapping my temple. "Like a steel trap."

In fact, I already knew both the fountain and the doors well, both here and in their original incarnations in Europe. Along with painting techniques my grandfather had insisted on teaching me the basics of Western Civilization, which somehow, in his mind, justified his forgery of the finest in Old Master art. Speaking of forgeries...

"Say, Wesley, do you happen to know the Odibajian brothers?"

Wesley stopped in his tracks and gawked at me.

"You can't just go around talking about people like the Odibajians."

"I can't?"

"Good Lord, no. How did you know Balthazar belonged to the Fleming-Union? The membership list is secret."

"It is?"

"Good heavens. Wait—I just assumed you knew he was a member, didn't I? I just gave it away. The brethren always tell me I talk too much. Don't you have any questions about architecture? I know all about architecture."

"I'd love to see inside the club." I was pushing my luck, but ol' Wesley was so easygoing I figured it was worth a shot. "Perhaps you could get me into the Fleming-Union for lunch sometime? As your guest? I'm happy to go in the back."

"Good Lord, I don't think so." He looked decidedly uncomfortable and avoided my eyes. "I know nothing about you. Could you even pass the background check?"

"They do a background check on prospective guests?"

"That's why they need twenty-four-hours' notice. Besides, you're not at all my type. We wouldn't fool anyone."

"Oh."

The last thing I wanted was to have Wesley Fleming the Third's love child, but all the same...I wasn't bad-looking, and I was awfully interesting. I looked down at my outfit. What would he think if he saw me in my overalls?

"Do you know about the reproduction of the Chartres labyrinth?" Wesley asked in a blatant attempt to change the subject, pushing his heavy glasses back up the thin bridge of his nose. "Let me show you."

He gestured toward the church, where a handful of shivering tourists, tricked by the day's earlier sunshine into donning shorts and T-shirts, admired the cathedral's soaring stained glass windows. Wesley insisted we mount the great flight of steps and then paused halfway up, pointing to the outdoor terrazzo labyrinth, a duplicate of the one created at Chartres Cathedral around 1220.

"Unlike mazes, labyrinths have only a single path. The twists and turns are symbolic of the course of a human life, and walking the labyrinth is intended to encourage contemplation."

Two boys jumped from one path of the labyrinth to the other, while a third raced through as fast as he could, arms held out airplane-style, as he emitted an array of engine noises. An eight-year-old's version of contemplation.

Wesley and I shared a smile at their antics, and I decided to try again to get my new pal to talk.

"So, Wesley, how come you're not in the woods with the rest of the 'brethren'?"

He turned bright red and pushed his glasses up his nose again.

"They didn't invite me," he mumbled. "Just said the place was closed for a few days for renovations."

"Surely they didn't mean to leave you out...?" I began.

"I've never...I mean, people don't like me much. They only let me in because of my name, anyway."

I suspected he was right, and he struck me as too intelligent to insult with soothing platitudes. Still, the look on his face put me in mind of an overly eager puppy that had just been smacked.

"It's not really my business," I said, "but if they treat you badly it doesn't seem like the kind of group you'd want to be associated with, anyway."

He shrugged and started back down the stone steps. "I certainly could use some coffee."

Following the Peet's Coffee signs, we entered the basement-level building adjoining Grace Cathedral and followed a long, institutional maze of white, windowless hallways. The muffled sound of children's laughter and the squeak of rubber soles on wooden floors evidenced the church's school for boys was at recess in the basketball court.

At last we came upon the coffee stand, right next to the gift shop.

"Mocha caramel Freddo, please," Wesley ordered.

"Double non-fat latte for me, thanks," I told the apron-clad young man behind the coffee cart.

On the counter was a display stand with silver pendants in the shape of the Chartres labyrinth, but I told myself *no*. Cheap, interesting jewelry is a weakness of mine. Up to this point in my life I had never had enough expendable income to figure out whether expensive, interesting jewelry would be equally intriguing to me.

I turned back to Wesley. "This place is so different from the cathedral. It reminds me of a really white cave."

"I love caves. Do you?"

"I haven't given it much thought, but sure, I guess so."

"Do you like bats?"

"Excuse me?"

"Bats. I'm the Batman. I love bats. And caves."

"Dude! Me, too," interjected the young barista. His shiny hair swept across his forehead, nearly obscuring his eyes. It was a hairstyle I would have associated with the most hopeless nerd in high school, but according to my nephews it was now considered fashionable in a kind of metrosexual way.

"I go spelunking every chance I get," said the young man as he dumped ingredients into a blender. "You ever check out those bat caves where you can't even go in without a special breathing apparatus, like a scuba diver? Awesome. And hey, they're not caves but *dude*, they say there used to be some tunnels between the mansions here on the hill before the big quake. Not as cool as caves, but still. I've never found 'em, though."

"Really?" The thought of tunnels in the seismically shaky Bay Area brought out my inner claustrophobe. "Tunnels in San Francisco?"

"They probably caved in during the '06 earthquake," added the barista. "You want extra whipped cream?" he asked Wesley.

I paid for our coffees...and bought a silver pendant. I'm not great at impulse control.

Savoring my blessedly strong caffeine-conveyance device, I followed Wesley back through the tunnel and out into the suddenly foggy day. I paused to take a gulp of coffee and spotted Michael engrossed in conversation with a buxom woman in a long black leather coat and fuchsia scarf. Her voice was loud and strong, and I heard her laughing all the way from the sidewalk.

Michael spied me, and made a beeline in our direction.

"Michael, this is Wesley. Wesley, Michael Johnson."

"Oh dear," Wesley sputtered, looking at his watch. "I really must run."

He handed me his card and loped down the street toward the Fleming Mansion.

5

The artist is, almost by definition, a mischief maker....
Keep in mind the close associations between the words
art and artifice, craft and craftiness, artifact and artful-
ness. The great Aristotle philosophized that all art is imi-
tation; while some artists imitate nature, others imitate
art itself. And only then are they able to pay the rent.
                              —*Georges LeFleur, "Craquelure"*

I GLANCED DOWN at the card in my hand.

Cheap. The kind you can order online—the kind I had until Michael insisted on spending a lot of money to spruce up our image. Name, phone number, address. Picture of a bat. I flipped it over and read the back: ULTIONIS EST PATINA OPTIMUS SERVO GELU.

"Picking up strange men at Peet's again, eh?" Michael asked as he watched Wesley's lanky form walk away.

"Something like that," I said. "Do you read Latin?"

"Only on money." He held out his hand and I surrendered the latte. "You didn't get me anything?"

I shook my head. "I got myself a necklace, though."

"Nice." Warm fingers grazed my skin as Michael lifted the medallion, and I was hyper-aware of his lingering touch. His voice deepened. "*Very* nice."

"I'll go get you something," I said ignoring his gaze and my quickening pulse. "What do you want?"

"Do they have sandwiches? If not, get a half dozen muffins and croissants."

"What, did you skip lunch?"

"It's not for me." He lifted his chin in the direction of a small alley off Sproule Lane, where the nose of a grocery cart indicated the presence of an informal living situation. "The doorman at the Fairmont said a couple of homeless guys live over there. Said one in particular hangs out on the corner at night. Cathy says they're always hungry."

"Who's Cathy?"

"The dog walker."

"You know her?"

"I do now."

"Is there anyone you can't make friends with?"

"Your buddy Frank doesn't like me."

"Frank's a very perceptive man."

"So you keep saying."

Best not to pursue *that* line of thought. "Did the homeless men see anything?"

"That's what we're about to find out. Come on."

Ten minutes later we emerged from Grace Cathedral's basement loaded down with cardboard boxes containing paper cups of sweetened, creamy Peet's coffee, three muffins studded with plump blueberries, two cherry-cornbread scones glistening with icing, and two gooey chocolate croissants. Delectable enough to tempt even the most reluctant of informants.

Skirting Huntington Park, we made our way down Sproule Lane until we reached what was technically an alley but was really more of a deep dent between apartment houses. Leaning against one wall was an older African American man with a grizzled beard and red-rimmed, hollow eyes. He was dressed in a black knit cap, dirty Levis, and several layers of grimy sweatshirts, the topmost of which was emblazoned with a crest and HARVARD in gothic script.

The alley's other resident was a younger white man in a newish red-and-black jumpsuit, orange gloves, and a black ski mask. A scraggly blond mustache poked through the opening for the mouth, giving him the appearance of a masked walrus. He lay on his back, eyes closed and arms sticking up and bent at the elbow. It was an oddly infantile gesture, and I hoped he wasn't dead.

Personal growth notwithstanding, two corpses in one day were beyond my coping skills.

"How you doin'?" Michael asked in that easygoing way of his that made me want to confide in him, until I remembered he was a thief and a liar.

The man in the Harvard sweatshirt looked resigned, as

though expecting us to order him to abandon his little hollow to the rats.

"We have hot coffee and fresh baked goods," Michael said. "Hungry?"

Harvard nudged the thigh of his jumpsuited companion with the toe of a once-white athletic shoe. "Hey," he said in a flat voice. "Food."

Jumpsuit sat up immediately, blinked blue eyes as red-rimmed and empty as his companion's, and stared at us. Handing me the carton of food, Michael helped the younger man to his feet.

I offered Harvard coffee and a muffin, and smiled. He nodded his thanks but looked right through me. As always when confronted with homelessness, my heart went out to these men. What were their stories? How did they come to live like this? Why were people just scraping by, living in alleys in the richest nation in the world?

"You guys hang out around here?" Michael said as he handed Jumpsuit coffee and a croissant. The man peeled up his ski mask and took a huge bite, smearing chocolate on his chin.

Neither man said anything.

Michael's voice became relaxed, almost slurred. "Thing is, we're lookin' for some guys who were here a coupla nights ago and made off with the sculpture in front of the College Club, over on Powell and California. Know what I'm talkin' about?"

Harvard took another muffin. "*Hermes*, right?"

"Right."

"Tol' ya," he said to his companion.

"*Hermes*," murmured Jumpsuit, nodding and gulping his coffee.

"Tol' ya, ol' Hermie was the god of up-to-no-good. Whaddaya-callit, mischief. Yeah," Harvard said, his voice coming to life. "We got us a verifiable patron saint in *Hermes*. I loves that statue, man. A coupla times I slept in that courtyard they got there. Reminded me of home, know what I'm sayin'? People got no respect for art."

Michael nodded. "It was stolen last Monday. Did you happen to see anything?"

"Coupla guys with a crowbar." He nodded. "Came outta nowheres, those guys. Then another guy pulls up in a truck an' they loaded *Hermes* up."

"What kind of truck?" Michael asked.

"Dark-colored Ford. Full-sized, kinda banged up. Nothin' special. I *tried* to tell the folks at the club. Huh. Even put on my Harvard shirt for 'em, but them sumbitches wouldna talk to me."

"Sumbitches," Jumpsuit echoed.

"Did you call the police?" I asked.

For the second time that day, three pairs of male eyes stared at me, incredulous. Note to self: stop hanging out with guys.

Harvard shook his head.

"Did you happen to notice anything strange over at the Fleming-Union earlier today, or last night?" I asked.

"There was a woman there pretty late last night," Harvard said as he reached for a blueberry muffin. "Only reason I mention it is 'cause women aren't allowed in there, and she didn't look like no maid. But sometimes they got professional women goin' in there, if you get my meaning."

"Do you remember what she looked like?"

He shrugged and gestured towards his chest. "Well built. Today there were a bunch o' cops. I steered clear."

"About *Hermes...*" Michael gave me a "stay on topic" look. "Any chance you noticed the truck's license plate?"

"Sure," Harvard mumbled around a mouth full of muffin, crumbs and errant blueberries clinging to his whiskers. "Thought maybe there be a reward. But them sumbitches wouldn't talk to me."

A look of pleased surprise flitted across Michael's face, but he quickly disguised it with his customary mien of amused self-confidence.

"Sumbitches," whispered Jumpsuit like a Greek chorus.

"Do you remember what it was?"

"I *said* I did, din't I?" Harvard sounded offended, and Michael held up his hands in apology. "Mem'ry's not so good. Tha's a *fact*. I wrote it down." He reached into the coin pocket of his threadbare Levis and fished out a gum wrapper. "I been thinkin' maybe this be worth somethin'? Say, ten bucks... Or twenty? Git us a room wit' real beds and a nice, hot shower."

"Hot shower," Jumpsuit echoed dreamily.

"Sounds fair." Michael took a business card and two crisp twenty-dollar bills from his wallet. "There's more where that came from if you think of anything else."

Harvard nodded, exchanging the gum wrapper for the card and the cash. "Best get on it, ya hear? They be sellin' my man for scrap, and he be melted down before you knows it."

"Scrap?" Michael asked.

"Sure. Might could git forty, fifty cents a pound. Maybe more."

"Maybe more," Jumpsuit repeated.

As we walked back toward the top of Nob Hill, Michael's eyes slewed in my direction.

"All right, I'll admit it: you did well," I conceded. "Though I'd like to point out that if the members of the College Club weren't such snobs, they wouldn't need our services."

"Sumbitches."

We shared a grin, and I felt a dangerous sensation. Was it affection? Animal attraction was one thing, but affection was *dangerous*. It was the first step on the road to picking out kitchen curtains.

Since Michael refused to tell me where he lived, this would be highly complicated.

"So, Super Sleuth, how do we find out who the license plate belongs to?" I asked.

"Now, missy, don't you go troublin' your purty li'l head 'bout that."

Good idea. The less I knew about Michael's investigative techniques, the better.

"What's this sudden interest in the Fleming Mansion?" Michael asked as we neared the huge building. "Weren't you researching 'killer wallpaper' for that place? Don't tell me the Martha Stewart Cabbage Rose collection took someone out?"

"As a matter of fact, I was working there earlier today." I took a deep breath. "A man was murdered, and the crime scene resembled *The Death of Marat*. You know the painting by David? The victim was in a bathtub and everything."

Michael's jaw tightened. "I told you not to take that job. The members of the F-U can't be trusted. They have too much money and too much power. It twists people. They start to think the rules don't apply to them."

"Does the phrase 'pot calling the kettle black' mean anything to you?"

"We're talking about you, not me. Do as I ask, just this once? Tell them you can't finish the job."

"First off, it's not for you to decide what commissions I accept. You're my partner for the online business only. Period. And second, I'm not involved. I just happened to be in the mansion when the body was found. Inspector Crawford's on the case."

"Glad to hear it," Michael said grimly. "I thought you might do something stupid because your Uncle Anton—ah, hell."

I halted in my tracks. "What about Anton?"

"Don't you think it's significant that Hermes is the god of theft?" Michael asked, his tone buoyant. He shifted his weight from foot to foot and stared into the distance, an odd look on his face.

It was the first time I'd caught him in a slip of the tongue.

"Perhaps the thieves have an ironic sense of humor," Michael continued.

"Don't change the subject. What were you going to say about Anton?"

"It has nothing to do with anything."

"I'll be the judge of that."

Michael's gaze shifted to a point over my shoulder. I turned to see what he was looking at and saw Annette Crawford approaching. She did not look pleased.

When I looked back to Michael, all I saw was his back as he disappeared down a nearby alley.

"I thought you were headed home, Annie," Crawford said. "But look, you're still here."

"No, I'm not. I mean, I went to my studio, then came back here, but I'm not trying to get into the Fleming Mansion. We... I'm investigating a different situation."

"Situation?"

"I have a new art assessment business, and—"

"I understood you ran a website that dealt with e-mails."

"Um..."

"You're not impersonating a private investigator, are you? PIs have to be licensed, you know."

"I don't carry a gun."

"Thank the Lord for small favors," she said. "What sort of investigation are you mucking around with, and *please* tell me it has nothing to do with my murder investigation."

"The boys at the College Club lost their *Hermes*."

"Excuse me?

"You know the big bronze statue that used to sit outside their club? It was stolen last week."

"And what are you supposed to do about it?"

"Find it?"

"Uh-huh." An unmarked police car pulled up next to her and she opened the passenger door to climb in. "Annie, do us all a favor and stick to faux finishing. It's more your speed."

—

Back home in Oakland, I flipped through my mail halfheartedly as I mounted the three flights of stairs to my apartment up under the eaves in an old house–turned–apartment building.

As I neared the little landing at the top of the stairs, right outside my door, I slowed my pace and looked up. Something was wrong.

Yummy cooking smells. Emanating from under the door of my apartment. My stomach growled in appreciation. There was only one problem: there hadn't been any actual food in my kitchen since I broke up with Josh-the-wonder-chef-and-carpenter.

And my front door was ajar.

"Hello?"

"Annie!" The door flew wide open and there stood my ersatz uncle, Anton Woznikowicz, arms outstretched, a brilliant grin on his face. "I thought you would never arrive!"

"Anton," I said as he wrapped strong, pudgy arms around me in a bear hug. He smelled of garlic, onions, and turpentine. "I see you've started on the wine. You know, most people call before they break into someone's home to cook dinner."

"Bah." He waved me off. "Family doesn't stand on ceremony."

"LeFleurs sure don't." I wasn't technically a LeFleur, but then no one in the family was. Grandfather, a Brooklyn native, had made the name up in a bid to convince the world he was French. Unfortunately, his linguistic skills left something to be desired; in French *fleur* is a feminine noun, so the name should have been *La* Fleur. It was something of a sore subject with the old forger.

"Come in, come in, my darling," said Anton. "Tell me: how long has it been since you came home to a traditional Spanish *paella*?"

"Pretty much never."

"Then it's well past high time." He *tsk-tsk*ed, and handed me a glass of ruby red Rioja. We clinked glasses.

"To your love life," he said with a wink.

"To *yours*," I replied. Anton laughed heartily.

Lately Grandfather and his cronies had been waging a none-too-subtle campaign to marry me off. I wasn't certain of Georges's motives, since he also maintained I would come to my senses one day, chuck the boring law-abiding life, and move to Paris where he and I would forge beautiful art together in his atelier in the Place des Vosges. But I suspected Georges was hoping that if I did crank out a passel of kids at least some of them would inherit the LeFleur art-forger gene. And should Michael—whom Georges adored—be the father of said children, they'd also lack a moral center.

They'd be perfect, in other words.

"How did you get in?" I asked.

"Ah, Annie! You are so droll!" Anton did legal art restoration these days, but in his prime—and in his heart—he was an unrepentant forger like Georges. Breaking into my dead-bolted third-floor apartment was child's play to my uncle's ilk.

"It's been a long time," I said.

"That it has, that it has. Georges will be so pleased to learn of our visit!"

"Have you heard from him recently?"

"I've been reading his blog. Don't worry, he sounds his old self."

"Oh, I'm not worried." It would take a speeding Mack truck to fell my septuagenarian grandfather. I just hoped it was genetic.

I was surprised Anton had found enough pots and pans to work his culinary magic. I noted a cardboard box that he must have toted in. He had brought his own special *paella* pan, and a number of other items, including a chipped mug emblazoned LE PREMIER ARTISTE DU MONDE, or "world's best artist." I had made it for him in Paris when I was sixteen, when Anton, Georges, and I had spent our days "aging" paper and canvases, and our evenings strolling along the Seine as the men vied to tell the most outrageous tale of international intrigue and daring. Did Anton always carry the mug with him? Or was this a none-too-subtle reminder of our shared past, and the importance of loyalty?

The kitchen was a disaster area, and I wondered why good cooks seemed to think the dishes cleaned themselves. Still, the whole place smelled *great*. Saffron and olive oil and shrimp and sausage. What's not to like?

"What are you working on these days?" I asked as I set out two places.

"A little of this, a little of that. Restoration mostly. It is very boring work—a child could do it." I noticed splotches of paint on his hands, and a streak of vermilion on his bald head.

"I doubt that. By the way," I began, real casual-like, while I fussed with the silverware, "did you happen to forge the Gauguin the New Zealander's looking for?"

Anton spilled the olive oil he had been pouring into a shallow saucer, swore under his breath, and sopped up the mess with a paper towel.

"Cut up that baguette, will you, Annie?"

I did as he asked, but kept one eye on him. Anton had never before dropped by to cook me dinner; in fact, he had never come to my apartment without an invitation. He was right; we were practically family and did not stand on ceremony. Still, his out-of-the-blue appearance was cause for concern. Anton had something to tell me. But he needed to butter me up first.

We sat at the table and served ourselves. I let the richness of the saffron rice and olives bathe my tongue. Besides being delicious, *paella* is a feast for the eyes. I remembered Anton telling me that the deep orangey-yellow saffron, a subtle spice gathered from the stamens of crocus flowers, was a component of traditional paints. When mixed with egg yolk, it was often used by medieval painters to imitate gold gilding.

After taking the edge off my hunger, I sipped my wine, sat back, and contemplated my faux uncle.

"A man was murdered at the Fleming Mansion today, and the scene was arranged like David's *Death of Marat*. Ring any bells?"

Anton paled. "I never cared for the Neo-classicists."

"It's better to talk to me now than to be questioned by the police later."

He snorted. "It would break your grandpapa's heart to learn you are with the FBI!"

"I'm not *with* the FBI," I insisted, though I couldn't suppress a visual of myself as a *muy macha*, gun-wielding Special Agent. I sort of liked it. Plus, I imagined FBI agents had health insurance. Maybe even dental. "This is about murder, not art. At least, that's what I thought—until someone suggested you might be involved."

"I am not involved in murder, Annie."

"I never thought you were. How *are* you involved?"

"I have done occasional restoration work for the club. Also, I painted a charming reproduction for a Fleming-Union member, many years ago."

"How long ago?"

"Five, maybe seven years. I don't remember; time passes so quickly at my age that—"

"And this is the copy that showed up at auction recently? The one the Kiwi insurance guy is looking into?"

"Ah, you met him! *Such* a charming fellow. Smart, too. Interesting people, the Maori." He waggled his bushy eyebrows. "He's single, you know."

"Anton, just tell me: did you paint the forgery that came up at auction?"

He just stared at me, lips pressed together in a stubborn line.

"Might as well 'fess up. I'll know the moment I see the painting in person."

"There's nothing illegal about copying a painting." He muttered in Polish, took a sip of wine, and sighed. "It wasn't supposed to go into circulation. Believe me when I say this. My client was forced to sell the original but insisted he would keep my copy at home. He did not want to lose face in front of his friends by admitting he had to sell."

I'd heard that one before. "So your client was a 'he,' then. Was it Victor Yeltsin?"

"I can't say, Annie. You know that."

Anton and Georges were Old School forgers, which meant they lived by a strict code of personal and professional ethics that often baffled outsiders. The men were, after all, criminals. Near the top of the list, just below "What Happens in thy Studio Stays in thy Studio," was "Thou Shalt Not Squeal on thy Employer."

"But you're positive there *was* a genuine Gauguin?"

"Of course! She lived with me for more than a month while I worked. A rare beauty. I could have stared at her forever...." Anton's expression was wistful, as though recalling a bittersweet romance. Passion such as this puts the "love" in "art lover."

"Who did he sell the original to?"

"All I know is that it was someone discreet. I did think..."

"What?"

"I got the impression at the time that selling the painting was part of another deal, perhaps a trade rather than a sale, and that he needed the insurance money."

"And the secret message?"

"The client asked me to write it. To distinguish the copy from the original, I presume. I also acquired for him an EDXRF."

"An EDXRF?"

"Annie, I'm surprised at you." He gave me a disappointed look, as though the acronym were as common as toothpaste. "An energy-dispersive X-ray fluorescence spectrometer. So he could see the message on the spot, not confuse the two paintings."

"Did you tell all this to Jarrah Preston?"

Anton looked shocked. "He's practically a police officer!"

"Then why did you refer him to *me*?"

"Listen, Annie, I'm leaving town tomorrow. Wonderful news, my daughter is having a baby."

"Congratulations. But—"

"I am to be a grandpapa! Oh, to think that my dear sweet grandchild might one day turn out as well as you, my dear. That would be the greatest of blessings indeed. How I have envied Georges his relationship with you, his granddaughter."

Even though I knew full well that Anton was manipulating my emotions, and none too subtly at that, I got a little choked up. "You deserve all the best, Anton."

"I think I do."

"Now will you answer my question? Why did you refer Preston to me?"

He waved a hand airily. "I assumed you would recognize my

work, keep my secret, and find the real Gauguin. I thought you might as well get paid for it. Your old Uncle Anton is always looking out for you, eh?"

"The only surprise is that I was surprised." I reached for more *paella*.

Anton looked at me sternly. "It is critical that you find the missing Gauguin, Annie. I cannot bear to think it might disappear forever. "

"Yeah, that's me all right," I said glumly; as good as it was, *paella* did not have the magical frustration-fighting abilities of chocolate. "Annie Kincaid the First, Finder of Lost Art."

Dear Georges: Is it true that some of your forgeries sell for millions of dollars?

Dear Reader: Yes. But if I tell you which ones they no longer will.

—*Georges LeFleur, "Craquelure"*

AFTER ANTON LEFT, I knelt on my living room floor beside my stack of old newspapers. Digging down a couple of weeks' worth, I found what I was looking for: the front page article on the Odibajian brothers.

According to the reporter, the two had built an empire together, riding to unthinkable wealth on the wave of real estate fever that clutched the San Francisco Bay Area over the last two decades. With the kind of money-making intuition that always eludes folks like me, they had diversified just in time to keep the bulk of their assets safe in the recent economic decline. They now had significant investments in the pharmaceutical industry, oil concerns, and several lucrative high-tech startups, besides owning a good section of San Francisco's downtown. They were important benefactors to the San Francisco Opera, the symphony, the Legion of Honor and de Young museums. They'd bought the naming rights for the baseball stadium next year.

But the brothers had developed certain "irreconcilable differences"—differences in management style, it said here—and were untangling their assets. I got the distinct impression that the elder, Balthazar Odibajian, ran the show. He was the one who gave the majority of the quotes, and in the color photo of the two brothers "in happier times" he was slightly ahead of Elijah, looking larger, more confident, unsmiling. Elijah's face was hard to make out, looking off in the distance.

Another, smaller black-and-white photo showed Balthazar Odibajian standing with a crowd of well-dressed men and women whom I assumed to be the city's upper-crust party-goers. Balthazar had his arms draped casually around two glossy, well-endowed women, one on either side. Despite the arm candy, he looked unrelentingly stern.

So Balthazar Odibajian and Victor Yeltsin were "brethren" at the Fleming-Union. Maybe Victor knew Elijah through his brother, and had sold Elijah the Gauguin five years ago, giving him the copy instead of the real one. Then Elijah, under financial pressures because of the rift with his brother, decided to sell. And only then did he realize the painting was a fake. So could the man in the tub be Victor Yeltsin, killed by Elijah in a fury? And what happened to the genuine painting?

I glanced at the clock: 11:30. Too late to call Jarrah to see whether he'd managed to track down Elijah. I'd check in with him in the morning.

I tore out the Brothers Grimm article and put it into the case folder Jarrah Preston had given me, then took the folder into bed, fully intending to read up on one Victor Yeltsin. I flipped through the papers for all of five minutes. Police reports will put a person to sleep faster than a pill.

—

A friend of mine moved from New York City to the Bay Area last year and the first time he experienced what we locals call Casual Carpool, he called a New Yorker friend to exclaim that strangers were crawling into other strangers' cars, and it wasn't even something normal like a carjacking.

Casual Carpool is a unique Bay Area answer to inadequate public transportation. San Francisco-bound drivers want to avoid the Bay Bridge toll and the most congested traffic lanes by using the "diamond" carpool lanes, which require three passengers on the bridge—except for two-seaters like my truck. Passengers, meanwhile, wish to avoid the cost of gas and parking, or BART or the bus. Riders wait at designated Casual Carpool spots, and drivers pick them up to cross the bridge. Simple as that.

This morning there was a long line of cars outnumbering riders. The aroma of my Peet's French roast permeated my truck's cab as I waited, creeping along in line as cars picked up two passengers at a time.

I had already called ahead to Spenser Keating at Mayfield's auction house. I would go straight there to assess the ersatz Gauguin, even though I knew it must be Anton's forgery.
I doubted it would give me any more information than Anton
had himself, but I had to look at it in person, and while I was
there I would see if I could learn anything more from Keating
about Elijah Odibajian. I had even dressed as a respectable professional for the meeting: straight skirt, silk tank, soft cardigan
sweater.

Anton said he was going to drop out of sight for a while. That
was good; one fewer thing to worry about. On the other hand,
one more thing to try to keep from Inspector Annette Crawford,
who, while she wasn't out to get me, wasn't the sort to turn her
back on an obvious act of larceny either. With regard to the SFPD,
my basic game plan was to avoid contact for the next few days
until I figured a few things out.

Too bad I wasn't on better terms with Annette—or with anyone in the police department. I would love to know how things
were progressing with the murder investigation.

I pulled ahead one more spot, starting to chafe at the delay.
Why are there always more cars than riders, or the other way
around? The law of averages would suggest that it even out, at
least some of the time, shouldn't it?

Actually I had no idea what the law of averages said. Math
was never my strong suit.

I placed a call to Elena Briones. I hated to talk while driving,
but there wasn't any driving going on at the moment.

"Elena? It's Annie. I was just wondering whether you had an
update on Destiny's situation with the police."

"Actually, it looks as though she's going to be released today."

"Already? Good job."

"It's not anything I can take credit for. They made some assessments having to do with the body and the crime scene, and
let her go."

"What kind of assessments?"

"All I know is, the sword seems to have gone in postmortem.
The most she'll be charged with is 'unlawful handling of a deceased individual.'"

"Why would she stab a corpse?"

"She didn't stab anything," Elena, the lawyer, said in no uncertain terms. "She was trying to pull it out."

"Oh. Right. Thanks a lot for helping her out. I owe you."

"No problem. All my clients should be so easy. But if she can't pay the bill, I'll send it on to you."

She wasn't kidding. Unlike Pedro, Elena was very pragmatic when it came to her professional services.

I craned my neck to look down the street, hoping for more pedestrians to show up, briefcases in hand and ready to be productive members of society by shuffling money around from one account to the next. I've never figured out how the money ever does anything useful, but that probably explains why I never seem to have any at hand. As Michael would say, I don't grasp the fundamentals of capitalism.

Speaking of whom, I tried Michael's cell phone again. No answer. No surprise.

If he disappeared for another week, I was calling the FBI on him. For real this time.

I called Jarrah Preston to see if he had made any headway with finding Elijah Odibajian, but he didn't pick up either. I left a message and asked him to get back to me.

Finally, I got to the head of the line. My turn to pick up the next passenger. I fiddled with my new Bluetooth device, which always made me feel like a cyborg, not even looking up as a suit-clad executive climbed into the cab of my truck, snapped open the *San Francisco Chronicle*'s business section, and disappeared behind the newspaper. This was par for the course at Casual Carpool, where too much social interaction was generally frowned upon.

By the time we reached the toll plaza I noticed the man in the passenger seat smelled good. Really good. I'm not a cologne girl, but despite this–or perhaps because of it—I notice when men smell inordinately good. Must be a vegetarian.

There was a brief delay at the metering lights regulating the entrance to the bridge, so I tried calling Michael one more time. My passenger's phone also rang. I rolled my eyes at our brave new high-tech world, where we're more likely to chat with someone miles away than with the person sitting next to us. The businessman answered his phone just as Michael finally answered his.

"Hello?" the executive said as I heard Michael say, *"Hello?"*

I looked to the right. The executive looked to the left.

I cursed.

"You're not exactly a morning person, are you?" Michael smiled.

"How did you manage...never mind. Listen, partner, we have to talk."

We made it through the carpool metering lights to the span, then screeched to a halt once again.

"So talk."

"Why are you dressed like that?"

"That's what we 'need' to talk about? My wardrobe? Whatever you say. This morning I'm wearing an amusing little ensemble, a summery wool neither too heavy nor too light, but appropriate for all venues, from bedroom to boardroom to ballroom—"

I snorted. "You look like you're attending a funeral."

"I'm heeding your words of wisdom and am taking seriously my responsibilities as a small-business owner. We entrepreneurs are the backbone of this country, the epitome of the American dream. It is by the sweat of our lowly brows that this great nation was built. Do you know, we self-employed small-business owners pay ten times as much in federal taxes than all the corporations in America combined?"

"No, we don't." We rolled ahead at five miles per hour, still only halfway across the first span. It was going to be one of those mornings that drove otherwise rational commuters to fantasize about rocket launchers and jetpacks.

"You got me. I made that up. You're looking pretty spiffy yourself today, partner."

"Michael, cut the bull. You owe me an explanation. Where were you last week?"

"On a business trip."

"What *kind* of business trip? You mean business as in your old business, as in stealing something?"

He frowned at me. "Annie, I'm hurt."

"Not half as hurt as when I finish with you—or more precisely, the *feds* finish with you—if you're back to your old ways."

He leaned back against the door.

"You want the truth?"

"It would be so refreshing."

"I had some family business to attend to."

"Family? What kind of family?"

"What do you mean, what kind of family? I didn't think there were that many options."

"Flesh-and-blood family?"

"Yes."

"The people you share your DNA with?"

"Is 'family' a difficult concept for you?"

"Huh."

"What's that supposed to mean?"

"It's just—nothing. So, where does your family live?"

"All over."

"What did they need from you?"

"It's personal."

First he mentions a mother, and now a personal life. Next thing you know the man would turn out to be a real person instead of a demi-god, and things would really spin out of control. I had an intense craving for chocolate.

After a brief pick-up in speed, the traffic slowed to a standstill again. Out the window Alcatraz Island and the Golden Gate Bridge shimmered in the morning light. My eyes fell upon the dozen bright red mechanical cranes that were supposed to be rebuilding the eastern span of the Bay Bridge, though they never seemed to be in operation. The Bay Bridge is actually two bridges: the western span connects San Francisco to Yerba Buena Island, and the eastern span reaches from there to Oakland. San Francisco's half is attractive and in good condition. Oakland's half is ugly and seismically unsafe. A chunk of it fell during the last significant shaker.

Many Oaktown boosters find this symbolic, and more than a few whisper of conspiracies. Usually I'm happy to jump aboard the victimization bandwagon, but I find it hard to embrace conspiracy theories. In my experience, people are too self-centered to organize a decent block party, much less pull off a successful conspiracy.

"Maybe you should stop disappearing," I said, sipping my coffee. "It makes me question your reliability."

He laughed and reached over with his left hand to smooth

my hair, letting his hand rest on the back of my neck. "I am many things, Annie. Reliable is not one of them."

"I know, I know. If I want reliability I should marry Frank."

"I sure as hell wouldn't go that far. In fact, about your golden boy Frank—"

"I already know your feelings toward the man, Michael. My point is, this is your chance. Your shelf life as a thief is limited, you know. Surely you must be on your third strike by now. This is California. Despite our loosey-goosey reputation, we put people away for life for stealing candy bars on their third strike in California."

Traffic picked up and we zoomed through the tunnel at Yerba Buena Island.

"Shocking," Michael said. "Then again, sometimes you feel like a nut...."

"I'm serious."

"Careful, Annie. It almost sounds like you care."

"I..."

"Take the Embarcadero exit," said Michael as we reached the foot of the bridge and entered San Francisco.

"Here? Why?"

"I have a lead on *Hermes*. We have to talk with some folks."

"I don't feel like it. I don't like those clubby types, and they don't like me. I want to do something fun, like work on the sketches for my clients' living room. Besides, I have to go by Mayfield's to check on the Kiwi's painting."

"This will be quick. And it's practically on the way. And need I remind you, *you're* the one who accepted this job."

I pointed the truck toward one of the last affordable neighborhoods in San Francisco: Bayview–Hunter's Point. Crime rates are high, drug use rampant. On the up side, there is plenty of parking. I followed Michael's directions and pulled up in front of a run-down, two-story apartment building painted a bilious Pepto Bismol–pink that reminded me of the repurposed Motel 6 where I had lived in my senior year at college. The downstairs apartments opened onto the parking lot while the upstairs ones opened onto a covered walkway. In front of the former motel office was a small, kidney-shaped pool that had been emptied of water and filled with trash and broken furniture. A dusty neon sign with a palm tree declared the place to be "Aloha Court," though based on the number of crack vials littering the premises, "Sayonara City" seemed more apt.

"Who—or what—are we looking for?" I asked.

"I ran the license plate number the homeless guy gave us," Michael said, handing me a slip of paper with a name and address.

"The truck's owner is 'Perry Outlaw'?" I said, reading. "You have *got* to be kidding. A man named 'Outlaw' becomes a criminal? If he had any sense of irony at all he'd have become a judge."

Michael chuckled as we climbed out of the truck.

"You guys cops, or Social?" a scrawny young woman called out to us, and I surmised our business-themed attire screamed "outsider." She was dressed in jeans and a bright yellow T-shirt, her shaggy hair an unnatural arterial-blood red with dark roots.

"Something we can help you with?" Michael asked.

"Bitch stole my money!" she fumed, flinging her arm toward the squat building. "Apartment Two."

"What happened?"

"I gave her twenty bucks and she gave me a hunk of plaster!" On her outstretched palm sat a small white chunk of plaster. We looked at it, at her, and then at each other.

"What do you want us to do about it?" I asked.

"Get my money back!"

"You think we're cops, and you want us to get your drug money back?" I said, not sure I'd followed the conversation.

"Hey, she *stole* my twenty bucks! This is America! *Do* something!"

"I'm afraid we're on another case, ma'am," Michael said. "But if you'd like, I'll be happy to call in some backup and you can explain to the nice officers that you want your drug dealer arrested for selling fake crack cocaine."

The woman stared at us, mouth open, before turning away with a look of pure disgust.

"I think we've shattered her faith in the system," I said softly as we walked away.

"That's what she gets for seeking justice from a forger and a thief," Michael replied.

"*Former* forger."

"*Former* thief."

"Fine."

"Good."

We shared a smile.

"So how do we handle this?" I asked.

"Let me lead. I'll be the bad cop. Jump in when you think you should."

"Okay, but be careful—impersonating a police officer actually is a crime."

We reached Apartment Six, on the ground floor, and Michael knocked briskly. A skinny, pale young man in his early twenties answered, dressed in nothing more than a pair of tighty-whities that were more gray than white. After my initial impression I tried very hard not to look.

"Perry Outlaw?"

"Who wants to know?"

"I'm Johnson. This is Kincaid. We'd like to ask you a few questions."

"You from Social?"

Michael inclined his head.

Outlaw stepped back and we walked into an apartment that looked like a cheap motel room: to the left was an unmade double bed flanked by a pair of generic faux-wood nightstands, and to the right a dresser was pushed up against the wall. Atop the dresser a television set was chained to a bolt in the wall. The floor was carpeted in the common brown-and-tan mottled shag favored by tightwad landlords wanting to disguise suspicious stains. The room smelled of stale cigarette smoke, fried chicken, and spoiled milk.

A thin blond woman, resembling a strung-out Kate Moss with bad skin, perched on the room's only chair, a towheaded toddler in her lap. The child pointed a bright green laser-type gun at us and pretended to pull the trigger.

"We're doin' okay," Perry said. "Erin's just fine, aren't you, sweetie?"

I smiled at the child, who turned back to the cartoons that nipped and squawked on the TV.

"That's not a real gun or nothin'," Outlaw said ingratiatingly. "Her uncle gave it to her on account of she wouldn't stop crying.

But it don't shoot nothin'. Listen, we're clean," he insisted, dropping his voice but speaking in a determined tone. "Ever since Melissa got outta jail the last time, we been on the straight and narrow, swear-to-God. I know this place don' look like much but—"

"Where were you last Monday night?"

"Monday?"

Michael nodded.

"I...uh...let's see. I guess I was here. Yep, I was here. I come home straight after work."

"When's the last time you were on Nob Hill?" Michael asked.

"Downtown?"

Michael nodded.

"Nah, man, not for years." He shook his head.

"Your truck was seen there."

"Ah, *maaaaan*." Outlaw clutched at the top of his head with both hands and blew out a breath in a dramatic move. "I *told* those dudes to stay clean. What'd they do?"

"There was a sculpture stolen."

"Naaaah, *dude*, they just borrowed my truck."

"Who?"

"Dude, I don't even know, man," Perry moaned.

"Listen, bud," I said. "Your scumbag friends stole an extremely valuable sculpture that belongs to someone with a whole lot of juice and not much patience, understand? If we don't get it back for him the legal way, he'll hire someone who will get it back the hard way. A real sick S.O.B., let me tell you. "

Michael looked amused, and I remembered I was supposed to be the good cop.

Outlaw looked genuinely stricken. "I'm telling you, they just borrowed my truck! I had nothin' to do with it, I swear!"

"Names and addresses. Now."

He continued to protest as he wrote down the information. "I got me a job, a legitimate job. Don't pay much, but I'm legit. Here."

He handed Michael a piece of paper with two names, Alan Dizikes and Skip Goldberg, and an address in Crockett, a small city on a northern finger of the bay about half an hour's drive.

"Hey, I can't get in trouble for lendin' them the truck, right?"

Outlaw pleaded. "I didn't know what they was up to and I wasn't there, man. Hey, maybe I got somethin' you could use for another case. Go ahead, ask me anythin'."

"We're just interested in the sculpture, Mr. Outlaw," Michael said. "Any idea what they'd do with a sculpture like that?"

Outlaw rubbed his jaw, the stubble making a *skritch*ing sound. "Sell it. Ain't like none of them wants it for his garden."

"Sell it where?"

"Dude, anywhere they can."

"Anything else?" I asked. "Now's your chance to do the right thing. Because if I find out you held out on us, I'm gonna take that as a *personal* insult. Johnson, tell Mr. Outlaw here what happened to the last lying low-life who insulted me."

"Well, now, that's hard to say, seeing how the body was never found."

Outlaw's jaw dropped, but no sound came out.

Michael handed him a business card. "You think of anything else, just give me a call."

"Sure. Sure I will. You can count on me."

Michael and I walked in silence to the truck. The sights and sounds of the Outlaw apartment had given me a dull headache and a nauseated feeling in the pit of my stomach. I felt the urge to go paint. Yes, I whined about the pitiful state of my bank account, but as an artist I could consider myself bohemian rather than just plain poor. Aloha Court was *depressing*.

"I don't think I'm cut out for this investigating gig," I said, climbing into the driver's seat and leaning across to unlock the door for Michael. "First snooty club types, now this. How can people live like that? And with a kid? Maybe my grandfather's right. Maybe I should go back to forgery."

"They're not as bad as some. At least they're trying, and that counts for a lot. So: off to Crockett? We could swing by Mayfield's first."

"I don't know...maybe we should split up on this one." I pulled onto busy Third Street. "We could get more done."

"It's more fun together," Michael said. "Besides, you just want to go hide in your studio and paint. Admit it."

"That *is* still my main job, you know."

"You've seen how lucrative some of these gigs are, Annie. We wrap this one up, plus that Gauguin gig, and you'll be able to put money down on that new truck you keep talking about."

My cell phone signaled an incoming call with an electronic version of *Flight of the Bumblebee*, which Mary put on it last month after I demanded she remove the annoying rap tune she had previously uploaded. Rooting around for my Bluetooth was enough to make me frantic; the frenetic music was not helping.

"Hello?" I answered, barely evading the switch to voicemail.

"Annie? It's Jarrah Preston."

"Hi, Jarrah. Thanks for calling back. I wanted to ask you—"

"Listen, Annie. I don't know if you've heard but your uncle Anton," Preston interrupted. "Anton Woznikowicz—"

"Has he been involved in something? Is he in trouble?" *Lord*, I had *known* something was going on. *Damn*. I just hoped the bail wasn't set too high, because I really needed to buy that new truck.

"I'm sorry to have to tell you this, Annie. I stopped by his place this morning and found him on the floor. He's been poisoned."

7

The history of paint is the history of poison, judiciously applied.

—*Georges LeFleur, "Craquelure"*

"HE HASN'T BEEN able to tell us what happened." Jarrah greeted me when I burst into the ICU waiting room at San Francisco General. Michael had gone to park the truck after I jumped out in front of the emergency room. "When I found him he was conscious and mumbling, but just barely. The ER doctors said we have to wait and see if he regains consciousness."

I squeezed my eyes shut. I should have done more. I should have forced Anton, at the point of a palette knife if necessary, to tell me what was really going on. And then I should have hand-delivered the nefarious fellow to his daughter's doorstep.

"What's wrong with him?"

"Here's the doctor now."

The physician was dark-featured and petite. Notwithstanding the stethoscope hanging around her neck, the clipboard under her arm, and the spotless white lab coat, she looked all of fifteen years old.

"I'm Anton's niece," I said. "I'm his only local family. What's the prognosis?"

"We believe your uncle's been poisoned," she said with a slight Pakistani lilt. "It looks like arsenic."

"Arsenic poisoning?"

"We've begun a process known as chelation, which is a way to try to rid the system of the poison."

"How does that work?"

"We're administering a drug called dimercaprol every four hours. It's more toxic than succimer, but we don't have much choice given his acute condition. We'll do that for the first two

94

days, followed by two injections on the third day then one a day for the next five days."

"And what does 'chelating' do, exactly?"

"The chelating agents sequester the arsenic away from blood proteins, which is the most immediately damaging aspect of this kind of poisoning."

"Are there side effects?"

"Sure. The most important side effect is hypertension, and possible kidney damage later. But at this point we don't have much choice. I hate to be blunt, but your uncle's condition is considered grave at this time. Given his age...well, it's not an ideal situation. It's lucky his friend found him in time. Be assured we are doing everything we can. "

I sensed a presence behind me, and turned to see a large, square-headed man who looked like a caricature of a Polish Mafioso. In fact, he *was* a Polish Mafioso. Hipolit—Hippo to his friends; I could only guess what his enemies called him—was an Old School gangster, which meant he rained mayhem down upon the heads of his enemies but drew the line at their families, civilians, and cops. I wasn't sure how he and Anton knew each other—whether the connection was social, business, or cultural—but they were long-term associates. Most of the time Hippo's very existence made me nervous, but today I was glad to see him.

"I have my best man on it, Annie," he said, hugging me. He smelled of tobacco and Juicy Fruit gum. "You need anything, Anton needs anything, you let me know. Here's my private line." He handed me a business card engraved with his name and phone number.

"Do you know how to get in touch with Anton's daughter?" I asked.

"I've already called her," Hippo said. "But she won't be able to make the trip in her condition. She's in Milan, due to have her baby any day now."

Michael hurried in from the parking garage and put an arm around my waist. I leaned into him, grateful for his presence, and told him what I knew. He and Hippo acknowledged each other with a barely perceptible nod.

"Can I see him?" I asked no one in particular.

"He's this way," Hippo replied.

A short way down the hall I spied Anton through a window. I moved to stand next to my unconscious faux-uncle, who looked small and fragile in the hospital bed. A plastic tube was taped to his mouth, he was hooked up to an IV stand, and wires and electrodes connected him to a bank of monitors that made rhythmic beeping sounds. For the first time he looked every inch of his seventy-something years.

Michael took up a position on the other side of the bed and gazed at Anton, shock and sorrow in his eyes. In my own grief I'd forgotten that Anton was a big part of Michael's world, too.

I felt rage boiling up, threatening to spill over. There was no point in hanging around the ICU. There was a would-be murderer to find. I turned to Michael, who nodded in unspoken agreement.

We walked out of the hospital into the strong late-morning sunshine. The next thing I knew I was sitting on the curb, struggling to breathe as my head swam. Michael sat beside me and stroked my hair.

"I was with him last night," I said.

"It was an accident, Annie. A mistake. It happens."

"Accidental *arsenic* poisoning? Tell me how that's possible. Anton knows paint chemistry better than anyone—better even than my grandfather, and *he* knows more than most chemists. Anton taught me himself, when I was a teenager."

"He was also an absentminded fellow, Annie, you know that. As likely to put a tin of linseed oil on the stove to boil as the teakettle. And he's always covered in paint."

"Arsenic doesn't work that way. It's not easily absorbed through the skin—that kind of poisoning would happen gradually, after years of exposure. The only way arsenic kills quickly is if it's ingested. We had dinner together last night, and I feel fine."

"Perhaps he ate something else later."

I stood up abruptly.

"Where are you going?"

"To his studio."

"Annie, wait..."

I was already marching to the parking structure.

"At least let me drive," Michael said, trotting up behind me.

"Make it fast." I tossed him the keys.

We turned onto Anton's street in the Noe Valley neighborhood, and saw four black-and-white police cruisers, a hazardous materials truck, and an unmarked police car parked in the already cramped space in front of his house. A uniformed cop halted us at the gate to Anton's yard, and at my insistence, called over the investigating officer.

Annette Crawford.

"Annie, I'm so sorry—"

"Why would Homicide be here if this was an accident?" I challenged without preliminary.

Annette shot a concerned look at Michael. It made me angrier.

"Homicide gets called in on special cases to assess the crime scene," she said, her deep voice gentle. "It's standard procedure."

"I want to see his studio."

"You can't. The place was full of arsine gas. Hazmat is in there now, cleaning up so we can assess the scene."

"Arsine *gas*?" I asked.

Someone dressed in a moon-suit shouted to Annette, and she nodded. "Listen, this isn't even my catch. I was checking out a possible link with the Fleming-Union. There have been some... developments that I need to speak with you—the *two* of you— about. I'll call with an update and we can arrange a time to meet, all right?"

"But—"

"Later, Annie. I promise."

I became aware of Michael's firm grip on my upper arm, and allowed myself to be turned toward the street. Halfway down the block, beyond the clump of emergency vehicles, I spied Anton's cargo van parked at the curb. Its tan paint was dented and scratched, its windowless sides advertised SULLY'S CARPET CLEANERS. It was the sort of vehicle that appeared unlikely to contain a functioning radio much less valuable artwork. Glancing around to be sure the cop at Anton's gate wasn't watching, I headed straight for it.

"*Now* where are you going?" Michael said, chasing after me.

"Open it," I demanded as we reached the van.

"Why?"

"It's Anton's. I want to check it out."

"Forgive me for stating the obvious, but if this wasn't an accident we should tell the cops about the van. It may contain evidence."

"You heard Annette, Michael. They think it's an accident. No one's interested in what really happened. They're only too happy to blame the crazy old artist. Besides, even if the cops do rule it an assault, the closure rate on homicide in San Francisco is, what—thirty percent? Not good enough. Nowhere *near* good enough."

"It's not a homicide, Annie. Anton's still alive, remember?"

"For now. But it was *meant* to be a homicide. And if anyone's going to get to the bottom of this, it'll have to be us." I was in a fever of needing to do something, anything. If I didn't keep going I would have to think about the fact that Anton—*Uncle* Anton— the talented, gossipy old artist, might never again bug me about my love life in his funny Polish accent. "Now, will you open the damned van or do I get a new business partner?"

Michael hesitated for a moment longer before trotting back down the street to my truck. He scrounged in back of the seat for a minute, returning to the van with a couple long strips of thin metal.

"Act as lookout," he said. I kept an eye on the bored cop guarding Anton's gate as he chatted on his cell phone, oblivious to the breaking-and-entering a hundred yards away. Michael slid a metal strip between the driver's door and the weather stripping and yanked up, popping the lock mechanism. It had taken at least three seconds.

"After you." Michael gestured.

"On second thought, let's drive around the corner so we can search it in peace."

"No keys, love."

"So hotwire it."

"You want me to *hotwire* it?"

"You expect me to believe you don't know how to hotwire a car?"

"I know how to hotwire a damned car," Michael bit off, casting a glance back toward the marked police presence half a block down. He climbed into the driver's seat and started kicking at a panel under the dashboard. Leaning down, he fiddled with wires, working by touch while keeping his eyes fixed on me. "In case you're wondering, I'm imagining what my poor parole officer will say when I'm busted for Grand Theft Auto."

"I know exactly what he'll say," I replied. "'Practice your breathing.'"

Breathing was a big part of Doug-the-parole-officer's philosophy of How to Fix the World and Find One's Place in It. He had explained it all to me over a vegan meal of flaxseed, tofu, and shredded carrots in a raspberry-melon vinaigrette at the Gratitude Café in Berkeley. The meal was memorable mostly because I grew weary of chewing long before my hunger was sated, which I imagine would be an excellent dieting technique. According to Doug, the secret to inner peace was to breathe with intent, inhaling anger and exhaling compassion. Or maybe it was the other way around. I got it mixed up.

At the moment I was both inhaling *and* exhaling anger and misery, with nary a hint of compassion.

The old van coughed to life, and I ran around to the passenger's side. Michael executed a twelve-point U-turn on the narrow, choked lane, took a right on Twenty-third, a quiet residential street, and maneuvered into a tight spot in front of a fire hydrant. I climbed in back and started poking around the cargo area in the dim light from the front and rear windows.

"Find anything?" Michael asked.

"Not yet. So far it's pretty much like his studio. Just, you know, without the easels."

One thing seemed out of place: I picked up a pack of sparklers stapled to a fireworks catalog.

"Does this seem strange to you?" I asked, handing him the fireworks.

"Why? Do you think I'm not a patriot?"

"I never actually thought about it."

"Hey, I'm as American as...the next American. I'm a *big* fan of John Philip Sousa."

"Why would Anton want fireworks? Fireworks are illegal around here, aren't they? Too great a fire risk."

"I'm fairly certain Anton would not be deterred by something as minor as fireworks being illegal," said Michael. "Wait a second. There's something written on the catalog."

I looked over his shoulder. Sure enough, Anton had scribbled a phone number and "Chan—Cameron House, two o'clock."

"What's Cameron House?" I asked.

"Beats me. Let's keep looking."

I leaned against the side of the van and picked up a brown grocery bag stuffed with papers, fearing it was only trash Anton had intended to toss in a recycling bin. Old ATM receipts, junk mail, a Publisher's Clearinghouse Sweepstakes entry, take-out menus for pizza restaurants—and a newsletter from Cameron House.

I handed it to Michael. "Look at this."

The front page of the newsletter featured a black-and-white photograph of Anton surrounded by a dozen kids, everyone grinning happily. The accompanying article was a laudatory piece describing how Anton Woznikowicz, "an internationally famous artist and CH benefactor" had restored a mural in the Cameron House entryway.

A siren blared, and we jumped. "I'll check it out," Michael said.

While he scoped out the scene, I pawed through the rest of the junk. Plastic milk crates held cans of turpentine and kerosene; sealed bottles of different kinds of oils; boxes of powdered pigments; brushes of various sizes and shapes; more boxes of artists' crayons and charcoal, pencils and chalk; a cloth bag of clean rags—the usual effluvia every working artist carts around. Nothing distinctive or suspicious about any of it.

I crawled to the front and slipped into the driver's seat. If I were an elderly Polish art forger who drove a piece-of-crap van any half-wit could break into, where would I put something valuable? In the molded plastic well between the front seats were some crumpled papers, including a coupon for five dollars off an oil change, two Golden Gate Bridge toll receipts dated several months ago, and a piece of heavy sketch paper on which was written "Victor" and a hand-drawn map to an address in Sausalito. Another piece of paper had a sketch of a brick-lined tunnel labeled "tunnel vision." On yet another scrap he had written "Fleming-Union" and a time, and jotted down a reference to Balthazar O.

A fresh wave of tears stung my eyes. Anton had never mastered the finer points of the criminal life, such as not writing down incriminating information. Dear, silly old man. If he weren't already in Intensive Care I would be tempted to send him there myself for doing whatever he had done this time.

"Anything?" Michael asked through the window.

"Some notes," I said.

"Isn't it possible this was an accident, Annie? I thought lots of artists suffered from toxin poisoning. Didn't van Gogh manage to poison himself with paint?"

I sat back, and tried to dredge up one of Anton's many lectures about the toxic potential of paint. I could practically hear the talented forger pontificating about one of his favorite topics:

"The history of paint is the history of poison, Annie. Lead, mercury, chromium, cadmium, manganese...and Emerald Green, such a lovely hue, is only achieved because of the arsenic in the pigment. The genuine shade was outlawed years ago, which is why a clever painter must mix it himself, of course! No modern green can compare to True Emerald. You know, Annie, art is but a metaphor for life: a little poison, judiciously applied, makes all the difference."

Interestingly, Emerald Green was one of Gauguin's favorite paint colors.

"Daily exposure can mess with your system, true, but that's over the long run," I said. "When I was a kid in Paris Anton insisted I wear latex gloves anytime we worked with dangerous pigments."

"Somehow I doubt Anton took his own advice. He was always covered in paint."

I nodded. Artists hate protective gear. Feeling the paint is part of the joy.

"The thing is," I said, "Anton was poisoned by arsenic *gas*. Arsenic green could be the culprit, but not only is it banned in the U.S., as far as I know it comes in the form of a powdered pigment, a solid. Why would he turn it into gas? It doesn't make sense." I wished I had paid more attention to Anton's lectures.

I needed to talk to someone who understood the chemistry of paint.

What had Anton said last night? Several years ago, he forged a copy of the original Gauguin painting for an F-U member. The forgery was supposed to have been kept private but for some reason was brought to Mayfair's Auction House. I was working from the assumption that Anton painted the forgery for Victor Yeltsin, the fellow who reported the Gauguin stolen and reaped a huge insurance windfall, which was why Jarrah Preston was investigating. Had someone tried to kill Anton to prevent him from admitting to the forgery?

That didn't make much sense. First, copying an artwork is not a crime in itself. Anyone who tries to pass that artwork off as genuine, however, is guilty of fraud. Forgers aren't normally a threat to their co-conspirators because not only are they also implicated in the crime but unless the forgery can be proved—which, when it comes to fine art and other original masterpieces, is much harder to do than most people realized—the law can't touch them.

Unless...a forger decided to indulge in a spot of blackmail. But successful blackmail required a degree of cunning and ruthlessness that Anton simply did not have. Anton was a criminal, to be sure, but he did not have a violent bone in his body. On the other hand, he was always talking about one last big score. Or could he have been working on a second Gauguin forgery? It wouldn't be the first time there were multiple Anton forgeries floating around. Could that be why he had arsenic-laden pigment in his studio? But why would he have needed another fake?

As much as I hated to admit it, this really *was* a job for the police. Michael was right; I needed to tell Annette Crawford the little I knew about Anton's possible connections with the F-U, and a copied Gauguin that had recently turned up at auction.

We returned to Anton's where, at my insistence, Annette broke away from her duties for a few minutes and listened to my vague suspicions and half-baked theories. The one time I decide to do the sane, legal thing and spill my guts to the officials, and all Annette had to say was: "I'll nose around, but chances are that it was just an accident. You're so close to it it's hard for you to see."

She also mentioned, again, that she needed to call Michael and me down to the station in the near future to discuss further "developments" in the Fleming-Union case. Oh goodie.

After that less-than-satisfying interaction with the police, Michael drove us back to the DeBenton studio building. Suddenly the X-man had become Mr. Law-and-Order, an obedient citizen arguing for allowing the wheels of justice to turn, telling me to let the SFPD handle it.

"I just gave the police all the information, didn't I?" I asked. *A fat lot of good that would do Anton,* I thought.

"Are you saying you'll let it drop?" Michael pushed me. "And the Preston case is on the back burner until we figure out how Anton's connected to that."

"I thought you knew that Anton was involved..."

"In what?"

"You let it slip that Anton was involved with the Fleming-Union. Remember?"

"That was something entirely different," Michael said.

"Like what?"

"A while back, Anton was doing some restoration work on an old mural in their wine cellar, and he happened upon something."

"What?"

"I don't know the particulars. You know how closed-mouth Anton could be. He thought he had discovered something relevant to the past.... He was asking the F-U for money for some community group."

"Do you know what group?"

He shook his head.

"Anyway," I said, "I just want to look up some of these names I found in Anton's van. Maybe one of them will shed some light on all of this."

"Look up some names, like 'Victor in Sausalito'? Didn't I hear you tell Annette that the man who filed for the insurance money was named Victor? And where did he live again?" He drove into the DeBenton building parking lot and pulled in next to Frank's shiny Jaguar. We were still arguing as we climbed out. "I'm serious, Annie. Leave this to the authorities this time. Just drop it."

"You are such a hypocrite," I said.

"Pardon me if I'm not looking forward to a repeat of last time."

Frank strolled out of his office, looking amused, hands thrust deep in the pockets of his gray wool trousers. "Everything okay out here?"

Michael glared at him, then at me, before stomping up the stairs.

"Lover's quarrel?" Frank asked with a ghost of a smile.

I burst into tears.

Dear Monsieur: Our school board cut the arts program in the elementary schools while increasing the budget for the sports programs. How can I make them change their minds?

Dear Madame: I regret to say that anyone who places a higher value on an inflated pig's bladder than on the spark of divinity within each of us, which is the very essence of art and beauty, is beyond redemption. It was for such as they that Dr. Joseph Guillotin invented Madame la Guillotine.

—Georges LeFleur, "Craquelure"

FRANK LOOKED SO appalled I almost started to laugh. But I was still sniffling when he wrapped his arm around my shoulders, gently led me through the door of his office, and sat me down in the leather chair he kept for visitors. He hitched a hip up onto the side of his desk, handed me a tissue, and looked down at me with a slight frown of concentration, as though trying to decide what to say.

"Annie, I'm not trying to tell you what to do"—that was news to me—"but I'm speaking as your friend. He's not good for you. It's as simple as that."

I sniffed loudly and looked up at him. "What do you mean?"

"Look at your life, at everything you've accomplished. He's part of your past, Annie, not your future. It's time you walked away. Just turn your back on him and everything he represents, and walk away."

"I can't do that. Not now, when he needs me most."

"You have to. You owe it to yourself."

"I can't just abandon him."

"He's gotten along without you all these years, hasn't he?"

"I don't care what legal troubles he's in. I still love him."

Frank let out an audible sigh. "All right then. I guess *I'm* the one who needs to walk away. Once and for all."

"Wait..." I saw muscles working as Frank clenched his jaw. He was furious. "Who are you talking about?"

"Michael."

"Michael?"

Frank spoke slowly, as if I'd lost my mind. "He's wrong for you. He can't give you—"

"You think I'm crying over *Michael*?" I croaked.

"I—"

"It's my Uncle *Anton.* He was found..." My voice wavered. "Hurt. Poisoned. He's been hospitalized."

"Anton Woznikowicz? I'm so sorry, Annie, I didn't realize—"

I stood and rested my head on his chest. He smelled of soap and a subtle male musk: pure Frank. Strong arms wrapped around me, one hand stroking my back slowly, and I let myself sink into him. It felt good. Really good. Safe. What would it be like to live in Frank's world, I wondered, a world where people you cared about never died under mysterious arsine-gas circumstances?

"I have to find out what happened," I said, sniffling. "Someone tried to kill him, Frank. I'm sure of it."

"This is a job for the police, Annie." Frank's voice was quiet and oh-so-reasonable.

"I realize that. I gave all the information I have to Inspector Crawford, remember her?"

"Then..."

"She says she'll look into it, but she still thinks it was an accident. But I think this might have something to do with the case I mentioned—"

"The case with Odibajian?"

I nodded.

"You have got to be kidding." His voice started to rise. "What did I tell you about him, not twenty-four hours ago? Why can't you leave things well enough alone?"

So much for soothing my worried brow. I pulled away from him. The good news was that I no longer felt like crying. The bad news was, it didn't look as though I would have much help in my quest.

"I'm an investigator now, remember?"

"You're *not* an investigator. Investigators need to be licensed, not to mention trained."

"That's only if they carry guns—"

"It is *not* only if they carry guns. You and your buddy-the-thief are supposed to be operating a simple Internet sting operation through an anonymous website, and the whole thing is meant to be overseen by the FBI to avoid precisely this sort of insane behavior. What is *wrong* with the two of you?"

"You weren't so picky when you hired me to find your stupid statue."

"That was a simple inquiry. I expected you to talk with some of your underground friends, not to go after shady billionaires with personal armies at their disposal."

"For your information, Michael's on your side about this one," I said over my shoulder as I headed for the door. "And as far as I'm concerned, you can both go to hell."

Fuming, I hopped in my truck and took off. I exhaled anger until I felt lightheaded and was forced to inhale a little compassion lest I keel over while driving.

Get a grip, Annie. Focus.

First stop: Mayfield's Auction House.

One of the reasons I had been a stand-out art forger while still in my early teens is because of my rare, some might say bizarre, ability to tell a faked work of art from the Real McCoy. I'm sure there must be some kind of intellectual process at work, but all I know is that when I stare at a piece of art an impression pops into my mind without conscious thought or effort. It isn't supposed to work that way; the determination of originality usually involves scientific tests for correct dating of materials, debates over proper brushwork and artistic technique, tedious research into the work's provenance, or paper trail, and a healthy portion of educated guesswork. I have no quarrel with scientific methods and esoteric debates, or even with educated guesses. But I don't guess. I know. Over the years a variety of skeptical artists, dealers, and experts have tried to prove me wrong. They failed.

Which is why I knew the instant I laid eyes on it that the Gauguin painting Elijah Odibajian had brought to Mayfield's Auction House was a fake, and that Anton was the forger. I didn't recognize every art forger's signature, but I had trained with the funny old Pole and knew what to look for: tell-tale brushstrokes, methods of shadowing, and an indefinable artistic "signature" that I would recognize anywhere.

Did you leave me any secrets, Anton? Holding the painting in my white-gloved hands made me feel close to him. If only a picture really were worth a thousand words, I thought, I would have a few choice questions to ask it.

The folks at Mayfield's weren't able to tell me any more than I already knew: Elijah Odibajian enlisted the auction house to sell the painting. The provenance papers appeared to be in order, but when they checked the Art Loss Register they found the painting listed as stolen. As required by law, Mayfield's notified Augusta Confederated, which now owned the painting since they had reimbursed the original owner for his loss. Elijah had dropped out of sight, and the auction house was now trying to keep the incident under wraps. Great forgeries have an undeniable cachet among the general public but don't do much for an auction house's reputation.

I left Mayfield's, wondering what my next step should be. I needed to tell Grandfather the news about Anton but he rarely answered his cell phone—he was convinced Interpol had tapped it—and, since he was somewhere in North Africa at the moment, e-mail was my only option. My computer was back at the office but so was Michael, and I was in no mood to deal with him. I drove to an Internet café in North Beach, ordered a double cappuccino and a chocolate croissant, and settled in at a table looking out onto Columbus Avenue.

I logged on to the free e-mail account I used on those occasions when I wanted to reach out and touch someone but didn't want that touch to be traced back to me. I got as far as *Très cher Grand-père* and stalled. How did I soften the blow of his learning an old friend had been assaulted and left for dead? I felt tears well up, gritted my teeth, and kept typing. I had to tell Georges before he heard it from someone else. The art underworld is one big gossip mill, surprisingly small and intimate, where everybody who matters knows everybody else who matters.

Still, even the forgery world changes over time. In the last decade or so, since international drug dealers and gun runners had gotten into the game, art crime had become more dangerous. The older generation of forgers and thieves despised the brutality of the new players, and liked to gather in out-of-the-way places and wax nostalgic about the good old days, when forger, thief, and buyer all knew each other and hardly anyone ever got killed.

...let you know the moment I learn anything new. Please, please be careful! You are not impervious to harm, you know. Je t'aime et je t'embrasse, A.

I hit SEND. My filial duty was done, and I felt like crap. Might as well ruin the day completely, I thought, and Googled "arsenic poisoning."

Arsenic, it turns out, is a naturally occurring mineral that converts to a gas when exposed to hydrogen. Arsine gas is colorless, though it sometimes smells like garlic or fish, and is often hard to detect because it is not immediately irritating. But it is intensely toxic. The gas is heavier than air, which means it sinks, and those lowest to the ground—children, pets, or anyone on a low bed or chair—are at greatest risk. The most common source of arsine gas is metal manufacturing, but art restorers can be exposed if they unknowingly apply solvents containing hydroxide to paints containing arsenic, such as True Emerald or Paris Green pigment. Sometimes simple mildew can be the culprit, acting upon the arsenic in paint pigments to release arsine gas.

Once released, the gas is inhaled and enters the bloodstream through the lungs. In acute cases arsine poisoning leads immediately to nausea, difficulty breathing, and abdominal cramps followed within hours by fatigue, loss of consciousness, liver damage, red blood cell damage, renal failure...and death.

I stopped reading.

The high-pitched wail of steam foaming milk for cappuccinos brought me back to reality. I hadn't touched the croissant; chocolate relieves frustration but is powerless against grief. Even the coffee tasted sour. The only thing that would help right now was to move forward. I took a deep breath, pulled my notebook from my backpack, and started another list.

1. *Get into F-U and talk to Balthazar Odibajian*
2. *Find "Chan" at Cameron House. Ask about fireworks?*
3. *Talk to Victor Yeltsin re: stolen Gauguin and Jarrah Preston*

4. *Forge my own damn Gauguin, sell it to the highest bidder, and*
   sail into the sunset with Michael and/or Frank bound and
   stuffed into the cargo hold for my amusement

"Have you ever heard of Cameron House?" I asked the young man in a striped polyester shirt from the 1970s who was busing the table next to mine.

"Sure. It's that big brick place in Chinatown," he said. "I forget which street. It's Presbyterian, I think."

"It's a church?"

"More like a community center or a mission or something. But there's some sort of religious connection."

"Thanks."

He nodded at my untouched plate. "If you don't like the croissant I can get you something else. Skinny thing like you needs to eat."

"Just out of curiosity, will you marry me?"

He grinned. "Sorry. I bat for the other team."

"Just my luck." I returned his smile.

I picked at my croissant while I called Pedro. "Do you have a home address for Elijah Odibajian?"

"Top o' the mornin' to you, lassie."

"You're not Irish and it's not morning."

"Whatever." I heard rapid-fire clicking sounds. If computer keyboards were souped-up cars, Pedro would be a NASCAR champ. "His official address was up on Pacific Heights, but it looks like he was most recently residing at the Fleming Mansion on Nob Hill."

"That can't be right. The F-U's a club, not an apartment building."

"It's not unusual for men's clubs. They rent rooms to members and special guests."

"According to the newspaper, Balthazar and Elijah are at each others' throats. Why would Elijah rent a room at his brother's social club?"

"The ways of the wealthy are mysterious, Grasshopper. What can I say? Looks like Elijah put his Pacific Heights condo up for sale recently, and he listed the F-U on the change-of-address form he filed with the post office. You're not planning to drop in on him, are you?"

"Nope." I was planning to drop in on Balthazar.

"Want the rest of the info you asked about earlier?"

"I'll call you back," I said.

The clock behind the counter said 1 P.M. Long past my lunch hour, but just right for the beautiful people. Would the F-U's kitchen have opened so soon after yesterday's tragic discovery? Was the bedroom still considered a crime scene? Annette Crawford said she would let me know when I could return to work but she hadn't mentioned anything when I saw her at Anton's....

One way to find out.

The Fleming-Union's parking lot was quiet. The police cruisers were gone, replaced by newly washed luxury cars. Feigning nonchalance, I marched up to the rear servants' entrance, said hi to the blond parking lot attendant, and tried to sign in, as I had for the past several days as I worked on the attic wallpaper project. Just another day in the life of a faux finisher, no matter than I was wearing a skirt and a silk top.

Blondie snatched the clipboard from me. "You can't go in."

"Sure I can. Remember me? Annie Kincaid? I'm working upstairs, in the attic."

"Not now, you're not. Not after..." Blondie's voice dropped and he leaned in toward me, as though we were sharing a secret. "Not after yesterday."

"Is it still an active crime scene?"

He shrugged.

"Then why can't I get back to work? I won't go anywhere near..." I dropped my voice, too. It just seemed right "...where we found him."

"Did the cops talk to you?" Blondie's eyes darted around and he shifted his weight from foot to foot. "They were looking for you."

"Yes, I spoke with Inspector Crawford. Several times, in fact. But now I have to finish the job. Are any of the...er...brethren around to talk to about that?"

"No," he said, his gaze turning up to the surrounding buildings. "They're not here."

"There are a lot of cars in the parking lot."

"Well, there's some but not the ones you need to talk to."

"Not to be rude, but how can you be so sure?"

"Thing is," he licked his lips, "I don't think they want you to come back."

"They don't want me to finish the job?"

He shook his head.

"Why not?"

"On account o' maybe you took the paintings."

"What paintings?" My mind flashed on the cheesy Western art and European hunting scenes that peppered the walls of the mansion. "I didn't take any paintings."

He shrugged. "Maybe you did, maybe you didn't."

"Listen, I could probably clear this up right now. Is Geoffrey McAdams here? He hired me."

"Maybe he is, maybe he isn't."

Blondie was really starting to annoy me. "What about Balthazar Odibajian?"

His blue eyes flashed. "Don't you go botherin' Mr. Odibajian!"

"So he is here, then?"

The attendant looked aghast at being outfoxed. He stomped over to his wooden kiosk, closed and locked the door, plugged into his iPod, and tuned me out.

Now what? Searching for inspiration, I spied yesterday's informants, Harvard and Jumpsuit, sitting on a park bench across the street.

"Hey there," I greeted them as I approached. "How's it going?"

"Beautiful day," Harvard said.

"Beautiful," echoed Jumpsuit softly.

"Either of you happen to know if the cops are gone for good across the street?"

"Dunno," Harvard said.

"Nope," Jumpsuit replied.

"So I don't suppose you'd know if they're open for business as usual?"

They both shrugged.

I sighed. It was a long shot anyway.

"Hey," said Harvard. "'Member how you was askin' 'bout if I seen anythin' unusual at the F-U the other day?"

I nodded.

"You see that lady over there? She walks her dog hereabouts a lot, so's I seen her."

"The woman with the full-sized poodle?" She was the one I saw talking with Michael yesterday. Same dog trimmed to within an inch of its life, same fuchsia scarf.

"Yup. She's the woman I seen go in the club."

"Okay, thanks a lot."

I sidled up to her. The woman had pretty blue eyes that crinkled up endearingly when she smiled, which she did almost constantly. She was not tall, only reaching my shoulder, but completely outclassed me in the va-va-va-voom department, sporting a pair of torpedo-shaped breasts that had either been surgically enhanced or bore witness to her ability to defy gravity. I estimated she was in her late forties, possibly older. It was hard to tell because her face had the oddly flat quality of an expensive facelift. Her hair was beautifully colored and cut, and her makeup was subtle yet striking. Large diamond studs adorned her pierced ears, and she played with a sparkling diamond tennis bracelet on one wrist. She reeked of disposable income.

"Beautiful dog," I said, putting my hand out to the animal to let it sniff, then stroking it under the chin.

"Isn't she just? And so *smart*!"

"I've heard that about poodles," I said. "What's her name?"

"Cuddles." She chuckled. "I didn't name her; she's a rescue and came prenamed. I probably would have chosen something outlandish, like Princess Napoleon Biscuit-Bottom or some such nonsense, so it's just as well!"

"Could you tell me, do you know anything about the Fleming-Union?"

She leaned toward me and whispered, as though offering late-breaking news. "It's a *very* exclusive place."

"Is that right. Are you a member?"

She laughed. "Well... I'm not supposed to tell anyone, but yes, my husband's a member."

She wasn't exactly a tough nut to crack.

"Is he on the retreat?"

"Yes, but it was cut short unexpectedly. How do you know so much about it?"

"I've been working there, doing some restoration. I'm a faux finisher."

"How exciting!"

One thing I had learned about the wealthy: they bore easily, and to keep themselves amused they renovate constantly. I had built a career on rich people's short attention spans.

"You're a faux finisher?" the woman asked. "This is wonderful! I've been meaning to have someone take a look at a project I've been thinking about. And here you are, out of the blue! It's fate, isn't it? Do you have a card?"

"I'm Annie Kincaid," I said, handing her a business card.

"Annie, it is just *lovely* to meet you. I'm Catrina Yeltsin. Call me Cathy."

"Nice to...meet you," I said, faltering as her name filtered into my brain. *Yeltsin?* "And your husband is...?"

"Victor Yeltsin. You don't happen to know him?"

"I may have seen him at the club, while I was working."

"Such a coincidence!" she gushed.

Wasn't it just? My mind raced. Did I dare ask her about the stolen Gauguin? I had meant to speak with the Yeltsins, but wasn't prepared and didn't want to blow it. Maybe it was better to follow up on her interest in hiring me as a faux finisher and figure out my next step later.

"And your husband's well?"

"Oh yes, he's in wonderful health! Aren't you a dear for asking."

Scratch Yeltsin's name from the list of possible dead blokes in the tub.

"It's *so* exciting, you working at the Fleming-Union," Cathy continued. "It's a beautiful place!"

"Yes, isn't it? The thing is, I have to complete the next step in the process. Faux finishing is a tricky business, you know, timing is everything, and that silly security guard won't let me in. I hate to impose, but can you think of any way I might get in?"

"Gosh, I wish I could help but even *I* can't go in!" she said with a huge smile. "I'm just waiting for my Victor to finish up a business lunch, then we're going home. Aren't we, Miss Cuddle-Cakes?"

The dog gazed up at Cathy adoringly.

"Aren't you allowed in sometimes?" I asked. "The other night...?"

Cathy was babbling high-pitched baby-talk to the dog and

didn't seem to hear my question. Either that, or she was ignoring it.

My attention was drawn by a pair of coverall-clad men arranging neon orange cones around an open manhole before descending, one by one, under the street. In a flash I had an idea for getting access to the F-U. One of my oldest and best clients divided his time between San Francisco and London, and paid me to keep an eye on things for him when he was out of town. One of my tasks was to schedule the annual testing and certification of something called a backflow prevention device. I had no idea what the device accomplished, but it didn't matter. When it came to bureaucracy and plumbing, nobody ever wanted to know the details.

"Cathy, it's been lovely chatting with you," I said. "Why don't you give me your name and number? I'll call and make an appointment to come look at your job."

Cathy waved gaily as I headed for my truck, which I'd parked out of sight on Powell. I flipped the seat forward and started riffling through the mountain of junk I kept there through sheer laziness. Sure enough, I found several things of use: worn khaki coveralls, a clipboard, a tube of hair goop, my tool belt, a pack of peppermint Trident, dusty work boots, registration forms from the local DVD store, and a black ballpoint pen with PROPERTY OF THE U.S. GOVERNMENT printed in gold. I stuffed everything into a canvas carryall, walked to the Fairmont Hotel, and made a beeline for their elegant, marble-lined women's room.

I knew exactly where it was; as the possessor of a tiny bladder I had long ago memorized the location of the rest rooms in all the nicer downtown hotels.

Ten minutes later I emerged a new woman: dressed in stained coveralls with my hair slicked down, braided, and wrapped around my head. I had scrubbed any vestiges of makeup from my face and removed my earrings. I looked plain, workmanlike. Utterly unmemorable. I tossed my nice clothes in the truck, slid the DVD store paperwork under the hinge of the clipboard, stuck the government's pen in my chest pocket, and cradled the clipboard in one arm. Now for the *pièce de résistance*: I crammed two pieces of gum in my mouth.

You're a cog in the wheel, I told myself. *Just another cog in the machinery.* I strode officiously up the Fleming Mansion's front steps, rang the bell, and commenced snapping my gum.

No answer. I peered in the side window, which opened into the office where a Diet Coke can still perched precariously on a stack of paperwork, just as it had yesterday when I met Wesley Fleming III. There was a man at the desk with his back to me, wearing a blue blazer that strained against his chubby shoulders. I banged on the window, held up the clipboard, and pointed sternly toward the door.

"Maintenance is in the back," he said through the closed window.

"Open the door," I insisted, ringing the bell again. I knocked for good measure.

At last the man came around to the front door and cracked it open a few inches, a radio crackling on his hip.

"Go round back," he said, and tried to close the door.

I put my boot-clad foot on the threshold.

"I gotta check your backflow prevention device."

"My what?"

"Backflow. Prevention. Device," I enunciated, eyebrows raised, my tone implying *duh.*

"Talk to Maintenance."

"Look, pal, this isn't brain surgery," I said as I put my shoulder to the door and shoved past him to step inside, speaking loudly. "Now I'm here it'll take, like, ten minutes. I just gotta do the annual check of the backflow prevention device."

A pair of well-dressed men descending the stairs glanced over at us, their expressions a combination of annoyance and contempt.

"I'm a card-carrying member of the American Backflow Prevention Association, the ABPA, if that's what's bothering you. Licensed and bonded, which is more than you can say about most people."

I waved the clipboard at him again, complete with the official-looking DVD rental agreement form. In my experience, a clipboard with paperwork is like a magic wand—people assume you're doing something official, and usually figure they don't want to be involved.

"Maintenance is in the back," he sputtered. "You'll have to go around and check in with them."

"All I know is, I gotta test the backflow device or your water gets cut off." I shrugged. "No skin off my nose, but I gotta lotta other people waitin' up to six weeks for my services." I flipped through the paperwork on the clipboard. "We scheduled this doo-hickey back on...yep, month and a half ago."

My cell phone rang. The readout said Annette Crawford. I pressed IGNORE.

"See there? My next customer. Listen, pal, you don't want me to come in, no problemo. I'll shut the water off at the meter and you can call to schedule to have it turned back on just as soon as you get your BPD tested. Shouldn't take more'n six, eight weeks. More if you run into a holiday." I turned to leave.

"Wait."

Gotcha.

He checked his watch. "You know exactly where to find this device?"

"Sure, I was here...lessee..." I made a show of flipping through the papers on the clipboard "...last September nineteenth. And the year before that, too. Gotta get recertified every year. They like to send the same folks out on account o' we know where to find the BPD. They're little buggers, but they're real important."

"Fine. Whatever. Just make it fast." He chugged back into his office, muttering into his radio.

I strode down the hallway as if I knew where I was going. The regal, oversized entryway was empty but for a few oil portraits of sour-looking old men, plush Oriental rugs, and the colossal staircase. I followed the muted sounds of silverware clinking against porcelain until I reached the dining room. Based on the hubbub it sure didn't seem like the members were in deep mourning for the man in the tub.

The dining room was a walnut-paneled extravaganza featuring a massive carved limestone fireplace in which a blaze roared despite the warm weather. Heavy brocade curtains and sheers dimmed the natural light. About half the linen-draped tables were occupied by well-dressed men, nearly identical with their close-cropped hair, starched white shirts, and plain business suits. I hoped none of them ever committed a crime in my presence because I'd never be able to pick one of them out of a lineup.

For several seconds everyone seemed so flummoxed by the sight of a woman—in coveralls, no less—that no one moved. I strode over to the man I recognized from the newspaper photograph: Balthazar Odibajian.

"Mr. Odibajian, I need to speak with you," I began. My confidence faltered when I realized his lunch companion, with his back to me, was none other than Frank DeBenton.

9

*During a lovely meal upon a terrace in Siena this eve-
ning, I pondered.... I have never trusted those who pur-
port to have a great love of art, yet profess no fondness
for the culinary arts. Palate and Palette—coincidence? I
think not.... Consider these indispensable items for the
chef, as well as for the forger: eggs, milk, bread, potatoes,
coffee, tea, olive oil, gelatin, flour...even the pastry board
and the kitchen stove.*

*On the other hand...as anyone who has ever dined
with a gallery owner will attest, there is still no such
thing as a free lunch.*

—Georges LeFleur, "Craquelure"

"AND WHO MIGHT you be?" Odibajian asked in a quiet voice as
he placed his fork and knife on the lip of his fine china plate as
his nanny must have taught him when he was a boy. Red juice
flowed freely from his steak, staining the roasted fingerling potatoes pink. His hazel eyes were cold and flat as they ran over my
outfit; his nostrils flared as though he were inspecting something
sticky and brown on the sole of his shoe. Authority and privilege
came off him in waves.

He lifted his chin, ever so subtly, and the muscled men who
had come up on either side of me backed off.

"I'm Annie Kincaid," I said, thrusting my hand out. He
looked, but did not shake. "Anton Woznikowicz is my uncle. Last
week your brother tried to hawk a fake Gauguin, painted—quite
legally I might add—by my uncle, and now Anton's been assaulted and left for dead. I don't think that was a coincidence."

"I don't understand your meaning, young lady. To what are
you referring? A fake?"

"An inspired fake."

"You're saying the Gauguin was a fake?"

I nodded.

"And now you're looking for my brother?"

"You'll do for the moment."

"Are you suggesting I had something to do with your uncle's misfortune?"

"I think it's a possibility."

Frank stood. "Annie—"

"You know the woman?" Odibajian asked Frank.

"She's my...tenant," Frank said. "Geoffrey hired her for the painting restoration upstairs. She's very upset about her uncle's accident."

"Of course," he said. His flat eyes held mine. "Family is so important, isn't it?"

Why did that sound like a threat? A chill ran through me. I realized why everyone warned me about him.

"Speaking of family, where *is* your brother?" I asked.

"In the morgue."

I gaped at him.

"The...morgue?"

"I believe you found him yesterday in one of the upstairs guestrooms. That was you, was it not?"

"Yes, it was. I didn't know he was your brother. I'm...so sorry. For your loss."

"And yet though you were by your own admission at the crime scene I have managed not to accuse you of playing a role in his murder. Perhaps you would be so kind as to show me the same consideration, especially since I've never met your poor uncle. I do, however, wish him a speedy return to good health."

His little speech sounded as sincere as that of a televangelist resigning from the pulpit after a video of him partying with prostitutes went viral on YouTube.

"What about the painting Elijah tried to sell? Did you have something to do with that?"

"I should say not. He spirited it away from the club's collection."

"The club's collection?" That was news. This whole talk wasn't exactly playing out the way I had imagined it. I was starting to feel sick to my stomach.

"It was donated to the club anonymously, years ago. The

provenance papers were in order. Suffice it to say that we had no way of knowing it was stolen when we accepted it."

"But it was stolen from one of the club *members*. How is it he never mentioned it?"

"Perhaps he never visited the gallery. Such a shame. Art is a gift to us all."

The half smile on Odibajian's face suggested he was toying with me.

"There's an international database of stolen and missing art. It's as simple as pie to check."

"And I will personally suggest to the board that we make it a policy to do so in the future. Ours is a small, intimate art collection. I'm afraid we're rather informal, not really up on the most current trends in art curation."

"I'd be happy to curate it for you."

He let out a loud bark of laughter. Everyone in the room seemed shocked at the sound.

"She is priceless, this one." The smile fell from his face and he gestured to the men hovering by my side.

One man grabbed me by each arm. My clipboard clattered to the floor.

Startled, I tried to pull away but I didn't stand a chance. They started dragging me toward the door.

"Hey," Frank protested, his chair screeching loudly as he jumped up. "There's no call for that. I'll escort her out."

While my captors looked to Odibajian, I decided not to wait and stomped heavily on one man's foot. He grunted and wrapped an arm around my neck in a choke hold. I reached for my secret weapon—a travel-size can of hairspray, as effective as Mace if used properly—and tried to aim the nozzle at his eyes but before I could fire off the first spritz Frank punched him in the nose, the other goon grabbed Frank, and two more oversized men joined the fray. One snatched the Lady Clairol from me but not before I smacked him in the face with the can.

All in all, it wasn't much of a fight. Without my chemical weapon I was useless, and Frank could only do so much against four musclebound men.

"Take them out of here," Odibajian said with contempt. "I wish to return to my meal."

We were hustled out of the mansion and tossed onto the sidewalk like trash. I lay on my back for a few minutes, rubbing my neck and imagining the size and color of the bruise I would soon be sporting on the hip that had made first contact with the concrete. When I worked up enough courage to sneak a peek at Frank, his shoulders were shaking.

My heart sank. Had I reduced Frank to tears? I sat up for a better look. No, my straight-arrow landlord was laughing. I was speechless.

After a few minutes he lay back, tucked his hands under his head, crossed his ankles, and gazed up at the cheerful blue sky. "I don't suppose it ever occurs to you, Annie, to think before you act?"

"You told me I should drop in on him over lunch."

He chuckled. "And you took me quite literally."

"I wanted to talk with the man. I don't know why he had to make a federal case out of it. What are you doing here, anyway?"

"Interrogating him in what I imagine would have had a far more productive outcome had you not interrupted."

"I mean this in the nicest way possible, Frank," I said, "but the way you phrase things makes you sound pompous from time to time."

"Having been summarily ejected from one of the city's most prestigious social clubs and currently lying on a public sidewalk in a twelve-hundred-dollar suit, I postulate I may be overcompensating for a certain loss of dignity." He got to his feet and brushed some dust off his pants, held out a hand, and hoisted me up. "Where's your truck?"

"On Powell."

"I'll give you a lift."

We walked to his gleaming Jaguar. It was parked in a visitor's spot in the club's lot and looked like a poor relation in a sea of six-figure automobiles. I think of Frank as wealthy, but it's all relative, I suppose.

The blond parking attendant confronted us and swallowed hard. "Uh, yes sir, ma'am. I'm to tell you not to come back. Ever. Because of the stolen paintings."

"Sure, sport. Whatever you say." I sank into the Jaguar's

leather-scented cocoon. As Frank roared out of the parking lot I asked, "What paintings is he talking about?"

"No idea."

"I didn't know the F-U had an art gallery. Did *you* know the F-U had an art gallery?"

Frank's face went blank.

"Oh, wait, let me guess. You installed the gallery's alarm system, didn't you?"

"I told you I did some work there."

"If it's your security system, and you're the best, then how did the paintings get gone?"

"Well, let's see. Bypassing the system I installed would take a thief with considerable skill and expertise. Know anybody like that?"

I ignored his question. "Where is this gallery?"

"It's private."

"The whole club's private."

"I meant, I'm not telling you."

"What's in the collection?"

"A few minor Impressionists, a couple of so-so contemporary pieces that may or may not appreciate much. Considering the membership's resources it's nothing special. Kind of rinky-dink, actually, as private art collections go. The Gauguin was by far their best piece. Until it turned out to be a fake, that is."

"When did the alleged theft of the other paintings occur?" For some reason, I was channeling Inspector Crawford.

"Earlier today was the first I've heard of it. Either they don't know or they won't tell me. Now that you've gotten involved, of course, I'll probably be accused of aiding and abetting a theft from a gallery whose system I installed."

"Surely it isn't that bad? They can't prove you had anything to do with it, can they?"

"Unless I find who did, I imagine I'll be the fall guy. I vouched for an art forger who's in business with a convicted art thief. I doubt that will reflect well on me."

"Who cares what the F-U thinks? They're a bunch of creepy, misogynistic old men."

"I envy you sometimes, Annie," Frank said. "The world you live in, where you don't have to deal with anyone you don't like.

But then again, I knew what I was doing when I gave them your name, so I only have myself to blame."

"What were you talking to Balthazar Odibajian about?"

"You."

"What about me?"

"I was trying to do you a favor. Feeling him out. My approach is more—what's the word? Ah, yes—*subtle* than yours. And as usual, when I try to do you a favor I wind up paying a price."

"I really am sorry. I'll take your suit to be dry-cleaned."

He shrugged. "It's almost a badge of honor to have Odibajian as an enemy. At least he'll keep things interesting. It's you I'm worried about."

"Don't."

"Too late. Just do me a favor. Don't go home tonight. Change things up, stay around people for the next few days. I don't know what's going on but I'm going to find out. At the very least I'll get some information on the paintings they claim were stolen."

"You don't believe them?"

"I think it's interesting they didn't mention it earlier. I want to see if a report was filed with the police, much less the feds. If they didn't know the real provenance for the Gauguin, perhaps the rest of the paintings are questionable, as well. They might not want the cops prying around."

"Good point."

Frank pulled in behind my truck, and as I turned to open the door he rested a hand on my arm.

"Annie...I'm sorry about earlier in my office. You came to me for comfort, and I wound up yelling at you."

"It's okay. I have it on good authority that I can be annoying."

Our gazes held.

Suddenly I was acutely aware of what I was wearing, feared how I must look. I could feel my curls corkscrewing out from my otherwise slicked-back 'do, I was a little sweaty from the scuffle, and I didn't have a bit of makeup on. I was a fresh-faced, street-brawling grease monkey.

Frank, on the other hand, looked great. I loved his mussed-up look. I saw it so rarely.

"You drive me insane, you know that?" Frank spoke in a low, intense whisper.

"I—"

"Come here."

"What?"

"Come over here and kiss me."

So I did.

He was hungry, demanding. I matched his ardor and then some, melting into him, the pain and fear and frustration of the day's events dissipating in the face of desire. Finally I pulled away, clamping down on the impulse to crawl right into his lap.

I was startled by a face in my window.

It was Jumpsuit, giving me a thumbs-up, wearing his ski mask like a hat. I sketched a wave in return, and he and Harvard ambled on down the sidewalk.

"Friends of yours?" Frank asked, his arm still curled around me.

"Sort of. Informants, actually. They gave us a lead on your *Hermes*."

Frank raised his eyebrows. "That was fast."

"They said they tried to talk to the management at your club, but no one would speak with them."

We watched the men push their grocery cart past homes whose mailboxes were worth more than all the pair's worldly possessions.

"I'm sorry to hear that. Had I been there—"

"I know." Frank could be stuffy, but he was not a snob.

"Stay with me tonight," Frank said softly.

"For my protection or for...?"

He chuckled. "I know I'm a Type-A personality, but that is one area of my life I don't like to plan. Let's play it by ear, let nature take its course."

We fell silent. I don't know about Frank, but I was thinking about nature taking its course. That was followed up, almost immediately, by the horrifying knowledge that I hadn't shaved my legs in more than a *week* and that I was wearing my plain-Jane underwear, boring cotton briefs. Oh, and I didn't have a toothbrush or—

"We could have dinner," Frank said. "Make it a real evening."

"You mean a date?"

"What the hell, Annie, we've known each other for, what—two years? I say we throw caution to the wind."

"Whatever happened to your girlfriend?"

"Who?"

"Hildegard. Svenska? Something Swedish."

"Ingrid. And she's not my girlfriend."

"You're sure?"

He smiled. "Very. Tell you what: I'll even tell you all about Ingrid. I know you've been curious."

Hairy legs be damned. I could pick up a disposable razor, take a quick shower to freshen up and rinse out the hair goop, and be good to go. I was never one for primping. "What time?"

"How about now? We'll play hooky. That way I'll know you're safe."

"Oh... I, uh, have to do a couple of things first."

"Like what?"

"Talk. To...some people."

"Drop the *Hermes* case. It doesn't matter. Or better yet, just give me whatever you turned up and I'll hand it over to the police, help them with their own investigation."

"There are a few other things I need to follow up on...."

Frank's eyes narrowed. "You're going to keep at this Anton thing, aren't you? Even though he nearly died last night, Inspector Crawford's on the case, *and* you've thrown down the gauntlet to one of the most powerful men in Northern California?"

I avoided his eyes. What could I say? The man was right. As high as my blood was running, I couldn't stop thinking about Anton. I had to pursue this.

"Annie, I'm dead serious. You'll be lucky to survive the night if you go traipsing around accusing a man like Balthazar Odibajian." His voice dropped. "And what would I do without you to annoy me all day, every day?"

I leaned forward and kissed him again. For a long time. When I spoke, my voice was husky. "Thanks for worrying about me. I'll annoy you tomorrow. Promise."

And hopped out of the car.

———

My hormones were stuck in overdrive. Before getting into my truck I stopped in at a corner store and bought comfort chocolate: a Snickers bar and Reese's Peanut Butter Cups. What was my problem? Frank was smart and funny and a successful professional. My mother adored him. My sensible friends were fond of him. My looney-tunes friends thought he was a riot. He kissed like...well, like Frank. He made me tingle and my heart race. I was scared to say it, but the truth was, it was easy to picture a future with a man like Frank.

The problem was that this future included a lot of him telling me what to do—or more precisely, what *not* to do. Maybe I had lived on my own for so long that I didn't know how to negotiate with anyone. I like things on my terms. I'm not any good at taking orders; hell, I'm not very good at taking broad hints. So did that mean I was destined to wind up alone; a lonely, sad lonesome loner? Wouldn't I have to learn to spin if I were to become a spinster?

I devoured the Snickers and licked my fingers. A *rotund* spinster.

Then again, if I was happy with my life the way it was, why was I fretting?

One thing I knew for sure: I couldn't deal with Anton's assault *and* pursue a romantic relationship with my stud-muffin landlord at the same time. Best to concentrate. Forget Frank's kisses. All of them. Right.

I polished off the Reese's Peanut Butter Cups, because they were, after all, Reese's Peanut Butter Cups, grabbed the carryall from my truck, and headed back to the women's room at the Fairmont Hotel to change into my street clothes. The doorman saluted as I breezed past.

Next stop: Cameron House.

Leaving my truck in its precious parking space, I hiked to nearby Chinatown. Within the space of a few city blocks, Nob Hill's fine homes and apartment buildings give way to storefronts selling lumpy root vegetables, bunches of leafy greens, salt-dried shrimp and fish, myriad varieties of mushrooms—inelegantly advertised as "fungus"—and twisted, unfamiliar fruits that to all appearances had been cultivated on an alien planet. Commerce was alive and bustling in this part of town, and crowds thronged the sidewalks clutching bags of fresh produce or bakery boxes full of delicacies such as sesame balls or pork-filled buns called *char siu bao*. San Francisco's Chinatown is a perennial favorite for tourists but is also home to thousands of immigrants and their American-born descendants, and the community is vibrant with cultural variety. In some alleys off the main drags, one could imagine being in a foreign country altogether.

I wandered aimlessly for a few blocks, up one alley and down another, hoping to spot a sign for Cameron House. Chinatown wasn't that spread out; how hard could it be to find a big brick Presbyterian mission?

Harder than one might think, so I gave up and popped into one of the hundreds of souvenir shops that were jammed with mementos of San Francisco, disposable cameras, sets of embroidered silk pajamas, cheap plastic shoes, and carved jade chess sets. A woman behind the counter obligingly directed me up the hill to the corner of Sacramento and Joice.

The pediment was inscribed OCCIDENTAL BOARD PRESBYTERIAN MISSION HOUSE, but it was more familiarly known as Cameron House. It was an imposing, square brick structure in a city without many brick buildings because, as any California schoolchild can tell you, when you live in earthquake country, mortar is not your friend. Either Cameron House had held up remarkably well over the years or it had been built after the 1906 earthquake and fire that leveled most of the city's brick edifices. I took a moment to appreciate the beautiful masonry. At regular intervals the bricks were misshapen: twisted, bubbly, and blackened. Intrigued, I ran my fingers over one, slick and glass-like.

"Those are called clinker bricks," said a young woman coming down the front steps. She wore her glossy black hair in a loose knot at the back of her neck, and a bright quilted backpack was slung over one shoulder.

"They're different," I said. "How did they get this way?"

"When bricks are fired some will melt and twist, and are considered throwaways." She spoke with the breezy confidence of an experienced tour guide. "These bricks became clinkers because of the explosions and intense heat of the fire in the wake of the '06 quake. The firefighters dynamited the original Cameron House, and much of this section of Chinatown, to save the mansions on Nob Hill."

"It didn't work."

"No, it didn't. Kind of ironic, isn't it? Cameron House survived the natural disaster but not the city's elite."

"That's a depressing commentary."

"I sometimes wonder if the architect who rebuilt Cameron House used the clinker bricks because she liked the way they looked, or as a reminder of how they came to be that way."

"Who was the architect?"

"Julia Morgan."

Morgan was also architect of famous Hearst Castle, halfway down the California coast. She rebuilt the Fairmont Hotel after the fire, and the Chinatown YWCA a block away from here, as well as dozens of stunning Italianate Gothic Revival homes and buildings across the bay in Berkeley and Oakland. Not long ago I had done some restoration work in Oakland's historic Chapel of the Chimes, another Morgan masterpiece. The woman got around.

"Do you work here?" I asked.

"Used to. I practically grew up in this place, along with half of Chinatown." She held out her hand. "I'm Laurene Chan."

We shook. "Annie Kincaid. Actually, I was looking for someone by the name of Chan. I thought they might know my Uncle Anton."

There was no sign of recognition. She shook her head.

"Good luck." She smiled. "Chan's a common surname, the Chinese equivalent of Smith or Jones. I have about forty cousins named Chan in the neighborhood, and that's not counting all the Chans I'm not related to."

"Oh." This wasn't going to be as easy as I'd hoped.

"I even married a Chan, so technically I'm Laurene Chan Chan. Sounds like a dance from the Roaring Twenties, doesn't it?"

"It does," I said with a smile. "I'm trying to find someone who might have spoken to my uncle recently. He was...assaulted. Hospitalized."

"And you think someone named Chan did it?"

"Not at all. But he mentioned meeting with someone named Chan at Cameron House, and I was hoping he or she might be able to help me figure out who did hurt him."

She glanced at her watch. "Come on in, I'll introduce you.

My cousin Nicole is working today, maybe she was the one he met with."

We walked into a dark wood-paneled foyer in the spare, sturdy architectural style of the Arts and Crafts movement to which Julia Morgan belonged. A stairwell dominated the ample entry, beyond which a pair of pocket doors opened into a large hall with a small stage at one end. Surrounding the pocket doors was a beautiful mural depicting the history of the neighborhood and Cameron House.

Laurene poked her head into a small office near the foyer. "Hey Nic, this is Annie Kincaid. She's asking about a man named Anton."

"Anton Woznikowicz?" She said without hesitation, though I still had a hard time pronouncing his name. "He's not here today."

"He's in the hospital," Laurene put in.

"I'm so sorry!" Nicole said. "What happened? I just saw him the other day."

"When was that?"

"Thursday...Friday, maybe. He's been giving us some advice on preserving our mural. He's a sweetheart. The kids love him."

"That's all he's been doing here? Working with the kids on the mural?"

"Pretty much."

"Did he mention anything about fireworks?"

"We don't sell fireworks," Nicole said. "We offer services to the community. Not fireworks sales, which are illegal, by the way."

"I didn't mean to imply... It's just that I think he was looking to buy some."

"Why?"

"I don't know. When you saw Anton did he say anything, do anything unusual?"

She shook her head, pensive. "Not that I remember. He did ask for a tour of the place. I think he was interested in the tunnels."

10

*Today finds me in my adopted city (are you listening,
Interpol?) The city of my heart and dreams: Paris. Ah, is
there any splendor that compares? The cafés, the opera,
les musées...even the subterranean secrets. Except for
the smell, the arched brick sewers of Paris are among
the most beautiful passages in the world. And they have
proved most handy when outrunning Nazis...or Interpol,
for that matter.*

　　　　　　　　　　　　　—Georges LeFleur, "Craquelure"

"WHAT TUNNELS?"

"I'm afraid I have to run," Laurene said, heading for the door.
"I'm sorry about your uncle, Annie. I hope he's feeling better
soon. I'll leave you in Nic's capable hands."

Nicole waved good-bye and turned to me. "Let me guess: you
want to see the tunnels?"

"If it's not too much trouble."

"Nah, that's okay. One of the downsides of working in a historic building—people want to see it. Just don't be surprised if
I hit you up for a donation to the building fund. Let's start with
some history to get you up to speed, shall we?"

Nicole led me to a display case containing an exhibit of sepia-
toned photographs from the late 1800s and early 1900s. Groups
of young Chinese men, dressed in traditional clothing and with
long braids, paused in their labors to peer at the camera, unsmiling. Photo after photo illustrated the challenges facing the
immigrants.

"Anti-Asian sentiment was strong in the U.S., especially in
California, which drew most of the Asian immigrants in the nineteenth century. Conditions were brutal for the Chinese in San
Francisco in those days. The 1882 Chinese Exclusion Act ended
legal immigration from China, which meant married men could

not bring their wives and families over, nor were unmarried women permitted to immigrate. The result was an illegal trade in young women and girls. Their futures were bleak in China, but when they arrived here they were forced to work as prostitutes. Young girls were sold as domestic servants called *mui tsais*, though many were also forced into prostitution. Most survived no more than five years."

"That's appalling."

"Not everyone ignored what was happening. In 1895, Donaldina Cameron came to work as a sewing teacher at the Occidental Mission Home for Girls, as Cameron House was then known. A few years later she became the home's superintendent. When she learned where some girls were being held, she and a few strong men armed with axes would stage a raid in the middle of the night, grab the girls, and bring them to Cameron House."

"Wow."

"The girls called her *Lo Mo*, Beloved Mother. Occasionally the girls' 'owners' bribed the police to attempt a 'rescue.' The girls hid in the tunnels until Donaldina Cameron could persuade the police to leave."

"Do the tunnels still exist?"

"There's an entrance, but it's been sealed off. We store sports equipment there now. I can show you if you'd like."

We descended a set of narrow, steep stairs into a bright basement, where half a dozen elderly Chinese were sorting and packing groceries into paper bags and cardboard boxes.

"Community food bank," Nicole told me. "Pardon us."

Nicole led me across the basement to a set of cupboards, and opened the doors to reveal a collection of soccer balls, basketballs, baseball bats, orange cones, and lacrosse nets. Immediately in front of us was a wall of concrete, the side of the street. On each end was clean white wallboard.

"That's it?" I asked.

"Kind of a letdown, isn't it?" Nicole asked. "When the original building was imploded after the earthquake, the tunnel was sealed off. That's assuming it was actually a tunnel; I don't know if it linked up to anything. It may have been more like a secret room. Look here." She opened another cupboard and we peered inside. At the top, near the low ceiling, was a gap about a foot high and two feet wide. "Here's another entrance. I think it must have been bigger back in the day."

"Where does it lead?" I asked.

One of the elderly women spoke to Nicole in Chinese.

Nicole nodded. "She says it leads to a coal chute. Big enough for kids to hide in."

The elderly woman was gray-haired and stooped, but unless she'd discovered a miracle cure for aging she was nowhere near old enough to have had personal experience with the tunnel. The woman spoke some more, and Nicole answered my unasked question. "Her mother was hidden there."

"When was that?"

Nicole translated. "Nineteen-oh-four or -five, she thinks. Her mother was rescued from a brothel. She was twelve years old and had been working there for two years."

I was speechless. I returned the old woman's smile and nod, but couldn't stop wondering what must it have been like for a ten-year-old girl to be taken from her family and village in China, smuggled across the ocean, forced to work as a prostitute for two years, seized by strangers in the middle of the night, and hidden in a dark tunnel? I silently thanked the powers that be for my life of privilege and my somewhat insane but always loving family.

"If the girls had been smuggled into the country—no matter that it wasn't their choice—weren't they in legal limbo?" I asked.

"They were, and the slave traders counted on that. But they hadn't counted on Donaldina Cameron. She used her social status and connections to petition sympathetic judges for guardianship of the girls. When the building was about to be destroyed in the chaos after the earthquake, *Lo Mo* ran back into the mission to retrieve the guardianship papers. She wasn't about to risk losing her girls."

"What a remarkable woman."

I thought about Julia Morgan, another woman who had accomplished great things during a time when there were so many barriers to women's ambitions. I liked the idea of Cameron and Morgan working together to rebuild Cameron House to make sure vulnerable children were safe and cared for. I also finally had a response for that cocktail-party conversation starter: If you could go back in time, with whom would you like to have dinner?

"Shall we?" Nicole started back up the stairs.

"You mentioned there might be other tunnels?"

"There are rumors of tunnels criss-crossing Chinatown, though I don't know if it's ever been proven. All kinds of rumors swirl about this community. Like, the Chinese will shanghai you and sell you into slavery if you're not careful. That sort of thing. Goes with the mysterious Asian stereotypes. You know, like fireworks."

I looked chagrined, but Nicole just laughed.

"You think the tunnels are a myth, then."

"Really can't say. Tunnel systems from this era have been found in Red Bluff and Portland, but those cities aren't as earthquake-prone as San Francisco."

"Red Bluff?" I asked. The small Sacramento Valley town wasn't far from where I grew up, but it was just as isolated. Hard to imagine Chinese immigrants landing there at all, but even harder imagining them building tunnels there.

Nicole nodded. "I'm sure their local historical society could tell you about them. Chinese immigrants were found in most early California towns, working in the mining camps, railroad construction, all sorts of things."

"Why would they build tunnels?"

"Lots of reasons, I'm really not the expert. And like I said, I don't even really believe it. But my cousin Will insists he's seen evidence of tunnels, especially when they take down old buildings. And he sees a lot; he runs a street-sweeping truck on the graveyard shift."

"Do you think he'd talk to me?"

"Are you kidding? He'll talk your ear off if you give him a chance. Will's a volunteer at the Chinatown Historical Society on Clay. I think he's there this afternoon."

"Thanks."

Nicole hesitated. "Listen, you really think this might have something to do with your uncle?"

"Someone tried to poison him. He wrote the name 'Chan' on the front of a catalogue where he scribbled something about tunnels." I took the fireworks catalogue I'd found in Anton's van from my backpack and showed her. "I don't know if they're connected or if they were random thoughts, but something strange is going on, and for Anton's sake I want to know what it is."

"Tell you what. Why don't I call Will and see when he's done at the historical society? Maybe we could have dinner. You like food?"

"Food?"

"Sorry." Nicole smiled. "Stupid joke—you call it Chinese food, but we just call it food."

I laughed. "I love food, Chinese food in particular."

Nicole made a phone call and told me to meet her and Will for dinner at a restaurant on Washington Street in an hour and a half. I meandered over to busy Portsmouth Square and perched on a slatted bench, pondering my next move. Clusters of old men played games and gambled, pigeons scouted for scraps, and San Franciscans of every age and stripe hustled in and out of the underground parking garage.

I called Pedro. *"Hola. ¿Qué tal?"*

"Your accent sucks."

"You should hear me speak French."

"This Jarrah Preston guy you asked about? Looks legit. You know, this little assignment didn't exactly test my computer skills. Preston not only works for Augusta Confederated, he's on their website. Photo and everything. Kinda cute, in an offbeat sort of way. You interested?"

"Why is everyone so invested in my love life all of a sudden?" I snapped.

"Whoa, sorry. We just want our Annie to be happy."

"I apologize, Pedro. It's been a rough day." I told him about Anton, and the Fleming Mansion, and what I'd found at Cameron House. He listened carefully, as he always did, and made soothing "There, there" sounds.

"And Elijah Odibajian?" I asked, hoping for news. "Find out anything more about him?"

"Turns out the Brothers Odibajian parted on bad terms. After what they so charmingly refer to as their 'corporate divorce,' Elijah disappeared. Seems he had a gambling problem."

"Serious?"

"I'd say it was pretty serious: he burned through his personal fortune—no small feat—and may have been skimming from the business. I imagine that's why Balthazar split from him. There are rumors Elijah was on the hook to some unpleasant people, which is pretty scary when you think about the Odibajians' reputation. We're talkin' *Terminator 2*-type nasty."

Pedro is a huge Arnold Schwarzenegger fan. It is a testament to our friendship that we work around his obsession.

"But you probably have better sources than I for that sort of thing," he said.

"What do you mean?"

"You know. *Sources*. Of information."

"Isn't that what I have you for?"

"You're telling me you don't know any bookies, loan sharks, or well-groomed men with a taste for gaudy jewelry?"

"Pedro, I'm an *artist*, not a gun moll. Good heavens. I hang out with people like you."

"You're a *special* type of artist, if I'm not mistaken."

"Hey, I let my membership lapse in the International Brotherhood of Forgers and Fakers years ago."

"And speaking of which, you asked about hidden messages under paintings? Turns out it's not that strange. A lot of artists do that. Who knew? Including your Uncle Anton."

"Yeah, I got that last bit already, thanks. But nothing on the phrase per se?"

"Squat-comma-diddley. Just that it seems to be a take-off on 'Revenge is a dish best served cold.'"

"What about Victor Yeltsin, the owner of the original Gauguin? I met his wife. She seems nice enough."

"Judging by...?"

"She was sweet to her dog."

"Yeah? So was Hitler."

"I didn't know that."

"Sure—loved his German shepherd, Blondi."

"That's...really creepy."

"Tell me about it."

"Okay, so what's up with the Yeltsins?"

"Let's see... Yup, got it right here. Catrina and Victor Yeltsin, Sausalito. About five years ago, Yeltsin started making a whole lot of money. Before that, he was well off thanks to his wife;

she inherited a bundle from her grandmother, a heartwarming rags-to-riches story. Brewed up shampoo and creme rinse in her kitchen during the Great Depression, branched out into moisturizers and makeup after World War Two. Made a killing. After fifteen years of depression and war, America wanted to look pretty. Marrying Yeltsin was a step down for Catrina, fortune-wise."

"What happened five years ago?"

"Dunno, but he started making a whole lot of money round about the time he joined the Fleming-Union. That's typical though—those guys throw each other work, seats on corporate boards, that type of thing. The surprising thing is that he'd be allowed into the club, though. They're pretty darned exclusive."

"What kind of work does Yeltsin do?"

"Consulting."

"What does he consult about?"

"Dunno. His business is called Yeltsin Consulting, Inc. Has one of those flashy, elaborate websites that look great but offer almost nothing in actual information. It's privately held, so there are no SEC filings that I can get my hands on without hacking into the feds' system. And that's a line I won't cross."

"I wouldn't ask you to."

"I would. But that's not why. I know a few tricks for getting in and out of the system without being detected, but there are only so many times I can play that card. I'm saving it for something special."

"You're secretly the mastermind of an evil criminal empire, aren't you, Pedro?"

"Well, I don't like to brag...."

"Thank you for the scoop on Yeltsin."

"Wish I had more for you. Want me to look up Catrina Yeltsin?"

"Sure. Any info is helpful. Oh, and the other name in the file, a guy described as their 'houseboy,' Kyle Jones."

The moment I hung up the phone rang: Annette Crawford. I hesitated, then decided not to answer. Suppose she wanted to talk to me about the Fleming-Union's missing paintings? I *hated* being questioned by the police at any time, but especially when I was a) innocent and b) didn't have the slightest idea what was going on. What would I say to Annette? That my business partner, a "retired" art thief, had been missing for an entire week during which the paintings disappeared? That I was working for a New Zealand insurance investigator who had hired me because I had a tendency to look the other way where the law was concerned as long as no one got hurt? That, yet one more time, I seemed to be caught up in some sort of criminal conspiracy?

I blew out a breath, frustrated. *Annie Kincaid, Crime Magnet.* Was it something in my DNA? Had the line for the "Catch a Clue" gene been so long that my pre-embodied self had settled for the "Freakin' Clueless" gene instead?

Maybe I should *commit* a crime so that at least once in my life I would understand what was happening.

I looked up at the monument to Robert Louis Stevenson, who in 1879 and 1880 used to sit in this very square, depressed, writing poetry while waiting for his beloved Fanny to divorce her husband and marry him. Failing to find that particularly inspirational, I looked down at my list of *Things to Do. 2....'Ask about fireworks?'*

That sounded simple. I could do that. I was in the heart of Chinatown, after all. And no matter what the upstanding citizens over at the Cameron House thought about it, this neighborhood was the mother lode for illegal fireworks. Even clueless lasses like me knew *that.*

I went into the first retail store I saw that sold a wide variety of items and asked about fireworks, receiving nothing for my trouble but wary looks and suspicious glances. In the next store, I made up a story about wanting fireworks for my children. Still nothing.

Probably I should have left my coveralls on.

I needed someone with criminal savvy. Someone with the face of a heavenly angel and the heart of a fallen angel. Someone who could talk others into doing things they would otherwise never consider. Too bad I wasn't currently speaking to Michael, my usual Plan A.

My usual Plan B was to call Anton.

I didn't have a Plan C. I had never needed one. Anton had always been able to—

Wait.

I clawed through my backpack and found the business card.

"'allo?"

"Hello Mr., uh, Hippo. It's Annie Kincaid. Any update on my uncle?"

"No better, no worse. Which is good news of a sort. The physicians are calling it 'wait and see mode,' which seems to mean they don't know what's going on."

"I am wondering if I might ask you a favor."

"For Anton's niece? Name it, and if I can help I will."

"I need to get my hands on some fireworks. Do you know where I might buy some? Oh, and the name of anyone who deals in stolen art?"

Twenty minutes Hippo called me back with a couple of contacts and addresses, and told me to use his name as a calling card. I could get used to having friends in high places.

"Before you go, could I ask whether you knew Elijah Odibajian?" I asked.

"Why are you asking?" His voice sounded wary.

"I don't know if you heard, but he was found dead yesterday."

"Yes, I did hear that."

"Did you also hear that he had substantial gambling debts?"

I heard a long intake of breath. "Yes."

"I'm not asking for any details. I was just wondering whether he thought he'd be coming into some money to pay off those debts?"

"Yes, I believe he was going to sell an asset, and pay on the balance."

So, one lonely night in the mansion, Elijah had crept down those wide carpeted stairs, made his way to the club's art gallery, disabled the security system, and snatched the fake Gauguin? Then he snuck it out of the club and took it to Mayfield's for sale, figuring since he had the provenance papers, it was no problem? Could he have taken the other paintings as well?

"Okay, thanks so much for all the information."

"Of course. But Annie? Be very careful."

"Yes, I know, I'm dealing with some scary people."

"No, they're actually lovely people. But you can lose a finger handling those firecrackers. Or worse. One of my nephews... Well, you don't want to know. Let's just say his friends call him Lefty."

"He blew his hand off?" I asked, appalled.

"It wasn't his hand."

———

The first fireworks supplier's address Hippo had given me led to a nondescript door opening off an alley. I banged on the door for what seemed like an eternity until a young man answered. Thin and short, he was not the typical bouncer; I had probably outweighed him by my tenth birthday. Feeling like a bad actress in a low-budget movie, I told him Hippo had sent me, and was escorted into a retail area jammed with a dizzying array of brightly colored packages. The place reeked of rotten eggs and Pine-Sol. I fought the urge to hold my nose and approached an old man behind the glass counter.

"I think my uncle was here recently." I showed him the photograph from the Cameron House newsletter. "Looking for fireworks?"

He nodded.

"You helped him?"

He nodded again.

This was going to be easy. "When was that?"

He turned stiffly to consult a flowery pink-and-red calendar from Dragon Land Bakery, and pointed to a day two weeks ago.

"Did he say what he wanted the fireworks for?"

He shook his head.

"Did he say anything?"

He shook his head.

"Nothing at all...? All right, thanks."

The newspaper article on the Odibajian brothers slipped out of the file. He tapped the black-and-white photo of Balthazar and nodded.

"What, you saw him, too?"

The young man came out from the back.

"He understands some English, but he doesn't really speak."

"Oh. He tapped the photo as though he knew this man. Could you ask him about it for me?"

The young man came and looked at the grainy newspaper image of Balthazar, and the newsletter photo of Anton, then shrugged.

"All old white guys look the same."

"Oh. So you don't remember either of these men?"

Grudgingly, he looked at the photos again, and tapped Anton's. "Maybe this one. Seems like he came in, said he was a painter."

"Why did he want fireworks?"

"We got Emerald Green, Paris Green, and Scheele's green. Different names for pretty much the same thing. Any kind copper arsenite, copper acetoarsenite. You can use it as a pigment, mix it for paint colors. Gotta be careful, though, it's poison."

"Do you keep records of when you sold it, who you sold it to, maybe?"

"Yeah, right." He laughed and escorted me out.

11

Dear readers, I have been asked many times, isn't it illegal to copy a painting? I shall clarify:

1. *Creating a new Old Master is not, in itself, a crime.*
2. *Pretending that the painting is a genuine Old Master, and therefore selling it for much more than it would have been sold as a copy, is a crime according to Interpol and the FBI.*
3. *Creating fake certificates of authentification or otherwise falsifying a trail of provenance, is always a crime.*
4. *To deprive the world of my masterpieces, my versions of beautiful paintings...well, this would be the greatest crime of all.*

—Georges LeFleur, "Craquelure"

WILL AND NICOLE were cousins who squabbled like siblings.

"Order," she demanded.

"You order," Will replied.

"Don't argue with me, William. I know where your bodies are buried."

"You really want to launch a cycle of revenge that can only end in tragedy?"

Nicole rolled her eyes. "I speak Mandarin, Will, not Cantonese. Order."

"Right. You grew up in Chinatown with Cantonese parents but only speak Mandarin. We're not buying it, are we, Annie?" Will looked at me for support, but I was staying out of it.

"I learned at college," Nicole explained to me. "Cantonese and Mandarin are the same written language but not the same spoken language. I can communicate in Cantonese just fine as long as I'm writing."

"So write already," said Will. "I'm hungry."

142

I got the feeling I was witnessing a Chan Family Smackdown. My money was on Nicole.

She stared at her cousin and raised one eyebrow.

He finally snorted and rolled his eyes. "Fine, I'll do it. But only because I'm starving." Will flagged down a waiter who soon returned with several plates of noodles, rice, fried meats, and vegetables. The scrumptious-smelling dishes were placed on the lazy Susan in the middle of the large round table we shared with others.

The cavernous room was filled with men, women, and children and loud with the clatter of dishes and the sound of people speaking, presumably, in Cantonese.

"So," Will said as we started in on the varied delicacies, "Nicole says you want to know about the tunnels."

"Do you think they really exist?"

"I know they do. I've seen evidence of them when they take down buildings, that sort of thing. PG and E knows about them, too."

"The gas company?"

"They know what's under the streets. Infrastructure. Pretty important."

"So if everyone knows about these tunnels, why are they still considered a myth?"

"Fact is, there's all sorts of weird stuff goes on under our feet: pipes, wires, cables, sewers. Did you ever hear about them finding old, wrecked ships sometimes when they excavate new building sites? But these might not be tunnels the way most people think about them. There were two and a half miles of brick sewer tunnels under Chinatown alone, back in the day, before the quake. They were big enough to walk in, and discharged into the bay."

"What were the tunnels used for?"

"Besides the sewage and coal they were designed for? Anything you didn't want people to know about. Gambling, smoking opium, smuggling. Maybe just a place to get away from the whites. No offense."

"Racial violence was a fact of life in old Chinatown," Nicole said. "Every once in a while tensions would flare out of control and curfews were imposed on anyone of Asian heritage. When bubonic plague broke out at the turn of the twentieth century, Chinatown was put under strict curfew. They may have needed the tunnels to move around after sunset."

"Or to get away from their wives," Will teased.

"They wished. Most of the men didn't have wives. That was the whole point of bringing in girls for prostitution: the whites didn't want the Chinese to marry, settle down, and start families, so they didn't allow marriageable Asian women to enter the country. Then somebody started bringing in Chinese girls to work as house servants, claiming they were here under 'three-year service contracts,' though they were usually forced into prostitution or domestic slavery. The authorities looked the other way."

Will gave the lazy Susan a spin and said to me, "Try the chicken feet."

"She doesn't want chicken feet," Nicole objected. "Why would she want chicken feet?"

"They're good!"

"Ignore him, Annie," Nicole said. "Nobody's feelings will be hurt if you don't eat chicken feet."

One of my strengths as a social being was the ability to eat almost anything, so I tried the chicken feet.

"What do you think?" Will asked, impressed.

"They're kind of...gelatinous. They're okay, but keep slipping out of my chopsticks," I said, dabbing at a spot on my silk blouse left by a swan-diving chicken's foot. "I like the noodles better."

"Who doesn't?" Nicole said, nudging her cousin.

"Allow me to continue my fascinating historical lecture," Will said. "A lot of the so-called 'dens of iniquity' that so intrigued non-Chinese were actually connected basements that were built to follow the contours of Chinatown's steep hills. Tourists thought they were several floors beneath the surface when in reality they were in a cellar just below street level. Same thing with the speakeasies during Prohibition. The subterranean mystique was good for business. Customers loved the thrill."

"How about under Nob Hill?"

"What about it?"

"Are there tunnels under there, as well?"

The cousins exchanged a look.

"There are stories about that," said Will. "Supposedly there used to be. But I don't know if it's ever been confirmed."

"Your Uncle Anton mentioned he'd found out something about that," Nicole said. "He was going to ask the F-U for some grant money to restore the Cameron House mural and other decorative pieces we inherited over the years."

"He intended to ask the Fleming-Union for money?"

"It seems only right considering their history. I'm not one to blame the living for the sins of the dead, but in this case some kind of reparations seem in order."

"What did they do?"

"Domestic slavery. Worse, maybe. Donaldina Cameron was never able to make much progress with them; they had more pull than she did. It's rumored the folks on 'Snob Hill' had their own tunnels connecting the homes of the wealthy so they could trade girls back and forth without anyone knowing. All the other mansions were destroyed in the earthquake, but the F-U kept the tradition alive."

By the time we parted, the city lights were coming on, making San Francisco look like fairyland. Nicole and Will wished me luck in my search and I hiked the several city blocks, mostly uphill, back to my truck.

What Nicole hinted at about the history of the Fleming-Union seemed to confirm my worst prejudices about all-male, exclusive refuges of the super-wealthy. Michael was right, that sort of milieu twists people. On the other hand, I reminded myself that I had a tendency to jump to conclusions. After all, a lot of organizations had shocking histories. And this in no way proved that anyone connected to the F-U had set out to harm Anton.

My stomach lurched when I thought of my uncle. I kept half expecting a phone call from the hospital, saying Anton had awakened and told everyone what the heck's been going on; either that, or a phone call saying he would never be able to speak to us again.

The current situation was ironic, really. Had it not been for Anton's being poisoned I might well be with Frank at this very moment, developing that love life Anton was so keen on.

I needed a serious distraction.

Surely the police would have cleared out of Anton's studio by now?

While riffling through the cab of my truck earlier, I noticed a respirator with a pack of fresh cartridges stashed behind the seat. I couldn't tell whether it was rated for arsenic, but presuming Hazmat had done their job airing things out, it wouldn't be an issue.

The street outside of Anton's place was quiet, with no police presence in sight. I slipped in through the gate and across the courtyard, then up the rickety stairs to Anton's atelier built over a garage.

At the top landing outside his door, I cut the police tape, used my old key to his studio, took a deep breath, pulled on my respirator, and started snooping.

Like most artists, Anton was a messy guy. Still, despite the general jumble and the aftermath of the police investigation, the studio did not show signs of having been ransacked. So whoever attacked him had either found what they were looking for sitting out in the open, or they were simply trying to silence the old forger. Successfully, so far.

I noticed that Hazmat had cleared out all toxic substances, which is saying a lot in a traditional artist's studio. Turpentine, mineral spirits, linseed oil, and of course any arsenic green they might have found. Normally Anton's shelves were crowded with dusty glass jars and bottles filled with enough toxic liquids and powders to rival nearby former Hunter's Point Naval Shipyard as a Superfund site.

In one dim corner stood a mannequin draped with an embroidered velvet cape and wearing a jaunty felt hat decorated with a large ostrich feather, à la the Three Musketeers. Mismatched bookcases, window ledges, table tops, and all other horizontal surfaces were cluttered with dirty wineglasses, half-empty cups of tea, cigar butts, wrinkled sketches, stacks of reference books, outlandish Mardi Gras masks, sea shells, goose feathers, flower pods, and teetering stacks of art supply catalogs hawking everything from gold gilt to terrazzo.

It was much like my own studio, except that the balding Pole's fondness for unfiltered Gitanes cigarettes made this place smell like a cheap French tavern on New Year's Day. Still, for an art restorer that could be a plus. Just as it does with the human body, nicotine speeds the aging process of paintings. It is an old forger's trick to tint new canvases an age-appropriate brownish-yellow by pumping cigarette smoke into sealed chambers.

I spotted a stack of unframed canvases leaning against one wall and wandered over. Shoving aside an insipid nineteenth-century landscape, I flipped through the paintings, which ranged in style from French Rococo to American Expressionism. None was worth much. Anton had probably picked them up for a song at estate sales and flea markets with the idea of recycling the vintage linen canvases and the aged wood stretchers dotted with authentic wormholes. A forgery painted on top of one of these would be good enough to fool most art dealers and collectors, the majority of whom decide on a painting's authenticity after a cursory inspection by the naked eye. More reliable testing methods, such as chemical paint composition analysis and spectrometer X rays of the underpainting, are expensive and are reserved for the most valuable works of art. A clever artist can make a good living, and avoid a prison sentence, by painting forgeries that sell for thousands of dollars instead of millions.

But Anton had promised me he hadn't been involved in anything nefarious lately. Supposedly he had gone straight.

A man appeared in the doorway.

I jumped and let out a scream, blessedly muffled by the respirator.

Jarrah Preston. "Sorry 'bout that. Did I scare you?"

I took off the mask. "Just a little jumpy, I guess. Let's talk outside."

We descended the wooden stairs and sat on a sad-looking concrete bench surrounded by a couple of tomato plants and straggly bushes that looked suspiciously like pot.

"I'm so sorry about what happened to your uncle," Preston began. "I had no idea this Gauguin thing would stir up a viper's nest."

"So you don't think this was an accident?"

He shook his head. "Do you?"

I shook mine in response. "But we can't be sure it has anything to do with the forgery, can we?"

"It would be awfully coincidental, if not. I wonder if Elijah—"

"He's dead."

"Dead?"

"He was the body we found in the bathtub at the Fleming-Union."

He looked stunned. "You're saying both the man who painted the copy, and the one who brought in the forgery for sale, are dead?"

"Anton's still alive." My voice shook slightly.

"Yes, I know. I'm sorry. I meant to say that they were both assaulted."

"Hardly seems like an accident, does it?"

He shook his head. "But why would they be harmed? What could they be hiding? What possible motivation?"

"What made you stop by this morning, when you found Anton?"

"He called and left me a message last night, saying he wanted to speak with me. I didn't get the voicemail until this morning, and I came right over."

We sat in companionable silence for a long few minutes, both lost in thought.

"Where to now?" Jarrah asked. I heard frank sympathy in his voice.

I shrugged, at a complete loss.

"It's late," he added. "A good night's sleep works wonders."

"I'm not supposed to go home," I thought aloud. Frank's warning rang in my ears. He was probably overreacting...or maybe he had just said that in an attempt to seduce me. Nah. Frank was more upfront than that. Still, the thought of climbing three stories to a lonely apartment, the one that still carried the fragrance of saffron rice cooked by the little Pole currently lying prostrate in the San Francisco General ICU, was too much.

Jarrah raised his eyebrows in question.

"I had something of a run-in with Balthazar Odibajian earlier today."

"What kind of a run-in?"

"I sort of broke into the Fleming-Union and...kind of accused him of being involved in what happened to Anton."

He gave a silent whistle. "I warned you Odibajian was a bit of a dag. But you really think he's a physical threat?"

"Probably not. But I promised someone I would lay low for a couple of days, let things cool off. Just in case."

"I've a suite at the Palace."

"What are you, visiting royalty?"

He gave me a wicked grin. "Expense account."

"I want your job."

"Sure, it looks glamorous, but the reality is traveling first-class to fabulous places, meeting fascinating people, and in general living the high life. How much can one man take?"

"Do you think Augusta Confederated would hire me to take your place, once I've served my time for killing you?"

He gave me a crooked smile. "How about a bribe to let me live? I can offer dinner and an expensive bottle of wine, and you're welcome to sleep over. There's a pull-out sofa in the sitting room. Can't imagine Odibajian would be able to track you down there."

"Really?"

"It'll be my first American slumber party."

"A real slumber party includes pillow fights."

"If you insist," he said with a slight leer. "But only if we do it in our jammies."

I laughed. "I'm afraid at this point, I might fall asleep in the elevator on the way up."

"Then by all means, let's get you to bed. And don't worry, no funny stuff."

Jarrah was true to his word. We ordered up room service, watched an appalling amount of cable TV, sipped a lovely Cabernet Franc, and then he tucked me into the sleeper sofa with a brotherly wink.

I really was going to have to visit New Zealand one of these days. Nice people.

—

Despite what my friends, enemies, and acquaintances seem to think of me, I haven't spent all that much time walking on life's wild side. I have never, for example, been in a street fight. I have never driven faster than eighty miles per hour, though in fairness this is because I've never had a vehicle that would go any faster. I don't have a tattoo. I have never danced naked in public. And never have I set foot inside a pawnshop.

Until today.

The store was in Oakland, on Telegraph Avenue. It looked like a cross between a regular retail shop and a high-end thrift store. Electronics and musical instruments lined the walls and took up most of the floor space, but there were also glass cases packed with jewelry, watches and guns, silver tea services and similar wedding- and anniversary-themed knickknacks, and, most disturbingly, numerous children's bicycles.

The man behind the counter was huge, dressed in a black leather vest over a Harley-Davidson T-shirt that was meant to either disguise or highlight his substantial gut. Greasy brown hair hung in lank clumps around his sallow face, his nose was vaguely porcine, and his bloodshot brown eyes bugged out in an unfortunate manner. He was, in brief, precisely what one expected of the proprietor of a pawnshop.

"Good morning," I said, ignoring his baleful glare and holding out the article with the photo of the Odibajians. "Do you by any chance happen to know these guys?"

He shrugged.

"Is that a yes or a no?"

"Vamoose, lady. I'm not good with faces."

"Did I mention Hipolit sent me?"

His prominent eyes got even bigger. Now he looked like a praying mantis. "Prove it."

"Call him."

"Don't have his number."

"I do." I pulled my cell phone from my pocket and flipped it open. "I'll be sure to mention you're not being helpful."

He grunted, glanced at the photo, and shook his head. "Haven't seen 'em."

"How about someone looking to sell a Gauguin?"

"A Gauguin? Like a real one?"

Either this particular pawnshop owner had taken a few art history classes, or he was a fence. I nodded.

"Coupla guys came in, askin' 'bout it a while back, two, three weeks ago."

"What kind of guys?"

"Two-bit hoods, not my usual clientele, if you catch my drift. I don't deal with that sort of thing much. Told 'em to get the provenance together and we'd talk. I'm no retard."

"Who were they? Where were they from?"

"We weren't formally introduced. Butler's day off."

I bit down on my annoyance. "What did the men look like?"

"One was kinda middle-aged, the other young, probably in his twenties. I told you, amateurs."

"White guys?"

He nodded.

"Hair color, height?"

He shrugged, buggy eyes focusing on a pair of teenage boys who had entered the shop and were admiring an electric guitar. "Like I said, I don't really know nothin'."

"Not even for Hippo?"

"Not tall, not short. Look, they didn't make an impression, okay? You want me to lie and say somethin' else, just tell me what. I'll do it. But I can't tell you somethin' I don't know."

It was a weirdly honest response. "How about a bronze sculpture? A life-sized sculpture of a Greek god. Anybody try to sell that recently?"

"That one? Sure. Those guys have tried to foist that thing off on every pawnshop from here to Sacramento. Coupla morons get drunk one night and snatch a—what? Five-hundred-pound? More?—big-ass sculpture off the street? How ya gonna move somethin' like that? Ain't no market for that sort of thing. Crazy-ass, shit-for-brains fuck-ups. Pardon my French."

"I think that's actually their legal name."

"You know, for a stuck-up bitch, you're all right."

"Thanks. Were those the same guys as the ones talking about the Gauguin?"

"What?" His attention was again fixed on the boys playing around with the guitar. "Oh, no. Different guys. Look, lady, like I said, I don't know nothin'. Okay? Hey, you two. Yeah, I'm talkin' to you. Watch it with that—that guitar's expensive...."

"All right. Thanks."

"Hey, any time. You be sure an' tell Hippo I cooperated, will ya?"

"Will do."

Seemed I now had a friend in the pawning business.

12

*I walked into an "art" store today, and was confronted
with hundreds of tubes of different oil colors! I simply
must protest. First, an artist should mix his or her
own paint. It is an act of devotion and love. Second,
if you must buy "off the shelf," consider the traditional
palette: 1. Flake White 2. Yellow Ochre 3. Venetian Red
4. Charcoal Black. Finis. From these, you can mix a pale
blue, an olive green, flesh tones, and a rich brown. From
these alone, such artists as Rembrandt and Hals created
masterpieces.*

—*Georges LeFleur, "Craquelure"*

AS LONG AS I was in Oakland, I decided to stop by the Piedmont Hills jobsite where my contractor friend, Norm Berger, was working. Norm had asked me to bid on the job last month, but the homeowner had low-balled it and I'd walked away. It was just as well; I never regretted losing those kinds of customers. Whenever a homeowner tries to save on remodeling costs by skimping on the subcontractors, it turns out badly.

From half a block away the annoying whine of a compressor clued me in to the jobsite. As I approached I saw dust wafting through open windows, plastic sheeting tacked across door frames, and scaffolding climbing the side of the Italianate Revival home.

"Well, well, well. If it ain't Her Highness, the Princess of Paint," Norm called out. With his dishwater blond hair, nicotine-stained teeth, and belly hanging over his dusty jeans, Norm could have been the pawnshop owner's brother by a different father. Today's T-shirt, tame by Norm standards, read REHAB IS FOR QUITTERS.

"Heya, Norm. What're you up to?"

"Oh, 'bout two hundred pounds," he said. "Hey, what the hell happened over to the F-U? McAdams called for another reference to finish up their job. I got Marisco on it."

"Mauricio, not Marisco."

"What's the diff?"

"*Marisco* means seafood, whereas Mauricio is actually a man's name. Like Maurice."

"And your point is...?"

"It's...nothing. So they hired him to finish the job I started?"

"Yeah. This sorta thing doesn't look great for me, ya know. Anyhoo, glad you're here. I gotta ask you about a gold gilt dealio in the master. *Mauricio—*" he enunciated in an exaggerated fashion "—is up there if you want to talk to him."

Upstairs we entered a huge room that served as the master bath. Mauricio was a young man with a slight build and a quick smile; he was covered in dust from sanding what may well have been lead paint, given the age of the house. We had all worked together a couple of months ago on a job in Pacific Heights.

We talked shop for a few minutes: I mixed a Venetian red base color for Mauricio, and gave him a few pointers on how to restore the gold and silver gilt on the bathroom mirror frames. The original base for gilding was clay, which was dampened and made slick and smooth as glass before the tissue-thin sheets of metal were applied. These days we use a poor substitute, red oxide acrylic paint, but if done correctly the overall effect is superb. The secret is to make the base as smooth as possible, and to "age" the final gilt surface with steel wool and a coat of burnt umber varnish or amber shellac.

Watch out, I thought, wrenching myself back from the paints and brushes and sample pieces laid out on a temporary work table. I yearned to stay and play, but I wasn't being paid, after all. And if I gave away all my faux-finish secrets to house-painters I'd wind up losing all my bids, and then I'd *have* to make my living as an investigator.

"So, you're working on the Fleming Mansion?" I asked Mauricio.

He nodded eagerly. "They told me it was a rush job. I been there all yesterday. Removed most of the paper but haven't started painting yet. I got two men there today just sanding and filling, doing prep."

"In the attic rooms?"

"And the second floor, too."

"The second floor? Where?"

"A couple bedrooms had water damage like in the attic."

"Do you remember which rooms? The numbers?"

"Two-twelve and two-ten, I think. Two-twelve was the worst. We were there all yesterday. I wasn't feeling that great this morning, so I came here instead."

"Do you have any of the wallpaper scraps?"

He gave me an odd look. "No, we took 'em to the landfill already. Cleanup's part of the job."

"Right. Did you wear masks?"

He shook his head.

"You and your workers should really wear protective gear, Mauricio. This sort of thing can catch up with you." I glared at Norm. "OSHA, for example, might have a few thoughts on the subject were it to stumble upon this jobsite after, say, receiving an anonymous tip from a good citizen."

"Yeah, yeah, okay," Norm gave me a glare. "Marisco, get some masks for you and the boys."

"Not just cheap dust masks," I put in. "You need respirators with cartridges that are rated for lead dust and fumes."

"Yeah, whatever the princess says," Norm grumbled before leading me out of the room and down the stairs. "You're a bleeding-heart-liberal pain in my ass, you know that?"

"That's why you like me so much," I said. "So, about the F-U boys. Anything about them seem odd to you?"

"You mean a bunch of super-rich guys playing house together? It's all weird, you ask me. They should just marry each other and make it official. That's legal now, ain't it?"

"Not quite. Did you know they had a private art gallery there?"

"Nah, but it weren't like they were giving me the grand tour. Alls I did was put on a new roof, a little electrical and plumbing, some finish work. And send them a huge bill."

Our conversation paused while we walked past a compressor drowning out all conversation with its ear-splitting wail. We went out the front door and Norm closed it behind us, quieting things down a tad.

"This one time I went in? Emergency call, leaking roof.

Flunky hustled me upstairs but not before I saw what they were doing."

"Human sacrifices?" I guessed.

"Nope. The men were all dressed in old-fashioned costumes and the women were all hoes. And get this: they were all sittin' round like they's at an indoor picnic. Weird."

"How do you know the women were hoes?"

"They were all naked. Butt-naked."

"Ah."

" 'Cept for some leaves."

"Got the picture."

He gave a wolfish grin. "The weird part was that they made, like, fake trees n' shit, and rolled out some sod—I'm not kiddin' you, real honest-to-God sod right there on the floor—and had set up a whole picnic. You wanna picnic, don't you go to Golden Gate Park or somethin'?"

"Not if you want the women naked."

"I guess you got me there."

"What did they do when you saw them?"

He shook his head. "They didn't see me. Figured they weren't in the mood to talk shop, so I just left."

"Did you ever meet Elijah Odibajian?"

"Oh, that the guy they found in the bathtub? I saw that on the news." He shook his head. "I dealt with McAdams, same as you. The only strange thing was, he asked for you by name."

"McAdams asked for me? I thought you gave him my name."

Norm shook his head. "I woulda, don't get me wrong, but he said he knew we'd worked together on the Garner place and asked for you. That's why I don't get why he wanted somebody else. Whadja do? Take a dump in the men's room and not flush?"

"Norm, you're something else."

He grinned, flashing nicotine-stained teeth. "Hey: I'm here, I drink beer, get used to it."

———

The upside to running afoul of the law over the past few years is that I now have a network of friends and acquaintances with useful expertise. Elena-the-lawyer, for instance, and Annette-the-cop, who, if she weren't suspecting me of crimes and whatnot, would be especially useful. But more to the point at the moment: I knew a chemist.

Brianna Nguyen was a graduate student at the University of California at Berkeley. We'd met only once, when her roommate got involved with some bad types at Oakland's historic Bayview cemetery. It was a difficult time, but I was pretty sure she'd remember me, and I needed her expertise. I drove up past the magnificent Claremont Hotel, through the university campus, and finally found a metered parking spot not too far from Hildebrand Hall, one of several buildings housing the College of Chemistry. I made my way to an institutional beige break room frequented by graduate students, and found Brianna almost exactly as I had the last time we spoke: huddled over a huge notebook, making notes in tiny, neat little columns of words and numbers.

"Brianna?" I said.

"Oh my God!" she said as she looked up, pushing long, straight, shiny hair out of her face. She looked all of fifteen years old in her fashionable jeans and gauzy floral blouse, and she spoke like a true California Valley Girl, but I knew from experience she was a knowledgeable scientist. "It's been, like, forever. Did someone else die?"

"As a matter of fact..."

"Oh. My. *God.*" She gasped. One hand flew up to her cheek, her jaw dropped, and her eyes widened. "I was just kidding! You have, like, the worst job *ever.*"

I could think of a few worse ones—cleaning out the sewer plant, for instance—but I saw her point.

"I was hoping you could help me. I need to know the specifics on arsenic poisoning. How long does it take? What are the symptoms?"

"I'm no expert," she said with a little shrug of her slim shoulders. "I mean, as far as I know arsenic poisoning basically involves the allosteric inhibition of essential metabolic enzymes, the ones that require lipoic acid as a cofactor, such as pyruvate and alpha-ketoglutarate dehydrogenase. On account of that, the substrates before the dehydrogenase steps accumulate, such as pyruvate and lactate."

I must have been staring.

"What is it?" Brianna asked.

I cleared my throat. "Sorry, I know you were speaking English but I have no idea what you just said."

She rolled her eyes. "It screws with your circulatory system and brain, causing neurological disturbances and leading to death from multi-system organ failure."

"Okay, that I get. How hard is it to detect?"

"Used to be hard, which is why it was so popular for killing your family members. White arsenic used to be called 'inheritance powder,' can you imagine? It's pretty standard to test for it now, though. In fact, they can find traces in hair so they can even dig up old bodies and run the tests if someone makes allegations of foul play after death. *Oh my God*, are you digging up bodies again, like you did in Bayview Cemetery?"

"I never dug up bodies."

"Grave robbery, then."

"No, I've never..." I sighed. What shreds of a reputation was I trying to salvage, anyway? "Never mind. I'm just trying to understand what happened to my uncle. He's still alive, but he was found—" it was still hard for me to get the words out "—poisoned by arsine gas."

"Arsine gas? Are you sure?"

"That's what they said."

"That's, like, a whole different deal than eating it. That hardly ever happens anymore. Does he work in a metal factory, some kind of manufacturing that mixes metals?"

I shook my head.

"That's weird then. Does he live in a place with really old wallpaper?"

Again with the killer wallpaper. "No. But how would that work?"

"Back in the day, like the late eighteen-hundreds, this Italian biochemist named Gosio figured out that when Scheele's green, a popular pigment at the time, is used in wallpaper and stuff, and it gets wet and then moldy, the latent arsenic in the green pigment can convert to vapor arsine, even dimethyl and trimethyl arsine. In these old homes, whole families were dying off, kids first since they're smaller and closer to the floor. The gas is heavier than air. Some people think that's what killed Napoleon when he was exiled on that island...what was it again?"

"Elba?"

"No...St. Helena. Anyway, he got exiled there and then got sick. Somehow they had a piece of the old wallpaper so they analyzed it to see if there was any arsenic green. By the way, the green darkens with exposure to oxygen, especially when it's degrading, so the paper might not *look* green. It goes kinda brown or gray. You can always find out by using an energy-dispersive analysis, like the Niton Portable XRF spectrometer. There's one around here somewhere. Want to borrow it?"

"Could I?"

"Sure. Just don't tell anybody you're not, you know, official UC. Want to test your uncle's wallpaper?"

"Actually, in his case I don't think there was any wallpaper involved. But he was an artist, and he might have been mixing a pigment he got from a fireworks distrib—"

I was cut off by Brianna's quick intake of breath. "Oooh, nasty. You can still get those colors, like Paris Green and stuff, and if they mix with any kind of hydrochloric acid you're in serious trouble. He's in the hospital? Are they chelating?"

"Even as we speak."

"That's good, then. He'll prob'ly be okay. It's a good thing he was found in time. Does he like garlic?"

"Garlic?"

"They say people who eat a lot of garlic don't absorb the arsenic as well, or pee a lot of it out or something. I read about it once. Arsenic's a real problem in the drinking water in parts of India, so a lot of the information comes from there. The scientists there are probably the most knowledgeable on the subject these days. It doesn't come up much around here, since arsenic has been outlawed from anything but rat poison for years. Oh, and fireworks."

———

After stopping for a quick garlic-based lunch at a small trattoria on Hearst, I pulled the Gauguin case file out of my satchel. Time to talk to Victor Yeltsin, victim of art theft...or perpetrator of insurance fraud. I still had no idea how he might be involved with Elijah Odibajian's fate, much less Anton's, but there was no time like the present to find out.

Cathy Yeltsin answered the phone and remembered our meeting in Huntington Park. I mentioned the remodeling project she wanted to talk about, and she invited me over to talk faux "right this minute."

Unfortunately there are no good traffic options to get from

Oakland to Sausalito on a weekday afternoon. One choice was to take the Bay Bridge to San Francisco, cross the city on surface streets, then head over the Golden Gate Bridge; alternatively, you could head north and cross the Richmond–San Rafael Bridge, pass San Quentin Prison, take surface streets through Larkspur Landing, pick up the freeway again and drive another twelve miles or so to the west.

I opted for the latter. It took me a good fifty minutes to arrive in quaint, tourist-clogged Sausalito, a small, historic fishing village on the bay just north of San Francisco.

Cathy had given me directions, but I'm better with visuals: I followed Anton's sketched map through the narrow, twisty roads etched out of the steep side of the mountain. The Yeltsins' house was a modern structure that clung to what appeared to be a sheer cliff. It offered an amazing view of San Francisco and the Golden Gate Bridge to the right, and Alcatraz and Angel Islands in the bay to the left.

So this is what undisclosed consulting work can get you, I thought. Maybe I should take up vague consulting for a career myself, and let Jarrah Preston keep his job.

The door was already opening as I angled my truck into the apron of the driveway, trying to leave enough room for cars to be able to pass on the narrow street. I noted an alarm service sticker in the window, right next to a Cal Bears placard.

A petite but perfectly muscled, tanned, dark-haired man with limited English skills stood at the door, beckoning me inside. Barefoot and wearing cut-off jeans, he looked like a pool boy in Acapulco—not that I would know from experience, not living the kind of life that allowed me to loll by pools in lush tropical settings. The case file referred to a statement from a "houseboy." Would this be him? Kyle something?

I followed the young man into the home, which featured plate-glass windows to take advantage of the view. Unfortunately, it was hard to notice the view because of all of the art, taking up every free inch of wall and floor space.

Normally I was in favor of such things. But this art...

There were wooden carvings from Africa with huge phalluses, and clay reproductions—or were they real?—of pre-Columbian artifacts with huge phalluses, and oils and acrylic paintings and drawings and etchings of everything from mythological satyrs to space aliens with huge phalluses. And everywhere in between were Indian paintings, sculptures, and woodcuts of couples enacting the *Kama Sutra*, and deities with huge phalluses.

I was sensing a theme.

I'm an art lover. And I'm no prude. But this stuff had me wishing I was tucked away in my studio or on some nameless jobsite faux-finishing banisters.

Banisters made me think of huge phalluses.

I tried to clear my mind.

"Annie!" Cathy wore black Spandex pants and a stretchy shirt that formed a V to point out her spectacular cleavage. Pedicured feet were stuffed into leopard-print backless pumps with a puff of red feathers on the toe. She rushed over to me and gave me a big hug, as though we were fast friends instead of virtual strangers. "I am *so* glad you could come! I've been telling Victor all about you, and he's beside himself as well. Wonderful, just wonderful. *So* glad you came."

I wondered if Cathy might be playing fast and loose with the Prozac. No one was this happy all the time.

"Ah, here he is now. Victor, lovey, come meet Annie Kincaid, the miracle worker who's going to transform our basement for us."

"Good to meet you," Victor said with a smile, holding his hand out to shake. Afterward, he held my hand in both of his, gazing into my eyes with a very warm welcome. Too warm. He was a powerfully built man in his early fifties, dressed in white pants and turtleneck, with a shining pink bald head.

Like a penis.

I looked away, desperate for someplace to rest my eyes without thinking about sex and nudity.

"Great view," I said, admiring the sights out the window.

"Please, come in, have a seat. Jean-Paul," he said in a deep, booming voice to the young man who answered the door, "get Annie a sherry."

"Oh, no thanks, I'm fi—"

Before I could finish my protest, a small crystal glass was held out to me. I accepted it.

Victor and Cathy took seats on a lipstick-red leather couch.

She perched with her short, shapely legs crossed demurely. He relaxed with his arms up on the back of the couch and his knees splayed open, wide apart.

I remained silent for a moment, trying to decide which approach to use. I'd had the entire traffic-clogged drive over here to come up with something to say, yet everything I had practiced seemed somehow inadequate when faced with Victor and Cathy in the House of Erotic Art.

"You're not here for a faux-finish job," Victor said, breaking the long silence.

"I'm not?"

He shook his head and gave me a half smile. Cathy looked at me, then back up at Victor, making a distressed little moue.

"Then what am I here for?" I asked. Heh. Frank's interrogation technique—refusing to talk—really did work well. I could be as noncommunicative as Frank.

"You're working with Jarrah Preston. You want to ask about the stolen Gauguin."

"Oh dear," whispered Cathy, frowning.

"How did you know that?"

"He told me you'd be calling. Why the subterfuge?"

"I just wasn't sure about the situation...and then I happened to meet Cathy in Huntington Park, and she asked me about the faux finish, and since that really is my main job, I thought I'd go with it." So much for playing my cards close to my chest.

"Kill two birds with one stone, eh?"

"Something like that."

Victor nodded his shiny bald head and stared at me.

"So," I said, pulling the case file out of my satchel. "Could you go over the basics of the case with me?"

"I believe my statements—both the one to the police at the time, and the more recent one to Preston—are in the report."

"Oblige me," I said, now trying to channel Inspector Annette Crawford. I even attempted to do her one-eyebrow-lifting thing, but I only managed to twist my forehead, which I felt sure made me look more crazy than intimidating.

"Cathy and I had gone out for the evening, it was a Saturday."

I glanced down at the file. "You were at the Power Play?"

"Have you been there?"

"*Me?* Um, no... Nope. Uh-uh. Nosiree..."

I really am not a prude. I love that the San Francisco Bay Area is one of the few places in the world where people are, by and large, allowed—encouraged, even—to explore their fantasies and pursue what is so coyly referred to as their "lifestyle." Still, there are certain aspects of said lifestyles about which I am just as happy to remain ignorant. It's sort of like thinking about your parents' sex life: you may know they have one, and are glad for it, but it's really best not to dwell on the specifics.

I was getting to know a little too much about Victor and Cathy already. I wasn't near ready for their club outfits.

"You should go," Victor was saying. "It would be an eye-opener. People unfamiliar with the lifestyle tend to think of us as sickos, aberrant. Nothing could be further from the truth."

He curled his arm around his wife. Their eyes met and held, and they shared a smile.

I cleared my throat. "So you were at the club until..."

"They close at two, so we probably got home about five."

"And the intervening time..."

"We joined some friends at their home."

"Oh." *Clear the mind, Annie.*

"When we returned, we found the place ransacked. It was terrible."

"It says in the report that there were signs of forced entry?"

He nodded. "A crowbar in the window."

"You owned some very valuable artwork. Why didn't you have an alarm system?"

"We did. This is a safe neighborhood, but the insurance stipulated we install a security system. But as you probably know, with a smash-and-grab job the thieves are gone long before the police arrive. The neighbors witnessed the whole thing, even saw a quick flash of the painting."

"Yes, I read that in the original report. How many people knew the artwork was here?"

"I told the police everyone I could think of. It was a long time ago, Annie."

"It would stand to reason that household employees would be high on the suspect list," I said.

"The only help we had at the time was our houseboy."

"And who was your...er...houseboy?"

"A young man named Kyle Jones. But the police cleared him. They searched his place and everything, but found nothing."

"Any idea where I could find Kyle?"

There was a slight hesitation. Cathy opened her pink-lipsticked mouth to say something, but Victor silenced her with a look. I thought I saw a strange flicker in his easy eyes.

"Kyle's often at the Power Play."

"At the...um..."

"The sex club. Right downtown."

"Oh, okay. Do you have any idea how Elijah Odibajian wound up with the painting in his possession?"

"Not at all."

"Do you know him?"

He shook his head.

"Aren't you both members of the Fleming-Union?"

Victor's eyes were growing more distant, his relaxed mien less so.

"No."

"No?"

"In any case, the members' list is private."

"I realize that, but we're talking about a crime—"

"It's not relevant. I have no association with Elijah Odibajian."

"How about Anton Woznikowicz?"

"Sure. Anton did some restoration work for me years ago."

"On the Gauguin?"

He nodded, then smiled down at a vague, distressed-looking Cathy, whose hands were tapping her knees. Victor put his hand over hers to stop their nervous fluttering. "You know, that painting was in Cathy's family for generations. Great-granddad Halstrom bought it in Amsterdam. We always hoped it would turn up somehow. And it did."

"You mean a forgery showed up."

Victor's gaze snapped up to meet mine. Already pale, he looked as though all the blood had drained from his face.

"A forgery?" he asked.

Oops. Was I not supposed to tell him that?

My phone rang again—Annette Crawford. I put it on Silent.

"Um, were you certain the painting was real when you owned it?"

"Of course it was real." He squirmed in his seat. "That's how we insured it for its worth. When can we get it back?"

"The insurance company owns it now, since they paid out for it."

"They don't want it. I do."

"You would have to return their money."

"That's not a problem."

"In any case, the painting that showed up at auction was a forgery, not the Gauguin you lost."

"That makes no sense," Victor protested, though his voice had lost its booming self-assurance.

"I'll leave those discussions to you and Jarrah Preston," I said, standing. I was anxious to have this interview over with. "Thanks for talking to me."

"Before you leave, don't you want to see the faux-finishing project?" Cathy asked.

No.

"Oh, right. Sure," I said. "That'd be great."

She and I descended a narrow flight of stairs into the basement. Intricate Indian tapestries adorned the walls on either side.

"I see you like Indian art," I said.

"Oh! I lo-o-ove it! It's so brash, so overtly sensual, don't you think? I spent some time there as a student. Even attended an ashram."

"Really? That must have been fascinating."

"Oh, it was. I traveled all about. Believe it or not, I was a science major in college, but after my time in India everything changed."

I wondered about access to drugs in India. Wasn't that what the Beatles discovered on their roads to enlightenment? Maybe that's why she was so happy all the time. On the other hand, I was awfully quick to attribute Cathy's perpetually sunny nature to chemical substances. Cynic. Maybe she was on a natural high, born from her activities at the Power Play. What did I know?

I looked around the unfinished basement. Spackled, unprimed wallboard and bare wooden beams gave it the look of half-done basements the world over. The space, though window-less, boasted a normal-height ceiling and an open floor plan that ran the full footprint of the house.

"Nice basement," I murmured. "Lots of potential."

"We never quite got around to finishing up in here. What I really want is for it to look like a medieval dungeon."

"A dungeon."

Her eyes twinkled. "Like a modern rumpus room."

"For the kids or..."

Her laugh practically echoed in the under-furnished space. "Good heavens, no! For our grown-up play. Could you paint it to look like stone walls, like an old castle? Gargoyles, maybe, and you could paint a flag with the colors on it, like old style? Like at the Renaissance Faire—do you ever go to that?"

"Um, sure." I had taken my nephews to the Ren-Faire last year. They wore plastic swords tucked into leather belts, and I dressed up as a tavern wench. It had been good, innocent fun. It would be hard now to see it in the same light. "I have to go...away now. I'll get back to you on this."

When we emerged, Victor was nowhere to be found.

"That's odd...Victor!" Cathy yelled as she ducked in and out of rooms. "Victor's so special. An artistic temperament, you know. I don't know where he could be. Oh well, fiddle-dee-dee."

Fiddle-dee-*dee*?

"Mommy!"

I swung around to see twin boys, about ten years old, both wearing blue-and-gold Cal sweatshirts, running in through the front door. They were followed by a sweet-faced toddler, also be-decked in UC style, and a bedraggled, plump young woman lad-en with an overstuffed diaper bag. I assumed she was the nanny.

"My angels!" Cathy fell to her knees and hugged the children to her. "How was the piano lesson? *Do* tell Mommy all about your day..."

I said a quick good-bye and slipped out the still-open front door. I had enough worlds colliding at the moment. I wasn't anxious to witness Catrina Yeltsin, Queen of the Dungeon, in Mommy mode.

13

Is there anything more beautiful than a well-rendered nude? There is no shame in such a painting; only beauty and metaphor and life.

—*Georges LeFleur, "Craquelure"*

WHAT NEXT? The last pinky-gold rays of the afternoon sun were lighting up San Francisco and making the red-painted Golden Gate Bridge appear actually golden. I supposed if I were ambitious, I could go straight on over to the Power Play and look for an ex-houseboy named Kyle. The police had cleared him in the original theft, but talking to him seemed like a logical next step.

Still, I needed company for a trip to a San Francisco sex club. Moral support. Even at my most impulsive, going into a sex club alone sounded like a classic example of a Really Bad Idea.

Speaking of bad ideas, Balthazar Odibajian's house was around here somewhere. I had the exact address from Pedro. I looked it up. Not far, in Belvedere. Surely I could drive by without being noticed, so long as I took a few precautions. I smeared mud on my license plates, removed my magnetic TRUE/FAUX STUDIOS signs from my truck doors, donned a pair of sunglasses, and set off.

I cast my mind back to the last time I was in this neighborhood, accompanied by none other than Michael X. Johnson. He had talked our way into a private residence in search of a stolen painting, and then he had abandoned me there. Ah, the good old days.

There were two kinds of vehicles found in this sort of neighborhood: wildly expensive, and work trucks. I rolled by Balthazar Odibajian's driveway, pretending to be one of the help on the way home. Odibajian's place was impossible to see from the road, sealed off with iron gates and an eight-foot stucco wall. I wouldn't be surprised if broken glass was embedded in the top of the wall. Balthazar seemed the type.

"I don't know. Maybe there's an obvious connection that would explain it all. Maybe there's a secret storage place."

"A storage unit down in secret tunnels? I think you're grasping at straws a bit."

"You're right, I know. But you have to admit I tend to stumble on to things, mostly by looking in places without any good reason."

She chuckled. "There's no arguing with that."

"So," my eyes slid over to her, "want to look for tunnels with me?"

"Nooooo. Nunh-uh. No thanks. Not my kind of thing. Finding a body in a bathtub was about my quota of excitement for the year. Or the decade, more like."

"I don't want to go by myself," I mused.

"I think that's wise. What about Michael? A thief like him ought to be able to ferret out secret passages, oughtn't he?"

"He's claustrophobic."

"Seriously?"

I nodded. "Got caught in a safe room once. Not a pretty sight. I doubt tunnels are his cup of tea."

"You know, the other, sane, idea is to talk to Inspector Crawford about all this. If there are tunnels, wouldn't the cops know about them? And if not, and there's a secret way in and out of the Fleming-Union, maybe they *should* know about it."

Good point. But that would require that I talk to Annette Crawford with her shiny SFPD badge. I know, I was working on personal growth and all, but this seemed like a bad idea, all the way around. Among other things, I didn't really know anything beyond conjecture and wild speculation with regard to the tunnels. That was plenty good for *my* unlicensed investigative standards, but official police types usually wanted something concrete to go on.

I stared into my rum.

"Anyway," Sam said, "tonight we both need to get some sleep. Reggie will be up early to make coffee and he'll probably rouse you. The man can't sleep past six o'clock, even on the weekends."

"That's okay. I've got a lot to do tomorrow, myself."

—

The next morning Sam's husband, Reggie, stumbled into the kitchen wearing sweatpants and a rumpled white T-shirt. He took in my presence on the couch with the aplomb born of awakening often to find children's college friends, relatives, and assorted Caribbean types sprawled upon furniture and pallets on the floor. Reggie brewed a pot of coffee with quiet efficiency and passed me a lopsided orange-glazed mug made years ago by their son. I joined him at the vintage green linoleum kitchen table. He handed me the Arts and Leisure section of the paper, tapped an article on the front page, and spoke for the first time.

"Check out the story about a new museum of erotica in Russia. You should paint erotica, Annie. You'd make a fortune."

"I'm not so sure what I find erotic is what other people find erotic."

"You paint naked people all the time."

"Not the same thing," I said, taking a deep drink of my coffee. "Naked's not always sexy."

"You're telling *me*. I ran the Bay to Breakers last year. There are *still* a lot of naked images I'd like to get out of my head."

The Bay to Breakers is San Francisco's major annual footrace, where world-class athletes run twelve kilometers from the Embarcadero, on the bay, to the breaking surf of the Pacific. Accompanying the more traditional runners are thousands of cross-dressers, samba dancers, people dressed like pirates, roller-skaters, naked strollers. As befits the City by the Bay, pretty much anything goes. Spirits are high, the mood is lighthearted, and fun is had by all.

However, as one of my mature-beyond-his-years nephews noted, the kind of people who like to get naked in public are rarely the kind of people one would *choose* to see naked.

Reggie rattled the paper. "All I'm saying is, sex is on everybody's mind all the time. I'm a trained social worker. I know these things."

Sam dragged in, sleepy and grumpy. One of the things I like about my Jamaican friend is that despite her typical equanimity, she is as cranky in the morning as I.

"There she is," Reggie announced. "My own little ray of sunshine. Make us some breakfast, woman."

"Oh sure, I'll get right on it," Sam said with a snort.

Reggie smiled at me and winked.

"Last thing they need in Russia is a sex museum," Sam muttered. "Like they don't need, say, an economic infrastructure first."

"Nothing wrong with a museum of any kind," Reggie argued. "And there's nothing wrong with erotica and healthy sexuality. You two are prudes, is all."

"That's me in a nutshell," I said.

"Prude is *my* middle name," Sam echoed, smiling at me over her steaming mug of coffee. "I'm still stunned we had children, Reggie my love."

Reggie ignored us and rattled his paper again. "Says here that local entrepreneur Victor Yeltsin is to donate a Gauguin."

I looked at the newspaper more closely.

"It's not his to donate." Looked like I should place a call to Jarrah Preston.

After a quick shower I asked to borrow fresh clothes from Sam. She offered me a brown-and-cream patterned African mudcloth caftan I had always admired on her tall, elegant form. On my average, slightly less chic physique it looked like I was acting in a play of some sort, or perhaps taking part in an experimental performance piece making subtle, cutting fun of the fashion-challenged. But since I had been wearing the same wrinkled clothes for two days, I decided it would have to do.

I met Jarrah at Caffe Trieste in North Beach. His dark eyes flickered over my outfit, but he remained politely mute. We took our creamy lattes to a small table in the corner.

"Victor Yeltsin contacted me, offering to buy the Gauguin back," Jarrah said.

"The fake one?"

"That's what the man said."

"Do you think he's trying to get it out of the country?"

"Seems like. He also mentioned that he was going out of town, and that he would be back in touch with me. He refused to meet in person. Truth to tell, he sounded scared."

"When I met with him yesterday, he seemed genuinely surprised to hear that the painting was fake," I mused. "But according to Anton, Victor hired him to copy it himself. So he must have known there was a fake. You think there was some kind of honest mix-up?"

"I doubt honesty enters into it in any form. Listen, I wanted to talk to you about something else: I've checked out Balthazar, and as much as it pains me to say so, he looks clean in all of this."

"Really."

"I know he's unlikable. Tell the truth, I was looking forward to busting him myself, but I'm afraid in this case he's innocent. It seems Elijah nicked the Gauguin from the club's collection one night, simple as that. Which means that the club had been given a forgery with provenance papers, and the real one is still out there somewhere."

"The club acquired the fake Gauguin around the same time as Victor was invited to join. Do you think his donation of the painting was what won him admittance?"

"Very possible. I think he probably had the painting copied with the intent to give the club the proper Gauguin, got mixed up, and instead perhaps sold the real one to someone else, or God forbid, destroyed it under the assumption that it was a fake."

If I were Catholic I would have crossed myself. A Gauguin masterpiece being deliberately destroyed was unthinkable, yet such things happened. Not so long ago a French waiter named Stephane Breitwieser had stolen hundreds of pieces of historic, one-of-a-kind artwork, including paintings by Watteau, Brueghel, and Boucher. While he was in jail awaiting trial, his mother attempted to destroy the evidence by shredding the paintings in her garbage disposal or tossing them into a canal.

"What about Anton?" I asked.

"It's possible that what happened to him isn't connected to the Gauguin at all," Jarrah said, sympathy playing in his dark eyes. "He has a sketchy past, a lot of enemies. Or there's still the possibility that it was an accident, after all."

Great. Now Jarrah Preston was jumping on the "it was an accident" bandwagon.

"I want to pay you for your time. You've really worked this case, Annie, we appreciate it."

"But I haven't found the Gauguin."

"At this point, the firm feels it would be throwing good money after bad. I'm just going to finish up a few things myself, then close the case."

"Why would Elijah Odibajian have been arranged to look like Marat in the tub?"

"I have no idea. But I have to be honest here: that's not my problem. It's not yours, either. That's an issue for the police. I was here looking for a work of art that looks lost...unless I can track Victor down and get the truth out of him."

"Another person of interest up the *boohai*? Did you check the other tubs in the mansion?"

Jarrah smiled ruefully and handed me a fat check. "Not yet. Still haven't been granted access. That's a tough place."

"You're telling me."

———

It was only midmorning by the time Jarrah and I went our separate ways. It dawned on me that I had been letting my regular work obligations slide for the last couple of days. I didn't have any current projects in progress, but there was always plenty of prep work to do. That was the thing about owning one's own business: the demands never stopped, no matter that my uncle had been poisoned and I had criminals to catch and a masterpiece to save.

I checked my pocket agenda, following the lines and arrows to figure out what I was supposed to be doing this week in my professional life. As Mary pointed out to me *ad nauseam,* normal business people maintain devices like BlackBerries or iPhones so they don't have to try to read through erasures and scratched-out appointments. But in this regard I take after my Uncle Anton, if not quite as bad as he: Anton is such a technophobe that he won't even leave a message on voicemail, much less install a machine of his own.

I called Mary and asked her to drop the new sample boards off with our client on Lyon Street; and to run the "ideas portfolio" over to a Russian restaurateur out in the Richmond; and finally to pick up the supplies I ordered from the San Francisco Gravel Company for a mural project that required traditional fresco: painting with dry pigments onto wet plaster walls.

While in North Beach, I figured I might as well take the newly painted rusty-railing sample over to the strip club off Broadway.

"Are you Fred?" I asked the big man standing outside the main doors, smoking. He looked about eight and a half months pregnant in his pale blue embroidered *guayabera*. An intricate tattoo ran up his bicep, disappeared under the shirt, and reappeared on his bulky neck. "I'm Annie Kincaid, the painter."

"Oh, right. You just called? That was fast."

"I was in the neighborhood. Here's the sample," I said as I handed it to him and brought out my measuring tape and camera. I took measurements of the short span and snapped a few digital photos. This was the sort of simple, quick job that would take Mary and me all of an afternoon to complete. I gave Fred a verbal quote for the work.

"Sounds fair," he said. "Management just wants it done fast. Come on into my office and I'll give you a deposit."

I loved it when people didn't want to bother with opposing bids.

Though it was only nine-thirty, inside the venue it could have been three in the morning: it was dark, the bass thumped, and the lights pulsed. I was surprised to see a woman dancing on the stage this early, and customers already hunkered down low over their drinks.

The girlie show put me in mind of what Norm had mentioned about the strange event with the "hoes" at the Fleming Mansion.

"This might seem like an odd question," I asked Fred as he handed me a check with my required fifty percent deposit, "but you wouldn't happen to know of any juicy gossip with regards to the F-U, up on Nob Hill?"

"Sure," he said with an unpleasant grin. "Some of the girls go up there from time to time."

"What sorts of things do they do?"

His pale eyes drifted over me as though assessing whether I could pass stripper muster.

"You ever hear of any strange parties, that sort of thing?" I asked.

"What's in it for me?"

"What do you want?"

"Carton of Marlboros."

"Deal." I was getting off cheap—I thought he was going to ask me to paint the railing for free. "I'll bring them by when I do the railing."

"Sure, they put out a call for girls every once in a while. Some weird shit up there."

"Weird?"

"Sometimes all they do is pose 'n' shit. Like it's some sort of living painting, costumes 'n' shit. Half those guys prolly can't even get it up anymore."

—

On my way out of North Beach I drove down Green Street. Not long ago I found out that my scalawag of a grandfather had been maintaining a *pied-à-terre* in a two-story stucco building on this street, not two blocks from Columbus. I love Oakland, but I would give my eyeteeth to live in a place like this, right in the heart of one of my favorite neighborhoods in San Francisco. I hadn't yet managed to get a key, but Michael, of course, doesn't let little things like keys stand in his way. He once took me there, pretending it was his place.

Since then, whenever I happened to be in the neighborhood, I drove by. No reason. Except that I was morbidly fascinated by the fact that Michael wouldn't tell me where he lived. He and my grandfather both swore he was no longer staying in Georges's apartment, but since I didn't know where else he was...

A tall dark-haired man was standing outside the building, laughing and looking down into the face of a very beautiful woman with shiny, thick honey-blond hair that fell halfway down her back. I rolled forward, not believing what I was seeing.

Michael?

14

Dearest Georges, Greatest Forger in the World: I want to be famous like you! What advice can you offer me?
— Yearning to be like Georges LeFleur

Dear Yearning: Give up. True fame comes only to those who do not seek it. But keep painting...always, always paint!

— Georges LeFleur, "Craquelure"

MICHAEL *NEVER* LAUGHED like that! Michael laughed in a cynical "I'm so much cooler than you'll ever be" kind of way. He was looking at this woman like...like he cared about her.

My stomach dropped. I stomped on the brakes and gaped.

Even though I turned the man down as frequently as twice a day, *I* was the one he was supposed to be sexually harassing. Who *was* this woman?

She was gorgeous, of course. Only a couple of inches shorter than Michael, with legs up to here and breasts out to there. No belly. Boyish hips. The face of a Madonna/whore, no doubt depending upon the circumstances.

They looked magnificent together: two demi-gods amongst the earthly gremlins.

I glanced down at the too-big African mudprint caftan I was wearing, thought of my wild hair and lack of makeup, and felt like something that had crawled out from under a rock.

Michael's face was split by a huge grin at something the woman said, and then he scooped her up in a big bear hug and twirled her around. My heart, already turning green, sank to my toes.

Suddenly Michael glanced up at the truck, and at me. Without missing a beat he put his hand on the woman's shoulder and escorted her quickly in through the front door, closing it firmly behind them both.

He had seen me, clear as day, and yet he turned and walked away. With a beautiful woman. Laughing.

I let the truck idle in the middle of the street for a minute, weighing my options. I could bang on the door and ring the door-bell, but given that Michael had just ducked into the apartment when he spotted me, I doubted it would do much good. I could call him and leave a threatening message. So far that tactic hadn't gotten me as far as I would have liked, either.

I could wait until he left and somehow pick the lock—or more likely, hire someone to break in there for me... Mary had an ex-boyfriend who was a locksmith—and ransack the apartment under the guise of looking for the F-U's stolen paintings. Maybe the unrepentant thief had them after all. Annette Crawford suspected him, as did Frank, so why was I so certain that he couldn't have them? And if I happened to snoop a little in bureau drawers looking for women's underwear or an extra toothbrush while I was in there, well, that would be part of the search for art.

Or I could be a grown-up about this whole thing, acknowledge that the man had a private life, and leave it at that. Respect his privacy.

Jeez, I hated being reasonable sometimes.

Fine. I blew out a deep breath. Best channel this energy into something useful, like trying to find stolen paintings.

The Fleming Mansion wasn't far. I wanted to get in and take a look at the room Elijah Odibajian had been found in. I had the XRF spectrometer Brianna had lent to me; I could check out whatever remained of the wallpaper, see if it contained arsenic, and get the information to Annette Crawford. That would be useful. And maybe I would stumble upon a secret cache of paintings the Fleming-Union brethren claimed were stolen.

Of course, the intractable blond guy wouldn't let me in, for sure, but they had to have another parking attendant/security guard from time to time, right? Blond guy couldn't be there every day, could he?

I was right: there was another security guard on duty today. This one was a fortyish, buff, Latino guy. Unfortunately, he was Alert and On the Job and knew all about little old me. There was even a grainy photo of me tacked up on the small bulletin board, no doubt taken by a hidden camera at the front door when I was insisting upon testing the Backflow Prevention Device. I did not look my best.

Unfortunately, I think I looked even worse today.

As I stood arguing with the stoic and unrelenting guard, the parking lot's ornate iron gates swung slowly open to allow entrance to a shiny red Aston Martin convertible.

Driving it was the man who had originally hired me for the attic wallpaper job, Geoffrey McAdams. And in the passenger seat was Destiny-the-maid.

McAdams left the car idling in the middle of the entrance. Before climbing out of the car he leaned over and said something to Destiny, who nodded and stared straight ahead.

"Annie Kincaid," he said as he oozed over to me and held out his hand to shake. His eyes flickered over my outfit, and once again I realized I wasn't making the best impression. McAdams reeked of old money and entitlement, and had a way of talking that was simultaneously all politeness yet made you feel like you were the tiniest pawn in his chess game of life. "What a surprise. How *are* you?"

"Hello Geoffrey." I nodded and shook his hand.

"Listen, Annie, did the police ever get a chance to speak with you further? There have been a few developments we all need to figure out."

"They've called, yes," I evaded. "A few times."

"This is a terrible affair, all of it. Very distressing to us all."

I nodded, but my eyes met Destiny's gaze.

"Hi Destiny," I said, ducking my head toward the passenger's side window. "How are you?"

"She's a little shaken up, but just fine," said Geoffrey, stepping in between us. "She insisted on coming back to work today, didn't you, Ms. Baker?"

Destiny Baker just nodded, remained mute, and looked away.

"Speaking of working," I said to Geoffrey, "I was wondering when I could get back to the attic job. No time like the present, I always say."

"The brethren agree that the project shall be put on hold for the near future."

Oh really? Except for having it done by a fellow named Mauricio...

"We have a contract," I reminded him, wondering how far he would take this.

"I assure you the terms of the contract will be fulfilled." He took a billfold and pen from the pocket of his costly double-breasted suit. "I have my checkbook with me now; would you like me to pay you for your services immediately?"

I must be doing something right, I thought. First I was hired on a no-results-necessary basis, and now people were paying me *not* to work.

I cleared my throat and glanced back at the mansion. The security guard was watching with avid fascination.

"Fifty percent is fair upon postponement of the project," I said. "If it's a cancellation, I'll have to ask for the full amount. I don't have the paperwork with me—"

"I happen to have the contract right here," he said, leaning in to the open window of his car to extract a sleek black leather briefcase. He took out the contract, handed it over, wrote out a check, and held it out to me. It was made out for the full amount of the original bid.

"It was lovely seeing you, as always," Geoffrey said as he moved back to stand next to the driver's side door and met my eyes over the roof of the car. "Now, please go away, and don't come back."

The frozen blue of his gaze chilled me to the core.

We stared at each other for a long moment. Overlong. I blinked first.

Destiny continued to stare straight ahead as Geoffrey McAdams climbed back into the driver's seat. How in the world did someone as sweet as Wesley Fleming hang out with these guys, ancestral home or no? More importantly, *why*? I watched as the gate slowly cranked closed behind the gleaming, vintage machine, which glided into the parking lot and came to a stop right next to the rear door of the Fleming Mansion.

The very door through which women and servants entered and exited, right alongside the groceries. And the trash.

As she climbed out of the car, Destiny looked over at me. Call me crazy, but it looked like a plea for rescue.

Not wanting the F-U cartel to think that I would just leave whenever they told me, I loitered outside the parking lot gates for a few minutes after McAdams had taken Destiny by the elbow and escorted her past the security guard.

Yeah, boy. Guess I showed them, sticking around for all of five minutes.

Ringing Nob Hill were several huge, 1960s-era apartment buildings. I remembered that Wesley told me he lived in one nearby, in an apartment with a view.

I still had his card in the pocket of my satchel. Couldn't hurt, right?

The entrance was on Clay Street at Jones. My heart dropped when I was met by a uniformed doorman in the glass-fronted entryway.

"I'm here to see Wesley Fleming. I'm a friend."

The doorman phoned upstairs and spoke for a moment.

To my surprise, Wesley invited me up.

"What are you doing here?" he asked as he flung open the door. "Come in, come in. I never get visitors here. This is a lovely surprise. Pardon the mess; what do they say at remodels at the airport? Pardon our dust? Quite literally in my case."

He wasn't kidding. I guess if you're a handyman without a garage, and you live by yourself, you make stuff wherever you darn well pleased. There were piles of wood scraps and small saws set up in what normally served as the living room area.

The apartment boasted incredible views of the Bay Bridge, Alcatraz and Angel islands, Nob Hill to one side, and Chinatown straight down the hill. And it overlooked the vast clay tile roof of the F-U.

"Great view," I said. "You can see right down to the Fleming-Union."

"Yes, I know. I've seen some funny things over the years. Down there," he pointed to the backyard of a house two doors down Jones, "lives a very old woman who still hangs her clothes out to dry herself. And I can see part of the Chinese New Year parade from here; I love the dragon, don't you? And do you know, the brethren take such great care of the Fleming Mansion that they even wash the roof? There were some workers out there just last week, making sure everything is spic and span."

"They wash the roof?"

"That's what it looks like. They go out every once in a while with hoses. Maybe they're cleaning out the gutters. A place like that keeps you up to your ears in maintenance—they're forever caulking windows or repainting rooms. That's why I like living in an apartment—it's someone else's headache."

I nodded, then gestured to his woodworking project. "What are you making?"

"Bat houses."

"Houses for bats? I thought they lived in caves."

He laughed. "Oh, they do, they do. When they can. But in urban areas it's hard for them to find refuge. Did you know, we're losing almost forty percent of our bat population in the U.S. due to habitat loss? These boxes," he hoisted a finished one up for me to see, "can be mounted on the sides of houses and apartment buildings, just anywhere."

It looked like the sort of flat, rectangular mailbox that was often attached to the side of a house, but the front was covered with closely placed slats. I tried to look in through the narrow openings.

"Neat."

"Aren't they, though? You mount them high on your exterior wall, near the roof. Can you think of anything cuter than having a little family of bats living right there under your eaves?"

"Um...real cute."

As the words came out of my mouth I noticed the series of framed photos covering one entire wall of the living room. Bat portraits. I walked over to read the brass plaques that were attached at the bottom of each one: CLEOBATRA, BINKY, ROCKY BATBOA, STELLA, MINI-ME, a brown ball of fluff named STICKY.

"I've adopted all those bats there," Wesley explained. He gazed at them with a father's adoration. "They're at a bat rescue center in Tulsa. Those are my babies."

"Cute names. Why 'Sticky'?"

"He was rescued from flypaper."

"Flypaper catches bats?"

"It can, depending on their size, and especially if they're immature. Sticky was tiny when they found him. Poor little buddy."

"Is this what you do, you know, full time? Work for the bat cause?"

"Pretty much. I'm lucky, I don't really have to work for a

living. Family fund, you know. If I watch my pennies, I can live off my interest. But I want to give something back to the world, obviously. This is my calling. Everyone should have a calling. I run a website for bat enthusiasts, and make bat houses to distribute, and try to educate people. There's a lot of ignorance out there about bats."

"I can imagine."

"For instance, *megachiroptera* are usually called 'megabats' while *microchiroptera* are usually referred to as 'microbats,' but despite the name, megabats aren't always larger than microbats. The main difference is that microbats use echolocation; they need it to help locate prey. Megabats mainly live off of fruit, pollen, and nectar, whereas microbats feed off of insects, blood, small mammals, and even fish sometimes."

"Blood? Like vampire bats?"

He gave me a disgusted look.

"Bats eat thousands of pounds of insects, you know. If not for bats, we'd all be eaten alive by mosquitoes. Think about that next time Count Dracula supposedly shape-shifts into a bat."

Good point. But I couldn't help but wonder whether even the lowly mosquito had a defender somewhere, like Wesley, building wee larvae habitats for the little buddies.

As I looked around I saw that Wesley's place was, indeed, the bat-cave. Except for being on the ninth floor, that is. There were bat pictures and bat replicas and bat books and a lamp that looked like a bat. I read another name off another picture of a bat.

"Is Bootsana Melonmouth a name or a type of bat?" I asked.

Wesley laughed as though I had made a joke. "Good one. Hey, can I get you something to drink? I've got lemonade."

"That'd be great," I said, trailing him into the small efficiency kitchen. "Could you tell me more about the tunnels you mentioned the other day? I was in Chinatown yesterday and it seems some people think there were tunnels there, too."

"You were talking about tunnels? To whom?"

"Just some folks there. Friends of a friend."

"You shouldn't really talk about that kind of thing."

"Why not?"

He just shrugged, taking two tall glasses down from a glass-fronted cabinet.

"Anyway, those were mostly coal chutes and sewer tunnels under Chinatown," Wesley said. He filled the glasses from a large turquoise plastic pitcher. "They weren't connected to the family tunnels."

"Family tunnels?"

"Oh dear." Wesley opened the freezer and pulled out an ice tray. "I always say too much."

"You can tell me, Wesley. What's the big secret?"

"The brethren don't like me to talk about it."

"Why not?"

"I don't know the details. There were some nasty things, in the past. You know, my great-grandfather built the place but he gave it to the club a long time ago. There were...events that... well, things have changed over the years. Values have changed."

"You think the club was involved in something bad in the past?"

"No...but times have changed. There's nothing like that now."

"I have to say, Wesley, except for you, I haven't liked any of the Fleming-Union brethren I've met."

Wesley turned around to look at me, ice in hand.

"Really? You've met them?"

"A few. Pretty creepy if you ask me."

"They're very powerful men. They own this city."

"Maybe that's the problem. They say power corrupts."

Wesley, realizing the ice was melting in his hands, dropped the cubes into the glasses of lemonade. He set one in front of me. Seemingly lost in thought, he pushed his glasses up on his nose, leaving a drop of water that trailed down and hung on the end of his nose.

"You're not really a student, are you?" Wesley asked.

"Not exactly," I answered. "I'm actually an artist, if you can believe that." I took a sip. "Good lemonade, thanks."

"Welcome." Wesley said. "Why's an artist asking all these questions?"

"It's pretty hard to explain. Something strange happened in the Fleming-Union just the other day, Wesley. Did you know someone died? Elijah Odibajian?"

"Yes, I heard about that. He wasn't really a member, he was just visiting. For a long time. But anyway, he died of natural causes."

"Who told you that?"

"He looked terrible. He'd been getting sicker over the last couple of months. No one could figure out what was wrong with him, even though his brother, Balthazar, brought in one of the best doctors. Up from Stanford Medical Center."

"Do you remember the doctor's name?"

He shook his head. "No, but Balthazar said he wanted only the best for his brother."

Wesley steered the conversation back to the lives and times of bats while we finished our lemonade. Afterward, I asked to use the bathroom and Wesley pointed me down a short hallway. There were more bat icons lining the corridor, but what stopped me dead in my tracks was a glossy reproduction of Jacques Louis David's *Death of Marat*, hanging on the wall right outside the apartment's sole bedroom.

"You like it?" Wesley asked, standing too close behind me.

I jumped. "Oh, uh, yeah. Sure."

"It used to hang outside some of the guest rooms in the F-U. One of the brethren gave it to me just the other day. I don't know why but I always liked it. Is that weird?"

I looked closer at the reproduction. On the simple frame was a brass plaque: NATURE MORTE.

"That means 'still life,'" said Wesley.

"I know. Why is it labeled that?"

"I guess it's the name of the painting."

"No it's not."

"You're sure?"

"Yes, I'm sure. Wesley, what does the Latin phrase on your card refer to?"

"Oh, that's the Fleming-Union motto."

"Do you know what it means?"

"Yes."

When there was no more forthcoming, I urged him on. "Could you tell me what it means?"

He looked wary and pushed up his glasses. "I don't think I'm supposed to talk about it."

"It's in Latin, Wesley, not Elvish. I'm sure it's not meant to be a secret."

"Oh, I don't know. The brethren always say I talk too much.

I'd feel much better about it if you just asked someone else who knows Latin. Didn't you need to use the bathroom?"

I did. Wesley was waiting for me right outside the door when I emerged.

"I'll walk you out," he said.

Hanging on the elevator doors was a handwritten note scrawled on a piece of scratch-paper: OUT OF SERVICE.

"Rats," Wesley said. "Let's take the freight elevator."

We let ourselves through a heavy metal fire door to a service corridor and waited at the freight elevator for another five minutes, but according to the numbered indicator, the lift never left the basement floor.

"Well, *this* has never happened before," Wesley said. "Good Lord. I guess we have to take the stairs. Good for our health, in any case, right?"

We started down. At the first landing we came to a man in coveralls, caulking a small window.

As we moved past him, he suddenly stuck his foot out, tripping Wesley and shoving him on the back.

Wesley tumbled down the flight of stairs, falling to the next landing, limp and silent as a marionette whose strings had been cut.

Until the advent of the signature, art was created to be used: as public history for the illiterate; in magical invocations when calling for rain or game; as the focus of religious reflection. The creator of the piece was invisible, allowing the art to speak for itself. As soon as attribution became important—especially now that it is all-important—forgery followed. It seems to me a law of nature.

—Georges LeFleur, "Craquelure"

THE MAN GRABBED ME from behind and yanked me back against his hard, muscled chest.

I threw my head back into his chin and stomped on his instep, gratified by the grunt I heard. Still, his grasp only tightened, pulling my upper arms back so hard I felt like they would pull out of their sockets.

Another man, in a ski mask, appeared in front of me. He slapped me, hard, across the face. Pain burst through my temple and cheekbone, sending more knife-edged shards of pain into my brain. He was speaking, but I couldn't focus, couldn't process the words. My sense of smell wasn't affected, though; the man holding me stank of sweat and the same pungent cologne worn by the goon who held me in the F-U dining room.

The ski-masked man slapped me again, across the other cheek. My ears rang, I tasted blood, and my cheeks felt on fire.

"...hear me?" he yelled in my face.

The guy holding me from behind leaned his head forward and bit me right on the fleshy part above my collarbone. The bite wasn't hard enough to break the skin, but I could feel it bruising.

"Yum," he said.

"You're a sick fuck, you know that?" said the goon in the ski mask to the guy holding me, who just laughed.

Ski Mask then held a knife to my throat. The shock of its sharp point brought everything into focus.

"This is your only warning, get me?"

I nodded vigorously, which made my head hurt. At that point I would have agreed to just about anything; all my concentration was focused on getting as far away from these men as possible.

Ski Mask took my bag, shook it out, grabbed the cell phone, scrolled through numbers, then threw it down the stairwell. I could hear it crashing on the cement steps below. Then he took my wallet, my money. Even my change purse, and my cheap silver earrings.

Then he descended the stairs and checked Wesley's pockets as well. Wesley's heavy glasses had been knocked into the corner; he tried to rouse himself, sputtering a protest, but after the goon showed him a fist he backed down.

"It's just terrible, someone getting mugged in such a nice building," The Biter in coveralls rasped as he pushed me to my knees. "What's the world coming to?"

They ran.

———

Time in the emergency room is almost as bad as getting interrogated by the police, so I decided to skip it.

I wanted Wesley to get his head looked at, but I was afraid my name would come up on the police scanner if I went with him. I used the lobby phone to call Mary—who was already out and about, running the errands I had sent her on—and asked her to accompany Wesley to the hospital.

One of the things I love about my assistant is that she doesn't ask a whole lot of questions. Wesley tried to protest that he didn't need any help until he saw her, all six-feet-blonde of her. She was wearing a particularly see-through black outfit today.

I slipped out before the police arrived, then limped on back to my truck and drove to the studio. Happily, Frank wasn't in his office. I had already reneged on my promise to show up and annoy him yesterday; if he were here now I was afraid I would collapse into his arms and ask him to marry me and take me away from all this.

I hurried into the bathroom to wash up.

The mirror showed that both cheeks were bright red from the vicious slaps I had received, but I doubted there would be bruising. It would look like slight sunburn to anyone who didn't know I'd been hit. Moving gingerly, I pulled the collar of Sam's dress aside to see a reddish-blue bruise developing above my collarbone, in the crescent shape of teeth. The bite hadn't broken the skin, and I knew a simple contusion wasn't a serious injury, but it creeped me out. The pungent smell of that aftershave and the weirdly intimate act of biting...ick.

I brought out a bag of frozen peas I kept in the tiny freezer compartment of my studio mini-fridge—a trick I learned from my sister, Bonnie, when she was the first-aid go-to gal for her sons' Little League team. Holding the peas to the bruise, I sat at my studio desk and started the rounds of phone calls to cancel my credit cards.

Unfortunately, navigating voicemail loops and sitting on hold with bad music piped into my ears did not succeed in getting my thoughts off what had happened in that stairwell.

Pedro had warned me. Frank had warned me. Even Odibajian himself had warned me. Was there anyone who *hadn't* warned me? And yet I stood talking to Geoffrey McAdams right in front of the F-U, then proceeded directly to Wesley's apartment. Those goons must have trailed me straight there from the club. Duh.

Looked like somebody needed to go back to spy school. Or at least learn to skulk properly. At the very least: manage not to take innocent bystanders down with me.

I felt terrible. Poor Wesley. He had been perfectly happy, just him and his bats, the monotony of his days interrupted by the occasional club function where he was no doubt teased and demeaned, but he still felt part of something historic and worthwhile...until Annie Kincaid, disaster on wheels, barged into his life.

I powered up the computer and Googled "Chinatown tunnels." There was a whole lot of information on the Broadway tube, and on Chinese-built tunnels in towns up and down the California gold trail. Fascinating. Still, the consensus was that tunnels under San Francisco were a myth. But I found a sole reference on a message board to a tunnel under a home on Nob Hill; the writer said his great-grandfather had lived in a mansion there, and that supposedly the tunnels really did exist. The man signed his name: The Batman. Wesley was a real subtle guy. At least it alleviated my guilt just a tad; even if I hadn't led them to

him, maybe the F-U boys would have gone after The Batman anyway. Surely they could use the Google search function if I could.

While I was on the Internet, I looked up the painting most
famous for juxtaposing nude females with fully dressed men.
Edouard Manet's *Le déjeuner sur l'herbe,* or "The Luncheon on the
Grass" is a large painting currently hanging in the Musée d'Orsay
in Paris. I downloaded a copy and faxed it to Norm with a note:
*Does this look like the party you witnessed? Also, please ask Mauricio
if he could save me a sample of the wallpaper he took from the Fleming Mansion, no matter how small. I'll buy you both a beer.*

Then I did something I should have done two days ago: I
called every scrap metal yard I could find in the phone book,
promising a reward, no questions asked, for *Resting Hermes.* I
wasn't going to spend much time and energy on the search, but
it seemed like the least I could do.

Next I called Pedro to see if he'd had any luck locating Kyle
Jones.

"He's not listed anywhere. He moved years ago from the address you gave me from the police report, and disappeared. I'm
doubting Kyle Jones is his real name, or else he moved out of
state."

"Rats."

"But here's something interesting: Catrina Yeltsin, née Watts,
was an excellent student at Cal until she took off on a student
exchange program to India, and never returned to school."

"I don't think it's that unusual. A lot of people get sidetracked,
don't finish up their degree."

"I guess so. Still, seems suspicious to me."

"Everything seems suspicious to you. What was her major at
Berkeley?"

"Chemistry."

That surprised me. "You're sure?"

"Yup. She even worked for a lab in India for a while."

The fax machine beeped. Still on the phone to Pedro, I picked
up the incoming message. A note from Norm: *FNA on the picnic
picture, nope on the wallpaper samples. You obsessed with wallpaper
now, or what?*

"Pedro, what do the initials 'FNA' stand for?"

"Fuckin' A."

"Seriously?"

"Yup."

One day I was going to have to join the modern world, before everyone I knew left me behind.

Okay, so what did I know at this point? Anton had painted a forgery years ago for a club member, Victor; then Elijah had tried to sell that forgery as authentic, and then was killed in the mansion while I was working there. Anton was poisoned, but I couldn't be sure there was a connection. There appeared to be tunnels running under the Fleming Mansion and perhaps connecting to old tunnels to Cameron House. Other paintings perhaps were stolen from the club while I worked there, despite Frank's security system, and Geoffrey McAdams had asked Norm to hire me.

All in all, this wasn't looking great for True/Faux Studios, much less Bacchus Art Associates. Or for Frank DeBenton's professional reputation, for that matter.

—

I felt the need to talk to someone keyed into the gossip of the City. My old friend Bryan Boissevain and I had been through quite a few adventures over the past few years, including tampering with evidence in a drug smuggling case, tracking down a Chagall he was suspected of helping to steal, and ruining a beautiful ball gown that had belonged to a gorgeous transvestite who, it turned out, held a grudge. But unlike me, Bryan both paid attention to, and remembered, stories about Who's Who in San Francisco.

Bryan works from home, so unless he's under deadline he relishes the chance to get out during the day. I made a phone call and invited him to a late lunch/early dinner.

An hour later we were sitting cross-legged on the floor of my studio in front of a sushi feast. Bryan, as was his wont, had brought a picnic basket full of rectangular ceramic painted dishes—white with delicate sprigs of flowers in blue—tiny cups, and chopsticks, along with a chilled bottle of sake and cloth napkins. He laid a beautiful steamer trunk–turned–coffee table.

"I thought *I* was taking *you* to lunch," I had told him when he arrived at my door with basket in hand.

"I had a yen for sushi. Get it?"

"Bryan, you keep 'em rolling in the aisles."

"Don't I though? Anyway, you know the sushi bar right under my apartment has the best spicy tuna in town, so I took the liberty of ordering for you."

I'm one of those people who love to have people order for me. Since I'm an equal-opportunity gourmet, I almost always appreciate whatever's put on my plate. And I'm a Libra, so I have a hard time making decisions, especially in times of stress. And I was feeling just a tad stressed at the moment. Bryan noticed my funk, but I put it down to being tired. He didn't believe me, but we'd been friends for so long that he didn't push it.

"What do you know about the Fleming-Union?" I asked as we started in on our meal.

"Oooh, that place. No women, no liberals, no reporters," said Bryan, "they take it seriously, God love 'em. I can see them now, bunch of wrinkly old white guys, smoking cigars and rattling their canes."

"Women aren't allowed through the front door."

"That's 'cause you've got cooties," Bryan said as he used his chopsticks to gracefully spear a glistening white rectangle of *himachi*. "And you're not the only ones. There's an old saw: if there were only five men left in the world, three would sneak out behind the house and form a club, and not allow the other two in. And I don't have to tell you which side of that wall I'd be on."

Bryan was gay and African American, and though he and his financier husband lived a comfortable life in an expensive city, they were neither rich nor powerful in Fleming-Union terms. "Three strikes, I'm out" was how Bryan usually phrased it. The only F-U membership qualification he held was being male, and since that applied to roughly half the world I suspected his engraved invitation to join had been lost in the mail right alongside mine.

"Do you know any of the members?" I asked as I helped myself to a disc of spicy tuna roll.

"The membership list is secret, though in many cases it's an open secret. Plenty of the city's movers and shakers, the older and more conservative the better. But there's a younger contingent, as well, I understand, the up-and-coming power brokers. I don't know anyone personally, if that's what you're asking."

"I need to find a way in there."

"Why?"

"It's sort of complicated."

"Uh-oh." Bryan put his chopsticks down on the edge of his plate and leaned back against the couch. "When you say something's 'sort of complicated' that usually means someone is going to post bail soon."

"Very funny."

"I'm not kidding."

"It's important. Too bad I didn't think to leave a window unlocked or something," I mused. "I was working there until a couple of days ago."

"What were you doing?"

"Stripping wallpaper in one of the attic rooms. I was supposed to reproduce the historical pattern in paint. But then they hired someone else."

"They kicked you off a job? What'd you do?"

"Why do all my loyal friends assume I did something to deserve having my services cancelled?"

He just gave me a Look.

"It wasn't my fault," I insisted, trying to keep the whiney note out of my voice. "I happened upon a body the other day. No one I had anything to do with."

"So why are you getting involved now?"

I told him about Elijah Odibajian, and Anton, and the Gauguin fake that turned up at auction. I left out the part about getting attacked by goons in the stairwell.

"I can't stop thinking that if I had a chance to look around the club, I would find something that would help explain things, maybe prove something?"

"Like what?"

Good question.

"Well...for one thing, I'd like to get the spectrometer up to the room Elijah was staying in and test that wallpaper, if there's any left."

"Let me get this straight: the place is full of a bunch of ethically challenged, incredibly rich men, and is also a current murder scene. And you want to poke around without even knowing what you're looking for?"

Bryan was loyal to a fault, loving and generous, and one of my dearest friends, but he was not what most people would refer to as the most level-headed of men. If *he* was doubting my schemes, maybe I really was going around the bend a bit.

"I—"

Mary flung open the studio door and stepped in, Wesley in tow, a small bandage placed over his left eye.

I jumped up. "Wesley, how are you feeling?

"No concussion," Mary said before Wesley had a chance to respond. "But we're supposed to keep him awake."

"Why?" I asked.

Mary shrugged. "That's what they always said at camp. Keep them awake."

"Did the doctors tell you to stay awake?" I asked Wesley.

"Not exactly, but that's okay," he said with an enthusiastic note in his voice. "I'll just stay with you, if you really don't mind."

"He's been threatened," Mary said. "He doesn't want to be alone."

"Of course," I said. "Hang out with us. This is my friend Bryan."

The men shook.

"Care for sushi? There's more than enough," Bryan offered. As Mary and Wesley joined us on the floor, Bryan looked pointedly at Wesley's bandage, then at me, but had the grace not to ask what had happened.

"Hey, you haven't heard anything about Michael, have you?" I asked Bryan.

"You mean Michael X. Johnson, as in your finer-than-fine business partner?"

"Yeah, where's he been lately?" Mary asked.

Bryan shook his head. "His name doesn't pop up much. He plays his cards close to his chest, as I believe you know from personal experience."

"Do I ever."

"I don't know why you two don't just sleep together and get it out of your system," Bryan said. "*I* would sleep with him if he were playing for my team."

Wesley gawked openly. Mary leaned over and whispered, *"Bryan's gay."* Bryan, unfazed, just looked over at the pair and winked. Wesley's eyes widened, and I wondered whether he was among the last people in the City by the Bay to become accustomed to alternative lifestyles.

"Liar," I said to Bryan. "You wouldn't sleep with Michael. You're too loyal to Ron."

"Yeah, well…if I *weren't* married to Ron, and I were a straight woman, you bet your boots I'd have slept with him already. Long time ago."

"That's what *I* said," Mary said. She leaned over to Wesley. "No offense."

"None taken," he said, looking up at her eagerly.

"You think that's the way it works?" I asked, busy chasing a slippery piece of plump pink tuna around my little rectangular ceramic plate. "Like if I slept with him, I would get him out of my system and I wouldn't have to think about him again?"

"Sure," Bryan said. "Maybe he's bad in bed."

I looked up at Bryan, and Mary looked over at me. We all started laughing.

"That's a good one," I said.

"Yeah, you're right," Bryan said. "One night with that man, presuming you survived, and you'd be ruined for anyone else."

The phone rang. I picked it up to hear Cathy Yeltsin's cheery voice.

"I found some wonderful design ideas for my basement!" she declared. She gave me a website address which I dutifully jotted down, but I made no promises as to when I would get back to her with drawings. It was going to take a much healthier frame of mind than I currently possessed to actually work on the design of a dungeon, faux or otherwise.

"Also, I have to tell you the strangest thing. My Victor seems to have gone missing."

"Really."

"I haven't seen him since you were here. Remember how he disappeared without saying good-bye? What do you suppose could have possessed him?"

"Has he dropped out of sight before?"

"Oh, no, never. Perhaps for a night at a time, but nothing like this. If you're going to the Power Play, could you keep an eye out for him? I would go myself but I don't have childcare."

"I wasn't really planning on—"

"Tonight's really your best bet to catch Kyle in action," she mentioned. "He's always there Thursdays."

I didn't like the sound of *that*. Or the visual, more precisely. On the other hand, trying to find a way into the Fleming Mansion might be too crazy, even for me. I was still moving slowly due to the bruises I had just obtained, and the goons' warning still reverberated in my battered brain. But Kyle-the-houseboy didn't have anything to do with the F-U directly, right? Surely tracking him down in the Power Play wouldn't be overly dangerous, beyond possibly seeing much more of him than I'd like.

"What does Kyle look like?"

"Late twenties, light hair, blue eyes, medium height. Pretty."

"Okay," I said. "I might go. And if I happen to see Victor, I'll tell him to phone home."

I turned back to my little group of friends, old and new: Bryan, Mary, and now poor smitten Wesley. My eyes alighted upon Bryan.

Bryan is a big, buff, gym-toned man, but given his gentle character and easy smile, it was easy to forget he could be formidable. I had seen him in action, however: when he wanted to be intimidating, it was an easy feat.

"Would you be willing to go to the Power Play with me tonight?" I asked Bryan.

"The Power Play?" Bryan said, nearly choking on a slice of *unagi*. "What, has all this talk put you in the mood?"

"Not exactly. I need to talk to someone there."

"Why does it have to be there?"

"I don't know where he lives, but he's supposed to be at the Power Play tonight. I really don't want to go alone."

He looked at me for a long moment, his mouth pulled tight with disapproval.

"I'll go, but under protest. Personally, I think you should reconsider this art investigation business. Faux finishes are more up your alley."

I'd heard *that* before.

"No way you're going to the Power Play without me! I wanna go!" said Mary. She leaned over and jabbed an elbow at Wesley. "You up for it, Wes?"

"Oh, I, er..." he sputtered.

"Great. We'll all go. It'll be an outing," said Mary.

I could use all the company I could get, but somehow I couldn't imagine Wesley in a sex club. I could barely imagine *myself* in a sex club. Mary, on the other hand...well, let's just say I wouldn't be surprised if she already knew the way there.

"Are you sure you want to come, Wesley?" I asked.

"I—"

"Of course he does," put in Mary. "After what he's been through, he needs to be with his friends. Don't worry, Wes, I'll look out for you."

Wesley remained mute, but looked over at Mary with eager adoration shining in his eyes. I had a feeling I now knew who Wesley's "type" was.

Just then our Bosnian friend, Pete, walked into the studio, flushed with happiness. "Evangeline, she said yes!" he said. "She will go out with me tonight!"

"No way," said Mary.

"Way," responded Pete.

"I could help you dress there, homeboy," said Bryan. "It'll be like *Queer Eye for the Straight Guy.*"

Pete looked worried. "What kind of eye?"

"Never mind," Bryan said with an encouraging smile. "On second thought, you're cute as a button just as you are."

"Speaking of which, what does a person even *wear* to a sex club?" I wondered aloud.

"You're going?" Pete asked. "When?"

"Tonight, say around nine?" I suggested to my Power Play entourage.

"Could Evangeline and I accompany you?"

"Are you sure?" I asked. "It might be a bit much for a first date."

"We will be with all of you. Please. That way I won't be so nervous."

The Power Play seemed pretty much like the opposite of their kind of place, but I guessed Pete didn't want to be left out. Besides, Pete was a big, hulking man, and Evangeline was no wilting waif herself. I could use the backup.

"Sure, come along. What the heck," I said, giving in to the absurdity of the situation. I had no idea what we'd find at the

Power Play, but given the excursion participants it was bound to be interesting. "The more the merrier. Anyway, back to the important stuff: what should we wear?"

Mary met my eyes.

"*Jeans,*" we said in unison.

"No easy access," Mary said.

"Amen to that."

"And boots." My assistant always wore boots, but that in no way diminished the wisdom of her suggestion. "*Big* boots."

———

We met on the street in front of the Power Play: Bryan and me and Wesley and Mary and Pete and Evangeline. Boy girl, boy girl. Bryan's partner Ron refused to participate, citing any number of reasons; chief among them, decency and sanity.

Clearly I wasn't the only one who decided jeans and boots were *de rigueur* at a sex club. Five of us could form a band. Only Wesley had dressed, as usual, in an ill-fitting tweed blazer and brown loafers. Meanwhile, typically mild, sweet Bryan looked like the quintessential sexy bad boy in his bulky black leather jacket, worn jeans stuffed into heavy black boots.

Perfect.

"Don't accept drinks from anyone," Bryan ordered, his agitation ratcheting up the closer we got to the entrance. He looked around and scowled. "You've all heard of roofies?"

"They don't serve alcohol here," I mentioned.

Bryan stopped in his tracks and gave me a horrified look. "We're supposed to get through this without a *drink*?"

Bryan's never been a big drinker, but I had to admit I was wishing I'd thought to have a shot or two of tequila before arriving tonight. It would help to have something to take the edge off, I thought as I noted the hand sanitizer dispensers mounted at frequent intervals on the wall. Next to them was a large sign that read: TOUCHING SOMEONE WITHOUT PERMISSION WILL RESULT IN IMMEDIATE EJECTION FROM THE CLUB.

"Well, see there? *That's* good news," I said with a falsely cheerful ring to my voice.

"Oh, look," Mary said, eyeing Pete. "Women get in cheap, but men have to pay more. Ya gotta love that. But guys get in for half-price if they take off their clothes and just wear a towel."

"Annie," Pete said with a sense of urgency, drawing me aside.

He was blushing; behind us, Evangeline just lurked, silent and agog. *"What kind of place is this?"*

"It's an S and M club, Pete. But we won't be doing anything, we're just looking—"

"What is this essenem?"

"A sex club," Mary interpreted.

"A *sex* club?" Pete exclaimed.

"What did you think it was?" I asked.

"A music club."

"Music?"

"Didn't you say sax? Like the instrument?"

" 'fraid not," Mary said. "This is a *sex* club, with all sorts of *sexy* stuff going on."

Pete and Evangeline didn't make it past the first bowl of free condoms. Stumbling over an excuse about having left clothes in the dryer, he and Evangeline fled without a look back.

"They're the only ones amongst us with brains," Bryan said wistfully as he watched them retreat.

As we entered the foyer, Wesley's nervous gaze kept sliding over to Bryan.

"Don't look at me, *I've* never been to a place like this," Bryan said. "We're not nearly as bad as y'all heteros. This is *her* doing." He jerked a thumb in my direction.

Since Bryan was the only one of this motley crew that I had actually asked to come on this ill-conceived venture, I had the grace to feel a tad guilty. Still, I wasn't above using my friends from time to time. This was important.

We approached the front desk to pay our entrance fees. Couples got in much cheaper than singles, so Bryan slung an arm around my shoulders, and Mary put hers around Wesley's.

"He's my boy toy," declared Mary. Wesley looked up at her with liquid, puppy-dog eyes.

"It costs more if you keep your pants on," said the bored-looking man behind the counter.

Wesley had a coughing fit. Mary slapped him on the back. Bryan glared at the receptionist, his eyes cold and dangerous. I stepped in between them, afraid for the first time in my life that Bryan might be moved to physical violence.

"We're good," I said as I shelled out several twenties to pay for everyone. It was the least I could do. "They like their pants. Do you happen to know where Kyle Jones is tonight?"

The man's eyes drifted over me, clearly seeing me naked and, no doubt, in an advanced *Kama Sutra* position reminiscent of a pretzel. My yoga hadn't advanced that far and, I hoped, never would. Unbidden, my mind flashed on the Indian artwork in Catrina and Victor's house.

"He's usually in the Dungeon, or the Pirate's Lair. But you could check the Jail Cells, or the Coffin Room."

Oh. Goodie.

Wesley paled. He would have left at that description, I felt sure, if Mary hadn't been latched on to his arm as though he were the big, bad protector of a woman two inches taller, and no doubt much fitter, than he. Mary had been taking kickboxing for years, and wore serious boots.

"Where do you want to go first?" Mary asked. "It would be faster to split up, but I think we should stay together."

"Oh, definitely," I said.

"None of you are leaving my sight," Bryan said, glowering at a clutch of young men entering the place behind us.

We started to look around. There weren't many people in the first couple of big, open rooms on the main floor. There was an empty rec room with Ping-Pong tables, a pinball machine, and foosball games. Kind of like camp for grown-ups. Another, smaller room was decorated like the great hall of a castle, complete with an iron chandelier and a huge wooden table. I didn't think much of the paint job, but the concept was kind of fun. Moving on, we found the Jail Cells, only one of which was occupied by a hopeful-looking young man who had already thrust his hands into the chains on the wall.

"Kyle?" I asked.

"I can be Kyle," he said with a smile. "What would you like to do with Kyle?"

Bryan stepped forward and steered me away.

A handful of men, most of them clad only in towels, meandered through the rooms and hallways as though lost. Most of these were middle-aged and paunchy, giving the Power Play more the air of an executive locker room at the gym than a sex palace. It seemed anything but erotic.

"Shall we check out the Dungeon?" I said, my voice unnaturally high.

"Unless we can go home now," Bryan muttered.

Wesley hadn't said a word since we first entered. As we descended the stairs to the Dungeon, I looked over to see him swallowing convulsively, eyes popping out of his head. His black-rimmed Mr. Science glasses were fogged up.

We paused at the bottom of the stairs. This was where all the people were. As on the first floor there were at least nine men to every woman, and most were wandering the hall, which skirted a cyclone-fence encircled area, where racks, frames, and lots of ropes and chains were set up. A woman dressed in black vinyl was spanking a man who was leaning over a leather horse. According to a tall, thin, purple-haired passerby, this was Stain, the resident masochist.

"You'd think they'd get someone else for a change." At my inquiring look, she added with a sigh, "He's here every week."

"Don't touch *anything*," Bryan told us in a fierce whisper. "Has everyone had their tetanus boosters?"

"Do you know a guy named Kyle?" I asked the young woman.

"Sure. Blond guy. Usually in costume."

"What kind of costume?"

"Thinks he's a freaking pirate. Thinks he's freaking Orlando Bloom or something."

A man tottered by in white pumps, wearing a pink Jackie O–style suit, complete with pillbox hat, white gloves, and vintage white patent leather pocketbook. It's not unusual to see transvestites here in San Francisco, but usually they were sexier and more feminine than half the women in town. This man, in contrast, had no makeup on, and had done nothing special with his short salt-and-pepper hair. He wore wire-rimmed glasses and a glum expression on his unshaven face. It looked for all the world like Murray from Accounting had lost a bet.

A group of at least half a dozen silent, watchful young men started to trail us, duckling-like, as we moved down the hallway past a series of fantasy bedroom situations. I was trying to imagine being willing to lie down on one of those beds; all I could think of was that TV show where they bring special lights and cameras to uncover the invisible cooties on hotel bedspreads.

Mary grabbed my arm and leaned into me to say something.

There was an audible gasp from the crowd. They circled around us.

"*Back off*, you freaks," Mary said. "We're not going to make out or anything. Ew."

One of the young men opened his mouth to say something.

"I said, back *off!*" Mary yelled, taking a step toward them.

Bryan glared at them, and they fell back. But when we continued walking, they followed at a respectful distance.

"We *are* in a sex club, Mare," I whispered. "It's not out of the question to assume we might be game."

"Freaks," she muttered, looking around malevolently. She put her arm back through Wesley's. He beamed.

We poked our heads into one room where a big-screen TV was playing porn movies, then entered a long, dark tunnel that led down one side of the basement. A few couples and trios were making out in the dimly lit corridor.

"Kyle?" I yelled, just to see. No answer.

Most of our loyal ducklings were still trailing us down the dim hallway.

"What this place needs is bats," said Wesley, finding his voice.

"Next time I'm bringing a flask," grumbled Bryan.

"I'm bo-ored," whined Mary-of-the-short-attention-span.

"Let's just loop around quickly and then we'll go on up to the second floor, couples-only. Then we can leave."

I averted my eyes as we passed the rack and a masked man with a cat-o'-nine-tails. The burly masked man came over to stand just on the other side of the cyclone fence.

"Good evening," he said as though a maître d', greeting us for lunch. "You ladies care for a turn? Giving or receiving, it's all good."

"Maybe later," I said, pulling Mary back before she could speak. I wasn't sure whether she would go for his throat or decide she was bored enough to give it a go—on the giving end, I was sure. Either way, we didn't have time for such things. We had work to do. "Have you seen Kyle, by any chance?"

"Second floor, I think. Couples only."

Our duckling entourage stuck with us up to the main floor, only dropping off as we ascended the stairs to the second floor, where men had to be accompanied by at least one woman. I glanced back at them. They looked crestfallen, standing at the bottom of the stairs in their towels. They appeared to be of every nationality and skin shade: Latinos, Asians, blacks, whites...it was like a dismal mini–U.N. convention of lonely men.

The couples floor seemed more like a regular club, with a dance floor and pounding music—complete with a stripper pole, of course—couches and benches, lots of couples around who seemed to be together and happy. One woman was dressed as a sexy Snow White, the man as the Woodsman. Another reclined in an Egyptian sarcophagus, with her attendant serving her needs.

The Pirate's Lair was decorated to resemble below-decks of an old-fashioned ship. A woman, naked from the waist up but wearing Victorian-style bloomers, was tied to a rack with tasseled silk ties, while a blond man in a Mardi Gras mask, ruffled pirate shirt, and black breeches whipped her with what looked like the floppy head of the industrial mop we used to use back in my maid days at the Olive You Motel.

The crowd ringing the couple stood silently, just watching. Indeed, the whole affair seemed more like a piece of theater— or performance art—than anything particularly threatening. I spent a couple of weeks roaming the streets of New York City last year, and in comparison it was all pretty tame.

Still, I think I was experiencing sensory overload. As I looked around, all I could think of was how I could do a much better paint job. I pondered Victor and Catrina's basement. There must be hundreds of rich people with a tendency toward kink. Just in case I didn't get any better at the *Annie Kincaid, Crack Art Investigator* role, I could develop a whole new career adorning Smut Chambers. Think of the possibilities: Stone walls and gargoyles and...

The tied-up woman moaned.

"Is she okay?" I asked, looking around at the avid bystanders. No one moved or said a word.

She cried out again, loudly.

"*Stop it,*" I told the man in breeches as I approached the tied woman. "Are you okay?"

Everyone looked at me like *I* was the freak. Apparently I had broken Power Play etiquette.

"She's fine..."

"Are you crazy?..."

"She didn't use her safe word yet."

The woman herself glared at me. The glare turned into a wide-eyed look of fear.

It was Destiny-the-maid.

"Oh!" she cried. "Cabbages! *Cabbages!*"

16

*Is erotica art, or pornography? Well as they say, it de-
pends upon the viewer. I believe that it is both, and that
the vast majority of us are better for having seen it.*
                              —*Georges LeFleur, "Craquelure"*

CABBAGES?

The man wielding the whip stopped short, brought her a
white gossamer robe, and wrapped it around her shoulders, murmuring to her as he released her wrists.

She turned her head and said something to him, her tone
urgent.

The man swung around to gape at me for a brief moment,
then took off.

I ran after him. Destiny chased after us, untied robe flapping
out behind her. I assumed the rest of my gang was following, but
my concentration was on the man in the mask and breeches,
running away. Kyle Jones, I presumed.

At the bottom of the stairs our ducklings were still milling
about, blocking access to the front door. Without pausing, Kyle
careened down the main hallway, toward the Dungeon. I glanced
over my shoulder to see Destiny behind me, Bryan, Mary, and
Wesley behind her, and now the ducklings bringing up the rear,
stirred up by the excitement or Destiny's half-naked body, it was
hard to say which.

Kyle fled down the stairs. By the time I reached the bottom,
he was nowhere to be seen.

"Which way?" I asked the crowd.

No one spoke.

Mary grabbed the first guy she saw with a shirt on, squeezed
the collar, and snarled: "Tell us which way he went or I'll kick
you in the balls."

"Promise?"

204

Mary rolled her eyes, and tightened her grip on his neck. "Tell me!"

He pointed toward the darkened tunnel.

Two hefty men wearing Power Play–logo T-shirts came up to us. "Everything okay in here? Everything consensual?"

"Yes, thank you, very consensual." We all stopped and smiled like kids caught running in the school hallways.

"Okay then. Let's keep it that way."

We hurried down the corridor. It was empty but for one couple; no Kyle.

I grabbed Destiny's arm and hustled her into a "private" room—it had walls and a door, but featured one very large viewing window. The ducklings jockeyed for position at the glass.

"Destiny, tell me what you really do at the F-U. You're not just a maid, are you?"

"It's not illegal or anything. I help set up the parties. I used to be part of them when I was younger, but now mostly I arrange them."

"What kind of parties?"

She hesitated.

"Come on, Destiny. These guys are hurting people. Help us understand what's going on."

"You can't tell the police. They'll kill me if they find out I talked to the cops."

"No police."

Destiny twirled a lock of blond hair around one long-nailed finger and shrugged. "They're like re-enactment parties. They choose a painting and then re-enact it. Usually paintings with naked women."

Big surprise.

"And what do they do at these parties?"

"What do you think they do? Have sex. But there's nothing illegal about it. People can have sex if they want to."

"So they re-enact paintings for their parties? Is that what they did with the dead man you found? Made him look like the painting, *The Death of Marat?*"

"I dunno about that, but somebody made him look like the picture in the hallway. I don't know why. I felt so bad for Elijah! He was always so much nicer than his brother."

"Balthazar?"

She nodded. "At first Balthazar said Elijah had to leave, he couldn't stay at the club anymore. But then he let Elijah stay as long as he didn't leave his room."

"That's the room he was found in?"

Nodding, she teared up. "Room two-twelve. It was dreary in there, wasn't it? It's one of the few rooms that hadn't been re-done yet. It got water-damaged from the leak in the roof. It was damned depressing, you ask me. I think that's part of the reason he got so sick. Depression is bad for the—whaddayacallit?—immune system. Poor Elijah had to stay in his room, wasn't even allowed to mingle with the rest of the boys."

"Even during the parties?"

"Especially then. Those are really exclusive-type-deals. Only the select membership gets invited to those."

"So Elijah stayed in his room for how long, all told?"

"Months. He hadn't felt well, so he just stayed in there, plus he was scared to leave the building, on account of he owed money to some scary characters. He only left once, last month, he went out for the afternoon when Balthazar was out of town. That's about it."

Out to sell a painting, perhaps?

I looked up to see a commotion with the ducklings. They had caught Kyle, and were hanging on to him for us, showing us through the observation window. While we hurried out the door, Kyle managed to pull away and ran through an emergency exit, blocking the door with a bunch of wooden crates. It took several of us to shove the crates out of the way. Finally it swung open onto a dimly lit brick alley smelling of trash and urine.

A single gunshot rang out.

We all hunkered down, hugging the wall.

Two more shots, then silence.

I looked up to see Kyle sprawled face down on the dirty concrete.

"Kyle! *Baby*!" Destiny cried out, running to him. She sank to her knees and turned him over. A large dark stain spread across his white pirate shirt. She took off his mask to show the young, handsome face of the Fleming-Union parking attendant-slash-guard. The one I called Blondie. Destiny hugged the man to her breast, rocking slightly, making an awful, pitiful keening sound. The sound of a heart breaking.

"Call 911," I shouted to Mary. I ran to Kyle's side, and felt his neck for a pulse. Nothing. I held my ear to his chest, his mouth, listening for breathing signs. More nothing.

Bryan and I jogged the rest of the way down the alley, which ended in a T. We hung back, then carefully looked around the corner, first one way, then the next. The alleyways were dim and shadowy, but empty. About half a block to our left was busy Gough Street. To our right the alley ended about forty feet down at a rear access door. We checked it. Locked. A dead end.

"Probably ran to Gough," Bryan said, his voice subdued. "Long gone by now."

"Yeah." I trotted down to Gough Street and looked both ways, not really expecting to see anything, but needing to look. And using the moment to regroup. I was nauseated, and shaky.

I dislike murder. I mean, *really* dislike it. And in the case of the blond young man lying dead in the alley, I had the uncomfortable and profound knowledge that if not for me, he would still be alive and whipping.

We returned to the dead man.

"I have to get out of here," whispered Destiny. She looked up at me and repeated with greater urgency: "*I have to go.* If they find me here with you they'll kill me this time for sure."

"*Who*, Destiny?"

"The brethren," she said, shaking her head and crying. "They'll kill me, too!"

"They won't, Destiny. We'll help you. We'll figure this out."

"They killed him," she said, gazing down at Kyle's lifeless form. "It wasn't his fault. He tried to be good."

The sound of sirens split the night. Destiny looked up at me in dismay.

"I can't talk to the police again! You promised you'd help me! Hide me!"

"You don't have any idea who did this?"

"The brethren! Duh!"

"Anyone in particular?"

"It doesn't matter! They take care of their own problems!"

I made a decision, for better or worse.

"Bryan, will you take her out of here?"

He looked almost as though he was going to balk, but then hustled her down the alley. Mary and Wesley followed.

———

"I haven't been in this place for years," Inspector Annette Crawford said, her perceptive gaze sweeping over our surroundings. We were sitting in the "private" booth where I had tried to interrogate Destiny not so long ago.

"You've been to the Power Play before?" I asked.

"I used to work Vice, remember?"

"Oh, right. Lots of problems here?"

"Very few, actually. In general this group is quite law-abiding, just want to be left alone to pursue their lifestyle, as they say. They have security on staff, safe words, lots of oversight, no alcohol...all night spots should be so sane. I imagine as a woman alone you'd be safer here than at your average bar."

I thought of the ducklings, who had been eager and interested but not aggressive, and decided she was probably right.

"Just like you came here tonight, all alone, right?" Annette's tone was casual, but her dark eyes had me in their tractor beam.

"I...uh..."

"Before you go too far with lying to the police you might remember that they keep records at the front desk. No lone women came in tonight. They would remember. In fact, Mr. Happy over there remembers you quite well, says you were with a 'buff black man' and another couple."

"I can explain—"

"I'm sure you can. I'm waiting. I'm tired of half truths, Annie. I want to know everything you know, and I want to know yesterday."

"Should I call my lawyer?"

"Have you broken any laws?"

I thought about that one for a long moment.

"I don't think so...but I think I might need a lawyer, just in case."

Annette stared at me for a long moment. "Talk to me, Annie. I'll stop you if you're about to incriminate yourself."

I told her that Kyle Jones had worked at the Fleming-Union, and what Destiny had told me. I didn't mention that Destiny had

been here not long ago and that I had a friend spirit her away...
so I guessed I really *had* broken the law. Sometimes it was hard
for me to remember.

"So Destiny used to be part of these bacchanalian festivals at
the Fleming-Union, and now she continues to help set them up
and provide the girls," Annette summarized.

"That's what she said."

"At least the F-U is offering her a certain amount of job security. Kind of makes a person feel warm and fuzzy inside."

Annette's humor was so dry it was sometimes hard to tell
whether she was kidding.

"Yeah. A lot about the F-U made me feel that way."

"And you have no idea where Destiny is at the moment?"

"None at all," I said. That was the truth. Pretty much.

"So you're thinking, what? That one of these parties got out
of hand and Elijah ended up dead in a tub like a painting?"

"No. I think he died of arsenic poisoning."

She shook her head. "According to his brother and friends,
Elijah Odibajian had been ill for some time."

"He may have been. But I think Balthazar put him in that
room, number two-twelve, on purpose. I think the wallpaper was
very old, and full of an arsenic-based pigment that reacts with
mold and mildew."

"You're losing me." Annette frowned.

"Old wallpaper manufacturers—even the famous William
Morris—sometimes used forms of arsenic green as a pigment,
as did painters in the old days. But damp plaster and water leaks
can create mildew, which reacts with the arsenic, causing arsine
gas. Whole families died from the effects."

"Gas like what we found in your uncle's studio?"

"No, this would have been much more subtle than that,
building up over time. But Destiny said Elijah was made to stay
in his room, and he was essentially a prisoner there for months."

"These are some pretty serious allegations," Annette said.
"And virtually impossible to prove."

"The Fleming Mansion's leaky roof was deliberately hosed
down from time to time. How strange is that? And now they've
fired me, and hired some guy who doesn't know anything to take
all the paper down, to get rid of the evidence."

"Why did they hire you in the first place?"

"I'm not sure. I think I was being set up as a fall-guy for something, maybe the theft of the Gauguin, something like that?"

Annette had her blank cop face on, but I could tell she was skeptical.

"Listen, just have Elijah Odibajian's body tested for arsenic poisoning. Apparently it's very easy to detect. I think he was poisoned, and then arranged postmortem to look like a painting."

"Why would someone take the trouble to make him look like that?"

"I have no idea."

"You're still not off the hook with the whole stolen-paintings scandal," Annette admonished. "Tell me about that."

"Sam, Evangeline, and I were working up in the attic. I swear to you, I didn't even know there *was* a Fleming-Union art collection. I still don't know where it is, or was. I think they're trying to pin it on me, or at least insinuate that I was involved to discredit me...or something."

Annette seemed to be mulling this over.

"From what I understand," I added, "the paintings weren't even particularly valuable. Frank said the club didn't report their loss to the FBI."

"That's true. It made me a bit skeptical, as well. Still and all, I need to chat with your business partner. He is one of the few with the requisite knowledge to overcome the security system."

"Besides the F-U members who had the code," I pointed out.

"Yes, besides them. But they were all in the woods when the theft occurred."

"Alleged theft."

Annette gave me a half smile. "Alleged theft. Anyway, I haven't been able to track Michael Johnson down, though I did receive a call from your handler at the FBI."

Michael and I had a handler. Like we were rare white tigers. That cracked me up. I think I was getting a little punchy.

"Okay, let's get you on back to the station, and you can call your lawyer."

"Are you serious?"

"I appreciate the information you've given me, Annie, but there are some serious holes in your story, especially concerning the friends you came in with tonight. I just want to make sure we have everything we need from you before I lose track of you again. It really bothers me when you don't answer your phone."

A mere two hours later Destiny was headed for a safe house; Bryan, Mary, and Wesley were off the hook; Elijah's body was being tested for arsenic poisoning; I had spilled everything I knew about everything; Elena told me she'd send me a hefty bill...and I was royally pissed off.

———

"Do you have any idea what time it is?" Mary asked over the phone.

"It's a little after one in the morning. You weren't asleep, were you?"

"Nah. You know me, never go to bed before dawn unless your mean boss makes you get up early."

"That's what I figured."

"So a visit to a sex club and a dead guy in an alley aren't enough for one night? You want me to crawl through tunnels with you? Right now?"

"Alleged tunnels. They might not actually exist, or we might not find them even if they do. Do you think you could get your locksmith boyfriend to join us?"

"*Ex*-boyfriend."

"Do you think he'd be game? We may have to do a little breaking and entering."

"Sounding better all the time. I can't think of the last time anyone's asked me to crawl through creepy old sewage tunnels."

We met a block from Cameron House, and walked toward the building together. The neighborhood was quiet at this hour, the buildings dark. I noted alarm service stickers in the street-level windows, but one thing I had learned from hanging around thieves like Michael was that if you were fast enough, alarms didn't much matter. In many cases, success had more to do with speed than finesse.

Mary's locksmith ex-boyfriend made short work of the basement door lock. He showed Mary how to jimmy it, then closed it up again. In the process they set off the alarm. That was no problem—I would have done it on purpose anyway. We hunkered down, observing the response time. From our hiding place behind a large ripe-smelling Dumpster, we could hear the phone ringing inside. It took the security guard a full four minutes before he made his way to the basement. Another nine until a black-and-white pulled up. A cop climbed out and spoke with the security guard, made a cursory inspection of the basement room, then left.

Once the security guard was settled back at his post on the main floor, Mary jimmied the basement door and set the alarm off again. Same procedure, but this time with a lot of grumbling about a faulty alarm system. It took the cops longer to arrive this time, for a total of seventeen minutes. The security guard was visibly irritated.

Perfect.

Committing felonies always made me think of Michael. Who *was* that woman he was with? *Push it to the back of your mind, Annie,* I told myself. Now was the time for breaking and entering, not romance.

"Here's the deal," I told Mary after her ex-boyfriend went home, leaving her with a small kit of locksmith tools. "We'll need to dash through the basement, over to a little cubby, then climb on something to get in the tunnel. Then we're all set. If the guard even bothers to come downstairs, we should be long gone."

"Then what? Do we know where the tunnels lead?"

"We don't. Not really. We might have to make our way out the way we go in, but again, I'm thinking the guard's already decided it's a faulty system. The alarm company's gonna have some 'splainin' to do."

"What?"

"'Splainin'. You know, *'Luu-cy, you've got some 'splainin' to do.'*"

Still nothing.

"From *I Love Lucy.* It's a classic."

"Before my time."

"It was before my time, too, but surely you've seen reruns?"

"Not really. I've seen reruns of *Three's Company,* though. It always makes me think of you, me, and Pete. One blonde, one brunette, one guy who's, ya know, gay but not really."

"All right, to each their own. Well, here we go. *Carpe diem.* Seize the day."

"*Carpe noctem,* more like."

I looked at her, eyebrows raised in question. "Seize the night?"

"Bingo."

"I always forget you know Latin." That reminded me... I pulled Wesley's card out of my pocket. "Can you translate this?"

She took the card and I watched her lips moving as she read it to herself. "It's kinda weird...something about revenge and cold food?"

"'Revenge is a dish best served cold'?" I asked.

"That sounds about right." She turned the card over. "This is Wesley's card?"

I nodded.

"That's a weird saying to have on your card, isn't it?"

I nodded again.

Mary opened the back door for us. No alarm went off this time. Maybe they turned it off, assuming it was malfunctioning. We snuck across the basement floor. I had a backpack, and for once in my life I had come prepared: flashlights for Mary and me, extra batteries, and an emergency backup flashlight just in case. Travel-sized hairspray, one for each. A box cutter, a small crowbar, a screwdriver set.

The alarm screamed.

I opened the cupboard door, pulled open a stepladder conveniently placed there, knocked paper towels out of the way, and scrambled up.

Mary stacked the paper towels neatly so no one would notice, and pushed me up by my butt.

This was *not* going to work. I'm no waif. There was no way I was going to make it through that opening, and if *I* couldn't, Mary couldn't. I looked at my watch. It had been two minutes.

"Let's try the closet." We moved the equipment onto the floor as quietly as possible, and I felt the wallboard. Depending on its thickness, this stuff was akin to sturdy Styrofoam. Easy enough to bash through. I even came prepared with a box cutter in my bag of tricks, but as I got really close to the wallboard, I noticed tiny hinges. I pressed the other side of the wallboard, and it swung open. A hidden door.

I shone my high-powered flashlight into the pitch-black rectangle. Then I crawled in.

This was a tunnel, sure, but it wasn't exactly what I had in mind: a rather romantic arched tunnel like the ample sewers of Paris, which made you think of the Paris Resistance movement, or lovers sneaking out for trysts. This was more like a tight, cement-and-stone animal burrow. We could pass, but only on our hands and knees.

I hadn't thought to bring knee pads and gloves. Rough cement shards, dirt, and gravel pressed into our palms and knees as we crawled. Even more fun were occasional bits of wire and scrap metal...and cockroaches.

"You okay, Mare?" I asked.

"Yup. Just keep going, 'cause there's no backing out of here."

It got much cooler the farther we crawled, dank and chill. After an eternity the tiny tube we were in opened onto a much larger space. About five feet tall by three feet wide, we still had to hunch over to walk, but at least we were on our feet. This looked like the old sewer Will Chan had talked about. There was a gutter in the center, and what was known as rat rails on the sides to walk along. The arched brick roof showed the skill of a bygone era. Other than a little murky water in the gutter, the sewer didn't seem to be used for anything anymore. It didn't even stink.

"Let's stop a second and try to figure out where we are," said Mary. "And where we're going."

"How are we going to do that, exactly?"

"Camp Good News survival training. They used to tell us that out in the woods, God will help you find your way back. Him and a compass and map, of course."

Mary started rooting through the equipment in my backpack. She looked at the compass, approximated the distance we had traveled, then consulted the map of the city, and came up with a possible location.

We continued on. My back was starting to ache from being hunched over for so long, and the creepiness of the damp, enclosed space was starting to give me the willies. I tried to distract myself by thinking of the evening's annoying police interrogation, and how Anton was doing, and why Jarrah Preston was giving up on finding the real Gauguin.

"You know, I was thinking," Mary said. "Down here, there's no one to hear you if you scream."

"Don't think, Mare, just navigate."

"Didja ever take that vampire tour of Nob Hill?" Mary asked.

"Uh...no."

We walked a few more yards in silence.

Great. Now I was thinking about vampires. Almost never did I think about the undead, and I certainly never gave them credence. But now that I was wandering down deep in the bowels of San Francisco, in the dark and the muck, they were harder to laugh off.

Finally, I had to ask: "Why?"

"It's just that...well...the guide said the vampires nested in the tunnels under Nob Hill."

"You're saying vampires live down here?"

"That's what she said."

"Wait. Isn't this the woman who insists she's a hundred-twenty-seven years old?"

"I think so."

"Does she look a hundred-twenty-seven years old to you?"

"Not really. I'd say thirty-fivish."

"Mary, you ever hear that phrase, consider the source?"

"Yep."

"I'm thinking vampires aren't the worst of our problems," I said, my flashlight picking out yet another fork in the tunnels ahead. I was getting the willies. What if we never found our way back out? "For instance, do we have any idea where we are?"

I waited while Mary hunkered down with the map again, moving her flashlight beam back and forth between the map and the compass.

"I'm pretty sure we're under Nob Hill now," Mary said as she stood and looked around. "We've been moving pretty steadily uphill, and I've been counting steps. I think if we take the tunnel to the right, we might actually wind up under the Fleming Mansion."

The opening to the right led to an unlocked iron gate, and beyond that it opened onto an ample nine-feet-wide, eight-feet-tall arched tunnel. We stood up and stretched.

"This is really wild," Mary said. "I *love* hanging out with you."

"Thanks."

"I mean, a sex club, a murder, and underground tunnels, all

in one night... Setting up a biker bar in Thailand was like a walk in the park. Hey—" She shone her flashlight on a section of the wall. "Check this out."

Scratched into the stone wall, as though by use of another rock, were Chinese characters. Their white lines were faint and chalky, but they were easy to make out.

"Chinese graffiti?" Mary asked.

"Looks like," I said, extracting my digital camera and snapping photos of the symbols.

We moved ahead, Mary taking the lead.

"Eeeee!" she screamed, dropping her flashlight into the water in the central gutter where it flickered briefly, then extinguished.

To view a great painting is to see something that has been loved; no artist can create a work of art without falling in love with every centimeter, every inch, every foot. Therefore a great artist must be a great lover.

—Georges LeFleur, "Craquelure"

"WHAT? *WHAT?*" I yelled.

"A rat! A *rat*! *Eee!* Another one!"

Mary was moving backward at a rapid clip, and I was scrambling so as not to be trampled. "Wait, Mare!"

She brought out the Lady Clairol and sprayed for all she was worth. Sounds of squeals and scurrying echoed off the tunnel walls. After a few moments, there was silence. I passed my flashlight beam all around.

"Where'd they go?"

There was a small hole in the wall, where brick didn't quite meet concrete, right at the base of a stairway leading up, with a solid iron door at the top.

I reached into my satchel, brought out the reserve flashlight, and handed it to Mary. "Don't drop this one." And started up the stairs.

"Do you think we're at the Fleming-Union?" Mary whispered, close on my heels.

"I'm not sure."

The soft soles of my sneakers sounded like boots on metal, the sounds were so magnified in the echoey tunnel.

I reached the doors. Over them was written a Latin phrase, the same as was on Wesley's business card. REVENGE IS A DISH BEST SERVED COLD. An appalling motto. These Fleming-Union boys were getting on my last nerve.

The old metal doorknob turned, but the door was stuck. I

put my shoulder into it and pushed. It started to give way slowly, creaking.

"*Annie,*" Mary said in an urgent whisper behind me. She handed me a crucifix she wore as part of her Goth outfit. "Take this. Just in case."

I tried to snort and roll my eyes, but the truth was, I half expected Count Dracula and his minions to be lurking behind the iron door, ready to pounce on me and make me an unwilling blood donor. Or maybe, I thought wildly, Balthazar Odibajian was actually a vampire. That would explain a *lot*.

I accepted the crucifix and held it in front of me as I pushed the heavy door open a few more inches.

Pitch black. The doorway had been covered with a velvet curtain. Pushing this aside, we stepped into another arched brick space. It looked just like Anton's sketch, "Tunnel Vision." Around the top of the walls, right under rough wooden corbels, was an intricate border that looked recently painted. The stone floor was swept clean. And there were racks and racks of bottles.

"This is awesome," Mary whispered behind me. "A wine cellar?"

There was a thick coating of dust and cobwebs on many of the bottles. I glanced at a few, and saw dates going back to the early 1900s. I doubted wine remained drinkable that long, but it was undeniably impressive. This was quite the historic collection.

I checked my watch. It was a quarter to three in the morning. No one would be up and around at this hour, would they? It was as good a time as any to sneak around, right? There must be some stairs that led—

A door opened. We heard far-off noises, sounds of a party. Voices, glass clinking, laughter.

And two men's voices in discussion, descending toward us.

"*Get back!*" I said in an urgent whisper to Mary. "Back to the tunnel!"

Mary and I careened back through the door to the tunnels. The lights in the wine cellar flipped on just as we slipped behind the curtain. We tried to close the door, but the heavy, stubborn iron was hard to budge, and creaked.

We left it ajar and ran down the steps, and around the corner, flattening ourselves against the wall. We could keep running, but our steps echoed in the tunnels. Presuming they had powerful flashlights, there would be nowhere to hide if they actually came down to investigate.

"Why's the door ajar?" A man's voice said.

He pulled back the curtain. Light spilled down the steps and pooled in the water of the sewer.

"I want this door locked at all times, understand me? What the hell's wrong with you people?"

It banged shut, and we heard the loud scraping metal-on-metal sounds of an iron bar being secured.

Mary and I stayed where we were for a few minutes, in the damp dark, catching our breath. Then we turned our flashlights on and snuck back down the tunnel.

We came to another iron gate, this one locked. Mary used her lock picks and opened it easily enough, but the area beyond it looked caved in.

"Is this the only way out, do you think?" asked Mary.

"It's hard to say," I equivocated. I was having a tough time thinking straight. Suddenly the walls felt like they were closing in on us. "Maybe we could retrace our steps."

"We'd probably end up explaining ourselves to the Cameron House security," said Mary. "Besides, we've been walking—and crawling—for more than an hour, and took a bunch of turns. We might get lost, make things worse."

"True."

"I sure would like to get out of here," Mary said. "It's cold. And I might talk a good game, but I really don't like vampires."

I flashed my light through the caved-in section. There was still enough room to pass. It didn't even look as narrow as the first stretch we went through from Cameron House, and it only went about ten feet before opening back up. The ceiling looked intact; the cave-in had come from the sides. I tapped the roof and a wall with the flashlight. It seemed secure.

"Okay, I'll go first," I said. "If I die, you get the business."

"Does that mean I have to do all the paperwork?" she whined.

"I'm facing death and you're worried about paperwork?"

"I'm just saying."

I took a deep breath and entered the space, crawling carefully on hands and knees. I held the flashlight awkwardly under my arm, wishing I had one of those miner's hats with the lamps on them. Ten feet stretched out, seemed like twenty. Thirty. I was feeling a whole lot of sympathy for Michael's claustrophobia about now.

At long last I emerged at the other end.

Mary's turn.

As she pulled herself through slowly, I looked around. My flashlight beam landed on a ladder that disappeared into a hole in the ceiling. As soon as Mary emerged from the collapsed section, we hurried over to it.

Metal rungs led up a vertical tube, to a round manhole cover.

Mary illuminated the shaft with her light while I climbed up. With a great deal of grunting and pushing, I finally managed to shove the heavy manhole cover up slightly and to the side. I waited for a moment, listening for cars: nothing. Finally I poked my head up, praying some Mack truck would not choose that precise moment to come whizzing down the street.

"I know you," said a voice. "What you doin' in the sewer?"

I looked around. Harvard and his jump-suited buddy stood staring at me, bewildered expressions on their faces.

Harvard offered me his hand and helped pull me up and out. His younger companion, meanwhile, took a broad-legged stance out in the street with his hands held out stiffly in front of him, keeping traffic at bay. Despite the fact that there were no cars on the street at this hour, I gave him points for good intentions.

Mary popped her head up, startling them both.

"Hey," Mary said.

"Hey," answered Harvard with a nod.

"Hey," repeated the blond man in the jumpsuit. "What up?"

The four of us just stood, somewhat awkwardly, for a moment. Hard to know what to say, really. Though it was dark, after the pitch black of the sewer Mary and I were blinking in the streetlights. We were right in front of the Fairmont Hotel, across Mason Street from the Fleming-Union.

"What you two doin'?" Harvard asked.

"Exploring, sort of."

"You sayin' *Hermes* is down there?"

"No, not that I know of."

"Find him yet?"

I shook my head.

"So you explorin' down in the sewers? Just the two of you? Woman shouldn't go down there by herself. Where's the man was with you?"

"He wouldn't go," Mary said, brushing herself off. "Scared of vampires."

"Duude," said Jumpsuit with a sympathetic nod. "Me, too. They totally weird me out. Supposedly they live right under Nob Hill."

Harvard snorted and rolled his eyes at me.

"Speaking of vampires," Mary said, "did you know that Chinese vampires hop?"

———

I dropped Mary at her apartment off Valencia in the Mission, then drove over the Bay Bridge, home to Oakland. I needed to shower and change, and I wanted to sleep in my own bed. It was well past three in the morning. Surely that didn't still count as night, did it? Besides, at this point I was thinking maybe I should just let Odibajian's goons put me out of my misery.

As I trudged up the stairs past the second floor landing, I noticed a tiny video camera near the ceiling of the stairwell. I had never seen that before. Was the building's normally hands-off management going high-tech?

I turned the corner at the landing and peeked up at my door. It stood wide open. This time it wasn't Anton with *paella*, that much was sure.

It was Frank. Looking rumpled and sleepy, shoving something into his jacket pocket. I glimpsed the butt of a gun.

"Is there something in your pocket or are you just happy to see me?"

He gave me a grudging smile. "You okay?"

"Sure." I walked the rest of the way up the stairs, and he stood back to let me pass. I noted a pillow and blanket on the couch, and perched on the coffee table was a small video player with a black and white picture of the stairwell showing on the screen. "Looks like you set up shop."

"You haven't been answering your cell phone."

"It sort of got broken."

"And you haven't been home for days."

"You told me to stay away, remember?"

"Since when do you do what I tell you?"

I shrugged.

"You sure you're okay?"

I nodded, not wanting to review the day, or the night, or remember pretty blond Kyle Jones lying too still in a filthy alley.

I pulled a bottle of vodka from my freezer and poured two shots, offering one to Frank.

"Listen, Annie, I need to talk to you about something." He reached for me, but I pulled back. In part because I feared I smelled like a sewer; in part because I thought if he touched me right now I would just melt right into him.

"I'm in desperate need of a shower," I said. "Could we talk after?"

By the time I came out, wrapped in my comfy robe, Frank had taken off his jacket and fallen back asleep while sitting up on the couch. I stood over him for a moment, and for the first time caught a glimpse of what he must have looked like as a little boy: pouty lower lip, long dark lashes. I had never seen him look vulnerable before.

As I watched him, his eyes opened.

He reached for me. This time I didn't back away.

As in the car, his mouth was ardent, demanding. I crawled into his lap, fully aware that the robe I wore was all that stood between him and me. All he had to do was push it open and—

"What's that?" he asked.

"What's what?"

"Here, on your shoulder." He traced the bruise gently with his fingertips. His eyes met mine, accusatory. "It looks like a love bite."

"It's, um..."

"Are you seeing someone? *Please* tell me it's not Michael, or whatever the hell his real name is."

"No. I'm not seeing anyone, least of all Michael."

Frank looked angry, hurt even. I didn't want to tell him the truth, but I was too tired, my mind too muddled to come up with any sort of plausible explanation. A doorknob? A crescent-shaped branch that somehow whacked me while on a hike?

"I...had a little run-in with a goon."

Frank froze. "A goon."

"I don't know what to call those guys. Guys who beat people up."

"Some goon *bit* you?"

"Kind of."

Frank shot up to his feet, dumping me unceremoniously onto the couch. He paced the living room, hands on hips. He finally turned back toward me, still breathing hard. When he spoke his voice was strained.

"When was this?"

"Earlier today...I mean yesterday afternoon. It's been a long day."

"Where?"

"In a stairwell. It really doesn't matter—"

"It doesn't *matter*? What else did he do?"

"They just—"

"*They*? There was more than one?"

"Two. One held me and the other sort of slapped me. No big deal, really, except for the bruise. It was worse for the fellow I was with, they pushed him down a flight of stairs. They just wanted to scare me, told me to back off and...What are you doing?"

Frank was pulling on his jacket and adjusting the pistol in his pocket.

"He's gone too damned far."

"Who?"

"Balthazar Odibajian."

"What do you think you're doing? Where are you going? It's four in the morning." He was pulling on his jacket and striding for the door. I ran to intercept him, putting my hands on his chest. "*Frank.* Stop it. You're acting as crazy as me. Stay. Here. With me."

Frank was livid, black eyes flashing, nostrils flaring, breathing heavily.

Suddenly I couldn't keep from smiling. My straight-laced landlord was like one big, blustery, ex–Special Forces sex machine. And I had him in my clutches. My hormones shifted into overdrive. Time to use my feminine wiles.

My smile gave him pause. But then his eyes dropped to where my robe gaped open, displaying one naked breast. If that's not a supreme example of feminine wiles, I don't know what is.

After a very brief moment, his mouth followed his gaze.

There was no more talk of goons, or Balthazar Odibajian, or retribution. There was very little talk at all, beyond moans and gasps and whispered nothings.

—

Far too soon I was awakened. Frank had already showered and dressed.

"Breakfast meeting?" I croaked.

"As a matter of fact, yes. I'm sorry about this." He sat on the side of the bed and pushed a lock of hair out of my face. "How do you feel?"

My eyelids felt like sandpaper. I glanced at the clock: just after nine A.M. As I sat up, any number of unfamiliar muscles cried out in protest. Were they from my active day yesterday... or the even more active night? Frank looked a little the worse for wear, himself. We couldn't have gotten more than a couple hours of sleep between the two of us.

Frank's lovemaking had been as passionately demanding, as gloriously insistent, as deliciously wicked, as his kisses had always promised. And I matched him at every step. Neither of us seemed able to get enough.

"Why don't you go back to sleep for a while?" Frank suggested. "I already called a guy to come watch your door."

"A babysitter?"

"A bodyguard."

"Frank—"

"Just let me do this. I'm older than you. My heart can't take the stress."

I smiled and kissed him on the cheek, hyper-aware of my morning breath.

He hugged me. Our eyes met. If my teeth had been brushed I would have kissed him, maybe tried to convince him to come back to bed.

"Frank, promise me you won't do anything crazy against Odibajian."

He smiled. "Thanks for reining me in last night. It's not like me to go off half-cocked."

"I'll say."

"Cute." He gave me a crooked grin. "I've decided upon a much better revenge. Odibajian will pay, believe me."

"Just as long as you don't get killed or hurt in the process."

"Now you sound like me. Let's both try to stick to that."

Frank kissed me on the top of the head, then cupped my cheek in his hand. When he spoke his voice was low, husky. "Last night was...incredible. Worth waiting for."

I just nodded, feeling suddenly awkward. After he left I tried to go back to sleep. Usually that's a real skill of mine. But now random thoughts kept flitting through my mind.

Among these was the fact that I might be falling in love with my landlord. He wasn't even trying to tell me what to do, or bend me to his will. What the heck was *that* about? Was this some sort of sneaky plan to lure me into his web, like a spider? Or could he really be just about the most decent man I had ever known?

My mind started replaying last night. The kisses, the caresses, the moans...

But then I started thinking. How was this going to work, exactly? Were we a couple now? He hated my business partner, and Michael would find it problematic to work with Frank. Plus, I still had no idea what was going on with Anton et al; and I think we all knew that I wasn't going to let that drop.

The vision of Kyle Jones's body came back to me, chilling me to the core, washing over me like a bucket of cold water. I had practically caused a man's death last night, then spent hours frolicking in bed. I was scum. Confused scum. Confused, horny scum.

All right, time for a quick shower, a stop at Peet's Coffee, and if I was very lucky I might even find a straggler at the Casual Carpool line.

There was one lone man waiting at Casual Carpool, but since I was the only car—other than the one containing Frank's man tailing me—I lucked out. I didn't even look over as a man in a cowboy hat and jeans with a huge belt buckle climbed in.

"What I don't get is, why you don't just call me if you want a ride," I said, maneuvering us onto the freeway entrance.

Michael-the-cowboy grinned. "This is so much more fun. And look how fast you caught on. I'm proud of you."

He leaned over and ruffled my hair. I pulled away. After the night with Frank I was fortified against Michael's charms.

"Hands to yourself, jerk."

"Whoa. What's up?"

"Crawford needs to talk to you. ASAP. You're casting doubts upon me *and* the business."

"I had Kevin, our FBI guy, call her."

"I realize that. She still needs to talk to you. In person."

He stared at my profile for a moment.

"That's not what's bothering you. Is it that you saw me with another woman?"

"What?" Truth was, it was the furthest thing from my mind. Funny how violence and passing the night in a police interrogation room and sewer tunnels could put things into perspective. Not to mention that I had spent the last several hours indulging in the lewdest sort of behavior with Frank, so it seemed a bit much now to act jealous with Michael. I shook my head and took a drink of my coffee. "A man died last night. Because of me."

"Who? What happened?"

"Kyle Jones. He was the parking attendant at the F-U, and used to work for the couple who originally lost the Gauguin. I think he must have stolen the painting from Victor Yeltsin in the first place," I mused aloud. "I just can't figure out why he was working at the F-U, especially if he had the painting. Unless, of course, it was a worthless fake. But even so, why would he hang around a club where Victor is a member? It makes no sense."

"How did he die?"

"Shot. In an alleyway, right outside the Power Play."

"You were at the *Power Play* last night? How did I miss out on this little excursion?"

I glared at him. "We're talking about a man's life, here, Michael."

"Sorry. Why do you say he died because of you?"

"I was trying to ask him some questions. I think someone stopped him from answering."

We were approaching the typical rush-hour traffic backup at the MacArthur Maze.

"Don't get on the bridge. Take 80 North instead," Michael said.

"Why?"

"I have my reasons."

"There *is* no 80 North. You mean 80 East?"

"It says East, but it's going north."

This is typical Bay Area signage. The freeway runs more or less north–south, following the edge of the bay, but the signs say 80 East and 580 West. So a person could go north, east, and west all at once. It seemed a fitting metaphor for my life these days.

After a brief hesitation I crossed six lanes of freeway, weaving my way through traffic with the skill born of near-daily experience dealing with this difficult, intricate intersection, to take the far-right off-ramp for 80. I noticed that the silver Honda Pilot tailing me didn't make it over in time. Poor guy. Looked like somebody was going to get in trouble with a Mr. Frank DeBenton.

"So you're saying that since you were trying to get some information from this Kyle fellow, and he was killed, now you're responsible?"

"He'd be alive right now if not for me."

"You don't know that."

Silence. I took a swig of coffee and savored the familiar, comforting smell and taste. Peet's French Roast is one of the few things in life I am utterly, completely sure about. I was grasping at straws, but there it is.

It was confusing to be with Michael so soon after Frank. I was beginning to yearn for the simplicity of last week, when my frustrating business partner was still missing and my sexy landlord was still refusing to talk to me. And my uncle was still well.

Traffic in the opposite direction was at a standstill, but 80 East is against the A.M. commute direction so we whizzed along, passing UC Berkeley's Campanile to our right, the bay and San Francisco to our left. The Golden Gate was socked in under a thick blanket of fog.

"Where are we headed?" I asked.

"Crockett."

"Why?"

"Remember Perry Outlaw? He gave us that Crockett address?"

I let out an exasperated breath. "I don't care about finding *Hermes* anymore, Michael. I have to figure out what's going on at the F-U. I have to find some way to talk to Balthazar Odibajian. I have to—"

"Turns out Perry has—*had*—a brother. Named Kyle."

18

*Pablo Picasso said that copying oneself is more danger-
ous than copying others, for it only leads to sterility.
Therefore, I feel free to copy others.*
                                    —*Georges LeFleur, "Craquelure"*

"KYLE *JONES*?"

"Née Outlaw. I guess in his line of work he felt he needed an
alias. Maybe he was the brighter of the two brothers."

"He couldn't come up with something more interesting than
Jones?"

"I'm thinking intelligent creativity wasn't his strong suit."

"You've got me there." So if Perry and Kyle were brothers...
was this yet another unlikely coincidence?

Crockett is a small industrial town on a northern finger of
the bay called the Carquinez Strait. Though I had seen the signs
for the town, I had never gotten off the freeway, just noticed it
as I whizzed by on the way to the Carquinez Bridge and points
north. From the freeway the most remarkable thing about the
town is a huge C&H Sugar plant sitting right on the water.

Once we exited and drove along surface streets, however,
Crockett was charming. It had been caught in a 1950s time warp,
and had the mien of a pleasant, slightly depressed Mayberry
RFD. The small main street had a number of boarded-up busi-
nesses, but there were still several shops and people on the sidewalks. Colorful banners batted around by the wind off the strait
announced an upcoming SUGARTOWN FESTIVAL AND STREET FAIR!

I pulled up to the curb on Pomona, the main drag. It was
early yet; folks were headed to their cars, newspapers tucked
under their arms, travel mugs of coffee in hand. Michael steered
me across the quiet street to an old-fashioned diner, where we
slid into an orange vinyl booth by a spotless plate-glass window.

"I'm not a breakfast person," I grumbled.

"Most important meal of the day," Michael said brightly.

The waitress came over, "Sandy," a middle-aged woman sporting a huge smile and orthopedic shoes. Michael ordered coffee and grapefruit juice for both of us, even though I was still clutching my travel mug full of Peet's. I leaned back into the corner of the booth, feeling listless. Elijah Odibajian, Anton Woznikowicz, Kyle "Jones" Outlaw...other than having complicated names, what did they have in common? Why had they been marked for death? Perhaps most importantly, how did I get myself wrapped up in these things?

When Sandy came over with our drinks, Michael ordered a Western omelet for himself and an English muffin, well-toasted, for me.

I stared out the window. Maybe I should move to Crockett. Seemed like a nice place. Slow pace, friendly people, cute houses. I bet people hardly ever got shot outside sex clubs here. On second thought, it wasn't nearly far enough away. At this point Siberia seemed like the better option.

Would Frank like Crockett, I wondered? My heart thudded. What, was I going to run out and purchase our first home? *You slept together once, Annie. Don't blow it out of proportion.*

While I was lost in thought, Michael struck up a conversation with Sandy. By the time I started listening in, she was eating out of his hand.

"Oh, sure, the Outlaw boys," she chuckled. "With a name like that, I guess it's no wonder that they were into mischief. Not bad kids, but lots of petty stuff, ran a little wild."

"And their friends...?"

"Alan Dizikes and Skip Goldberg. They were like our own little Crockett gang," she chuckled again and shook her head, "but like I say, they were basically good kids. Bored, is all. Not much to do here in town, so a while back Perry and Kyle moved to San Fran, but Alan and Skip stuck around."

"And they're up on Cherry Street?"

"That's right. Alan's folks passed away early on, so he inherited the house, rents out rooms. Skip lives there now, too. Corner of Tilden."

Michael gave Sandy one of his patented "you are the most fascinating creature in the world" smiles.

She melted. I wasn't sure Crockett was ready for Michael's megawatt sexiness.

"Thanks, Sandy," I said, reaching across the table and putting my hand atop Michael's. "I'm sure you're busy; don't let my nosy husband monopolize your time."

"Oh, sure, no problem," she said, picking up her coffeepot. A little bell tinkled as the front door opened, capturing Sandy's attention. "Well, look who just walked in. Speak of the devil...."

We looked around to see a short, paunchy man in wire-rimmed frames and a cheap brown suit walk in and take a stool at the counter. By his graying temples and jowly face I would guess he was in his mid-fifties. Surely this couldn't be one of the Crockett Boy Gang?

"That's Jim Stafford. He's their lawyer."

"Whose lawyer?"

"All of 'em. Every one of those boys has needed a lawyer at least once in their lives. Well, eat hearty." She hustled off to refresh coffee cups on linoleum tables throughout the small diner.

Michael and I looked at each other, and without saying a word we got up and each took a stool on either side of Jim Stafford, lawyer to the Crockett gang.

"Hi," I said.

"Um, hello," Stafford said.

"Good morning," Michael said.

Stafford swung his head toward Michael, then back to me. "Is...everything okay? Can I do something for you two?"

"We wanted to talk to you about a client of yours."

"Clients' information is entirely confidential."

"What about after they've been shot to death in a dirty alleyway?" I asked.

Stafford took off his glasses and looked at me. Up close I realized some of his puffiness probably had to do with the veins on his nose and in his cheeks, and the red rims of his eyes. He was a drinker. But I had the sense he was no fool.

"Who? Who died?"

"Kyle Outlaw. A.k.a. Kyle Jones."

"Kyle?" Stafford stared straight ahead, sipped his coffee, and shook his head. "I guess I'm not surprised. Kyle did have a way of living on the edge. I'm sorry to hear that, though."

"He was a client of yours, right?"

He nodded. "But I haven't seen him for some time. I was under the impression he was toeing the line, keeping out of trouble. I represented his brother's wife not too long ago, but Kyle and Perry have both been trying to straighten up."

"What about a few years ago? Kyle was working for a couple in Sausalito, and a valuable painting was stolen. Do you remember that?"

"Kyle was questioned by the police at the time, but he wasn't ever charged."

"When did you represent him?"

"It was shortly after that, actually. He got involved in a robbery, was driving the car, wasn't part of the heist at all, didn't even know what his friends were up to until it was too late."

Uh-huh.

"Would you happen to know anything about Kyle being involved with stolen paintings?"

His red-rimmed eyes looked at me, then over to Michael. He gave a mirthless chuckle and climbed off the stool, throwing a few dollars on the counter.

"Let's talk outside."

Michael settled up with Sandy and the three of us headed out to the street.

"Listen, I've got an ex-wife going for my jugular, prostate problems, and chronic heartburn. Last thing I need at this point is to get hassled over some dead kid's past." Stafford paused and looked up and down the street, as though searching for inspiration. "Tell you what. Kyle gave me something for safekeeping a while ago, against a later payment...which never came, thank you very much. You want it, it's yours."

The Stafford Law Office was just a few blocks away, housed in the front room of an old Victorian on a corner lot in a residential neighborhood. The lawyer brought us in, then marched upstairs to a small bedroom, pulled down a set of retractable attic stairs from the ceiling, and led the way up. He pulled on a string and a bare lightbulb lit up the cramped space: a few crates of Christmas decorations, an old footlocker covered with University of Washington stickers, random cardboard boxes and bags, and numerous white file boxes neatly labeled with names and dates.

"I got a bum knee on top of everything else," Stafford complained, his hands shoved into his pants pockets, jingling change. He looked around absently, as though he couldn't remember why he was here. "I tell you, I don't need the hassle."

"What are we looking for?" Michael asked.

"It's here somewhere...a black plastic Hefty bag..."

In the distance we could hear the phone ringing.

"That's my business line," Stafford said. "I'll be right back."

He descended the stairs, then slammed the apparatus shut and locked the trapdoor from the outside.

"Hey!"

We could hear him thundering down the stairs, and the front door slamming. I ran to the tiny ventilation window just in time to see Stafford run out of the house and climb into a dated red Cadillac, talking on his cell phone. He peeled out. *Damn!*

The window was far too small to crawl out, and I'm not good with heights, anyway. I pondered for a second. Calling 911 wouldn't do—there was no way I was going to deal with the police again. Besides, my cell phone was in pieces.

"Do you have your cell?" I asked Michael, hand outstretched. He handed it over.

I dialed Mary.

After she stopped laughing, she said: "I'm impressed, though. You had your cell phone, and it was actually charged. Awesome."

"Actually it's Michael's phone. Do you think you could borrow a car and come get us?" I asked.

"Are you *serious*? Michael the über-thief is with you, and you thought you needed my help to get you out?" She yawned loudly. "Annie, you have *got* to learn to take that man seriously. I'm going back to bed. You can't ask a girl to traipse through vampire tunnels all night, then get up with the birds."

I heard a crashing noise. I turned around to see Michael using a heavy candelabrum to bash at the attic door. He shoved a corner between the attic floor and the lip of the panel and fortunately seemed to be making progress prying the pieces apart. Wood whined and splintered.

The hatch finally popped open, hanging limply on one hinge.

"Good work there, chief, but now we can't use the ladder."

Michael had a relieved look in his eye, and I remembered

his claustrophobia. Probably he just needed to know there was a way out.

"Let's look through this stuff first," Michael said.

"What are we looking for?" I asked.

He hauled a couple of boxes to the side, then checked the date on one and looked inside.

"Goldberg was one of 'the gang,' right?" He pulled a file.

"And...?"

"Alan something. But Kyle's who we most want."

We found files for Perry Outlaw, Alan Dizikes, and Skip Goldberg...but nothing at all for Kyle, even though we ended up looking through each and every box. No mystery treasure in a black plastic Hefty bag, either.

"All right, I don't think there's anything here," Michael said. "Let's check downstairs."

Rather than try to use the now lopsided, perilous ladder Michael hoisted himself over the side of the opening, hung down by his arms, then dropped the rest of the way to the floor below. As easy as pie.

"Your turn."

"It's high. I don't like jumping from high places."

"I'll catch you."

"Yeah, right." I'm no lightweight. I could just see flattening Michael like a pancake, and then I'd have a paraplegic partner on my hands, one who would spend the rest of his life waxing on about his exploits before Annie-the-elephant landed on him in a rescue attempt gone bad. No thanks.

"Annie? You there?"

"Just stand to the side." I didn't even try to keep the irritation out of my voice. Gingerly, I sat on the edge of the opening, then turned over on my stomach, butt in the air, and ooched my way toward the edge. I hung briefly, but I didn't have great upper body strength. I finally made myself let go, and dropped to the ground, thumping and rolling. Luckily during all my machinations Michael had thrown some cushions from a nearby couch onto the ground, so I survived, winded but unbroken. I lay on my back for a minute to recover.

Michael stood over me, crooking his head, eyebrows knitted in confusion. "You okay?"

I nodded.

"You might want to work on your physical prowess a bit, there, sweetheart. In this business you occasionally have to jump all of three feet."

"It was a lot more than three feet."

"Four, tops."

"At least five. And I'm taking yoga, but I'm not as young as I used to be. And I don't like heights. And what 'business' are you referring to that requires me to study gymnastics?"

"Investigations."

"I've been meaning to talk to you about that. According to both Frank and Inspector Crawford, we're not investigators. Apparently a person *does* have to be licensed to call yourself a private eye, whether you carry a gun or not."

"So?"

"We're not licensed so we can't call ourselves investigators."

"Hmm. Maybe you should get on that."

"It requires forms to be filled out. Fees to be paid. And tests to be taken."

"Sounds like your strong suit, not mine."

"Not hardly."

Michael held his hand out to me and pulled me to my feet. "Let's get moving," he said.

We rummaged through Stafford's office for a bit, Michael standing at a big gray metal filing cabinet and me poking around his large oak desk.

"What is it we're looking for?" I asked.

"Hard to say. Usually it's a sort of 'we'll know it when we see it' scenario. There may be nothing at all, but Stafford's behavior seems rather unusual for an innocent man."

True enough. I riffled through his desk drawers: plenty of files and legal pads with notes; a bottle of The Macallan 18-year scotch; Xeroxed reference materials. And in one desk drawer, several auction catalogs for fine art. I hadn't noticed a lot of collectible art in the home; in fact, there was nothing on the walls beyond family photos and a decorative print or two.

"Find something?" Michael asked.

I shrugged. "Could be something, could be nothing. Art catalogs."

Could Stafford have been telling the truth, that Kyle offered him something in lieu of a retainer? Something like a valuable painting? Your average person would have no idea how to put a well-known painting up for sale. I thought back to the pawnshop fence I had spoken to in Oakland: he had mentioned a couple of white guys offering up a Gauguin, one middle-aged, one young. Jim Stafford and Kyle Jones?

"Why don't we check out Skip Goldberg's current address?" Michael suggested.

"You don't want to ransack this place, see if there's stolen artwork stuck in a closet somewhere?"

"We can look around if you want, but somehow I doubt he would have it just lying around, and left us in here with it. He must have known we'd be looking around once we got out of the attic."

"True. Let's go."

We hurried a few bucolic tree-lined blocks away to check out Goldberg's address. With my newfound knowledge about local disreputable lawyers and boy gangs, probably I should have been dissuaded from wanting to make my home in Crockett. But it sure was a charming town. Big trees shaded the streets and supported rope swings. The houses were relics of a more prosperous age, marching up the hillside, with views of the strait. Down closer to the water the train chugged by, blowing its horn. Cute as all get-out.

The Goldberg home was a simple clapboard saltbox. The driveway was empty of cars, and peeking in the windows we saw that the place looked abandoned. There was a fair amount of trash on the floors and cupboard doors gaped open, not in a ransacked way...more in a "we'd better get the hell out of here" way.

"Well. Crockett has been something of a bust," I said as Michael and I headed back toward the main drag of Pomona Street.

"Except that we now know Kyle Jones's lawyer and friends were in on something, or are afraid of something."

"Aren't we all."

I leaned against my dusty truck, waiting while Michael went back into the diner and worked his magic with Sandy. I could see him gesturing and smiling through the plate-glass window. He was so freaking gorgeous, so at home in his body, so confident. And the weird part was, I really believed that he liked me for *me*, not for some cleaned-up version of me. Then I thought of Frank and my stomach clenched. What did Frank offer? Escape? Or a trap? Could Frank really love me as I am, or would he expect me to stay on the straight and narrow?

Leave it to me to choose now to worry about my love life.

I was a mess.

I pondered moving to Siberia again, but I realized I would need a really good coat. We Bay Area folks don't really do coats.

"Stafford hangs out at Toby's Tavern," Michael said as he trotted across the street to join me. "Might be worth coming back tonight, asking around."

"Sure. Super. Can't wait."

Michael looked down at me.

"You okay?"

"No, I'm *not* okay. A man was killed last night, practically right in front of me. My Uncle Anton might not pull through. I can't figure out how Kyle is connected to a forgery, stolen paintings, and now a stolen sculpture. I put my friend Bryan on the line with the police to keep a maid safe...." I trailed off and looked down Pomona Street. No way was I going to mention that I'd slept with Frank last night. Instead, I took the offensive. "And *you're* an ass."

He leaned back against the truck and crossed his arms over his chest. To my great relief he didn't say a word, just stood there with me for a long couple of minutes. I closed my eyes and sighed.

"Why am I always so clueless?" I whined. "Why does all this stuff happen around me, but I never have any idea what's going on?"

He smoothed my hair back, resting his large palm on the nape of my neck and giving me a little massage.

"I think you're being a little hard on yourself, there, tiger. You do tend to attract trouble, I'll give you that, but it seems to me you always get your man—or woman—eventually. You just do it in your own special way."

"Why did you turn and walk away from me?"

"What?"

"You saw me clear as day yesterday in North Beach, and you turned and walked away from me."

"I have no recollection of that event."

"Who was that woman you were with?

"She's shy."

"She didn't *look* shy."

He smiled. "What did she look like?"

"She looked like a smart lingerie model. A nightmare to every normal woman in the world."

"You're adorable when you're jealous."

"Hunh. Jealousy would imply that we have some sort of relationship."

"I think we're dancing around one, aren't we?"

I shook my head. "Only a business relationship."

Michael put his hand under my chin again, and I met his gaze.

"You can't possibly be this obtuse. You know I want more, have wanted more since the day I met you."

"Sex, you mean," I said, pulling away.

"That's always a good place to start."

"It's a moot point, anyway. I don't believe in dating co-workers."

"That's easy enough: I quit."

"Besides, it's..."

"What?"

"Things have changed. Between me and Frank..."

He snorted. "Oh yes, your sainted Frank."

"Frank's a good man, Michael. You should give him a chance."

"Thanks anyway."

"I mean it. You two could be...friends, maybe."

He peered at me for a long moment, so intently that I looked away.

"You *slept* with him." It was more an accusation than a statement.

"I...uh..." Strictly speaking, there wasn't a whole lot of sleeping going on. But it seemed a sore point to bring up at the moment.

Michael stepped back, shook his head, and let out a mirthless chuckle. He ran his hands through his hair. "I can*not* believe this. I really can't. Among other things, when did you possibly find the time?"

"Don't be a such a hypocrite. You've probably slept with half the women in San Francisco by now."

"I don't judge you for having a love life, Annie. It's your choice I quibble with."

"I know he's law-abiding, but being a man of honor is considered a positive trait for most people."

"A man of honor. Oh, that's a good one."

"What are you talking about?"

"You want to know the truth? That woman you saw me with yesterday was my sister."

"Sister? For real?" No wonder they looked like a matched set of demi-gods. I could only imagine what their parents looked like—what kind of DNA must they be carting around?

"My sister, Ingrid."

"Wow, I can't believe you have a sister. Wait, her name's Ingrid?"

"She also happens to be your precious Frank's wife."

19

From the dimmest corner of the Kasbah, to the grittiest
New York dive bar, to the raunchiest bordello in Amster-
dam, never neglect humble establishments, for there is
some great art to be found. Believe me. This is the voice
of experience talking.

— Georges LeFleur, "Craquelure"

I COULDN'T SPEAK for a full minute. Michael was a habitual liar, but I couldn't imagine him fabricating something like this.

"Ex*cuse* me?" I finally croaked. "What did you say?"

"You heard me."

"I don't think I did."

"My father and I have been...estranged for a few years. I haven't been in close contact with my family for some time. I only found out about this recently, myself."

"But I don't understand...how could Frank possibly be married to your sister?"

"The world is a strange and frightening place."

And mine was tilting on its axis. I couldn't process this. Couldn't deal. Not with everything else going on.

"We'd better go," I said, pushing away from the truck. My voice sounded hollow to my own ears. "I want to get to the hospital, check on Anton."

—

I dropped Michael downtown before proceeding to the hospital. Anton was still sedated, but the doctors seemed pleased with his progress. The process of chelation would be completed soon, and then all that was left was to wait and see, hoping that Anton's prior health and spirit were enough to bring him back from the brink.

By now word had gotten out about Anton's condition. The ICU's waiting room was filling with a steady stream of Anton's

240

friends and associates, from artists and art aficionados whom he'd met at galleries and museums, to drinking buddies from the bars where he'd been a regular for twenty years. There were even a few upstanding citizens, for Anton was a man of cosmopolitan charm when he wanted to be.

I sat in the sole remaining chair, glum and uncommunicative. A cell phone rang, and for an instant I thought it was mine. Before I could stop myself, I hoped it was Frank calling. I blew out a breath, envisioning Frank's deep, espresso-brown eyes. The eyes that had always seemed, though guarded and often disapproving, brutally honest. And now this latest revelation.

What *was* it with me? Was I a magnet for lying, charming, worthless men? That *and* random crime?

To distract myself, I flipped through the case file Jarrah Preston had given me, it seemed a lifetime ago. I reread the article on the Odibajian brothers to see if I'd missed anything the first go-round. Nothing jumped out at me from the text, but in the black-and-white photo of Balthazar with a woman on each arm...one of the women was none other than Catrina Yeltsin. No big surprise. It could have been taken at any Fleming-Union function. Still, I remembered the old man in the fireworks shop tapping the photo. Could he have recognized Catrina rather than Odibajian? Or did all white women look the same, as well? Or was he merely a fan of spectacular cleavage?

"Annie?"

"Nicole, hi." I looked up to see my Cameron House tour guide standing in front of me.

"The kids made Anton a bunch of get-well cards." She held up a brown paper grocery bag. "I volunteered to bring them over. I wanted to see how he is."

"He's still sedated, so he can't really respond. But so far his vital signs look good. The doctors are hoping he'll be coming back to us soon."

"I'm so glad to hear that."

"He'll be cheered to see the kids' cards, I'm sure. Hey, I wanted to show you something." I fished around in my bag until I found my digital camera. I pushed buttons until I found the photos of the symbols etched on the tunnel walls. "Do you have any idea what these mean?"

"They're names, and dates, and the names of...villages, maybe? I only recognize one or two." Her dark eyes looked up at me. "Where did you get these?"

"I saw them written on a wall. In a tunnel."

"A tunnel. Where?"

"Under the Fleming-Union."

"You found tunnels? How?" She gave me a shrewd look. "Hold on, you didn't happen to break in last night...never mind. I don't really want to know. But tell me—you found this written on the walls, like graffiti?"

"Like very old graffiti."

"I have to see this in person."

"It's not all that easy."

"Do you have any idea what this means? The girls, the *mui tsais*, must have written this. I can look up the records, see how the village names correlate with the areas they were coming in from."

"Wouldn't the girls have been illiterate?"

"Most of them, sure. But many knew how to sign their names, at least. And a few of them might have known how to write, or just to copy the village symbols from their papers."

I took a moment to think about these youngsters, so far from home, brought through these tunnels to work as housemaids, or worse, as prostitutes. They had managed to leave traces of themselves nonetheless. And some of them had even survived, helped perhaps by Donaldina Cameron, or other characters lost to history, or through their own superhuman efforts. Some of their descendants had gone on to contribute to the crazy tapestry of humanity that is San Francisco.

"Do you realize how big this is?" Nicole asked, excitement in her voice. "This is proof of the Fleming-Union's past."

"It's remarkable, but I'm not sure it proves anything."

"Knowledge of these tunnels, along with the oral histories we've collected over the years, handed down from grandmothers, and these characters...at least it's enough for supposition. After all, this isn't a court of law, it's a court of public opinion."

"I guess you're right about that," I said.

"For years the Fleming-Union members have been denying any part in this sort of thing. Anton was looking into it when he got sick." With a determined look on her face, Nicole said, "There will be no more denial."

Could the F-U boys have come after Anton, simply because he had seen the writing on the wall? Surely if they had found it themselves, they would simply have destroyed it, wouldn't they? In any case, a few Chinese characters were pretty slim evidence, and they didn't prove anything. Unless Anton had further proof somewhere, somehow. Besides, Kyle might well have been shot by hired muscle, but Anton and Elijah—those seemed much more personal crimes, committed by someone who knew something about both art and chemistry.

I looked up to see Frank come into the ICU. Dressed impeccably, as always, he carried an expensive-looking bouquet of flowers and gave me a warm smile. It was hard for me to see anything but red.

I stormed down the hall, away from him.

"Annie?"

I whirled around.

"*Bastard.* Asshole. Piece of *crap.*"

"Sorry?"

"You bet your ass you are. A sorry character. So, Frank, buddy, how's the old ball-and-chain?"

He stared at me for several beats. I noticed his jaw clenching.

"It's been in-name-only for some time. Over two years now."

My heart sank. Though I really didn't think Michael was lying, I had been hoping against hope for some sort of explanation. Talk about your worlds colliding.

"Why do you think I've taken things so slowly with you?" Frank continued.

"Slowly. Is that what you call it? What I remember, with great clarity, is you telling me to break up with Josh, and then to stay away from Michael."

"I take it Michael's the one who told you?"

When I didn't answer, he cleared his throat and continued. "She had legal reasons to continue with the marriage. But we're divorced in any significant sense of the word."

"All except the eyes of the law." Speaking of eyes, I couldn't bring myself to meet his.

"Hey," he said, voice husky. "I'm still the same man. It probably sounds hard to believe at this moment, but I was going to tell you when I got you to stop moving for an hour. This isn't the sort of thing a person can blurt out at the office, or while being thrown out of the Fleming Mansion."

"How about while rolling about in bed?"

"You're absolutely right. I meant to, but you were naked under that robe... I got distracted. I'm only a man you know."

"I'm not so sure. A man would have told me the truth."

Frank inhaled deeply through his nostrils as though trying to calm himself down. "Could we talk about it now?"

"No. I've got to go faux a railing at a strip club."

"Is that a euphemism for something?"

"Yeah. It means I don't want to talk to you."

I stopped off to buy a carton of Marlboros for the doorman, then had Mary gather supplies and meet me at the club off Broadway. We "rustified" their railing in record time. Nothing like misery to spur on a work ethic, I always say.

———

That night I slept at Sam's again, hiding from Frank more than the threat of Odibajian. The next day Michael and I headed back to Crockett. According to Destiny, there was to be a memorial service for Kyle Jones at the Community Baptist Church, right on Pomona. Michael dropped me at the church while he returned to Jim Stafford's place. He thought he might find the attorney there, or if not, he could use the opportunity to look through the house with more care, just in case we missed something.

I stood in the back of the church while I listened to the preacher, and the call-and-response of the congregation, feeling like a fraud. I wasn't exactly one of Kyle's fans in life. Still, I was genuinely sorry for his passing, and couldn't quite shake the idea that I played a role in his death. Kyle's mother may have raised two no-good kids, but she was experiencing the kind of grief no parent should ever have to face.

I've been lucky so far; though I'd seen more dead bodies than anyone should have to, until now they had never been anyone I was close to. Until Anton. I said a little prayer for him. His age was a mark against him, but his love of life was a definite boon.

When the service wrapped up, I watched a newly shorn, suit-clad Perry Outlaw assist his weeping mother from the pew. She was soon surrounded by several aging women, and Perry extricated himself and headed for the door.

I followed, watching as his wife and daughter joined him. They exchanged hugs. Then the young woman took the girl by the hand and they wandered over toward the church garden.

"Perry," I said.

"Hi, oh, he-ey." He reared back from me as he drew out the last syllable, and I figured he was remembering where he knew me from. The smile dropped from his face and his eyes looked wary.

"I'm sorry to bother you, Perry," I said. "I know this is bad timing. And I'm really sorry about your brother. But I need to ask you a couple of questions."

"I, er..."

"Look, I'm not a social worker; I'm not a cop, either. I'm just looking into a missing painting, and I think it might have something to do with your brother's death."

Perry looked over at his mother, still surrounded by relatives. He then glanced at his wife and daughter, who were picking tiny daisies from the lawn and making a fairy chain.

"They look great," I said.

"They do, don't they? Fresh air and all that. You know, this whole thing with Kyle." He shook his head. "It's actually what decided me to try and straighten up, know what I mean? I mean, he was just getting so strung out over everything."

"What happened?"

"I guess it don't matter anymore. No more secrets, right?" Perry paused and kicked at a brownish weed in the sidewalk. "For years now, Kyle was always going on about some big score with a painting he lifted, but then it turned out he couldn't figure a way to sell it."

"They say that's the hardest part," I said.

"Yeah, right? Seems like the stealing would be tough, but seems like that's the easy part. Then you can't unload it."

"Did he ever mention anything about a forgery?"

"Like, a copy of the painting?"

I nodded.

"Yeah, as a matter of fact he did. Said his asshole boss had the painting copied, and wanted Kyle to 'steal' the copy and give the real thing to some men's club up there on Nob Hill. Up where Kyle works now...worked, until..." His eyes took on a faraway look. "Anyway, he even had a little X-ray gun thingie to tell which painting was real. Revealed a secret message and everything. He gave it to me for my little girl to play with, last time I saw him."

"But he didn't turn the genuine painting over to the club, did he?" I asked.

"He figured, why should his boss get any richer than he already was? And the copy was so good, nobody could tell but a museum, like. But then he gave the painting to his lawyer for safekeeping 'til he could find some way to sell it. Plus, he didn't have no cash and he needed Stafford to get him out of jail." He shrugged. "That was a different deal."

"Jim Stafford is the lawyer, right? He lives here in Crockett?"

He nodded. "Not much of a lawyer, but the best we could afford, I guess. Mostly he drinks. We even met him at Toby's Tavern, he liked it better than his office. Sometimes you could get him so sloshed he'd forget to charge you. But then again, sometimes he forgot what you talked about so you were back to square one."

The women were dispersing, coming toward us.

"I don't want to keep you from your family any longer," I said. "I appreciate you talking to me about this."

"You really think the shooting had something to do with that painting?"

"It might."

He shook his head. "I thought sure Kyle got away with it. So did he. 'sides, since he couldn't sell it anyway, it was just like, who cares? And it was years ago, before Erin was even *born*."

"I'm very sorry for your loss," I said. "Take care of that beautiful little girl of yours."

"I'm gonna. Got a new job and everything. Gonna move back here to Crockett. It's a nice town, my mom can see Erin more, help with childcare. Get us a nice place, maybe a one-bedroom."

"I like this town," I said. "Seems like a really nice place to raise a kid."

"Right?"

I smiled. "Right."

"Let's stop by Toby's Tavern on the way out of town," suggested Michael. He had failed to locate Stafford, or any other telling evidence in the lawyer's house and office.

"You really think Stafford's going to be sitting there waiting for us?"

"No, but we should at least have a chat with the bartender. Besides, you never know—drunks haunt their favorite bars. Creatures of habit."

Though smoking has been illegal in California bars for several years, Toby's Tavern still smelled of stale cigarettes and spilled beer. It featured roughly finished dark wood, zero natural light, and a multitude of knickknacks. Thousands of business cards and receipts had been tacked to walls and ceiling, many of them brown and crumbling with age. There were road signs and paintings and cartoons; old pairs of eyeglasses studding standing lamps; what looked like frilly bloomers atop a petite figurine of Bo Peep; and wrapped around the neck of a chipped, life-sized plastic Marlon Brando was a pink feather boa so dusty it looked like an oversized pipe cleaner.

A lone man with a straggly white beard sat at one end of the bar, nursing a beer. A young fellow stood at the jukebox, studying the music selections. And a burly bartender stood behind the bar, slicing limes. He ignored us as we took two stools at the counter.

We gave him a few minutes.

"Get for ya?" the man behind the bar finally asked, still not meeting our eyes.

"Sierra Nevada," Michael said.

"Gin and tonic, lots of lime," I ordered.

"You Toby?" asked Michael.

He nodded.

"You seen Jim Stafford in here lately?" Michael asked.

"I don't see nothin'," the nice bartender replied, turning to fill a pint glass from the tap.

Michael extracted two twenty-dollar bills from his wallet and laid them on the counter.

"Keep the change, maybe use the cash to get your eyes checked. Can't go around neglecting your vision."

The bartender scooped up the bills with impressive speed.

"I'll be right back," I said. I figured Michael might be more convincing one-on-one.

I headed toward the restrooms, which were down a very dark, narrow hallway decorated with a Polynesian theme, complete with Tiki dolls. The facilities were labeled DUDES and DAMES. A man was coming out of the Dudes' room, and as I scootched out of his way I almost sat on a sculpture in the corner.

Bronze.

Life-size.

Greek God.

Resting Hermes, treasure of the College Club, sign that San Francisco would rise from the ashes, victim of frat-boy pranks... was sitting right outside the Dames' toilet at Toby's Tavern.

Even more interesting: the man passing me was attorney Jim Stafford.

We gawked at each other for an awkward moment. Even in the dim light I could make out the signs of a recent beating: a black eye, a cut on the chin, vivid purple bruising along the cheekbone. Alcohol fumes wafted off him, filling the cramped space.

"What are *you* doing here?" he gasped.

"Hi there," I began, grasping his arm. "We need—"

He yanked it away from me, turned, and ran.

"*Michael!*" I shouted.

Michael nabbed him before the lawyer made it past Marlon Brando. He grabbed Stafford by the scruff of the neck and hauled him to a table in the corner, shoving him into a chair.

"Let's have a chat, shall we?"

"Look," Stafford said, "I'm sorry about yesterday. But you don't know what I've been going through, swear to God."

"Just tell us about the Gauguin," I said.

"I don't know what you're talking about," he replied. "I don't know anything about a painting."

Toby interrupted from the other side of the room, intrigued now by our discussion. "What about that painting you asked me to hold for you? The one you picked up earlier?"

Stafford rolled his eyes and hung his head in his hands. "Idiot," he hissed.

"Today?" I asked Toby. "When?"

"Just an hour or so ago," said Toby. "With some bald guy."

"Bald guy?" I turned back to Stafford. "As in Victor Yeltsin?"

"Oops," said Toby, picking up his knife and returning to his task slicing limes. I got the sense that Toby wasn't quite as slow-witted as he might appear. "Was I not supposed to say anything?"

Michael smiled and slipped the man another twenty across the bar.

"Okay, listen," began Stafford. "Kyle gave the painting to me years ago, but we couldn't figure out a way to sell it."

"How did Victor Yeltsin find you?"

"Few days ago, Victor found out that he gave the club the wrong painting, the fake, which means he's in deep shit. They take this stuff seriously. So he forced Kyle to tell him what he did with the real Gauguin. I guess then he must have shot him. I feel guilty as shit. Couldn't even go to the memorial service, face Kyle's mother." His voice took on a plaintive, whiny note. "Plus, he hit me. I tell you what: I couldn't even figure out how to unload the thing. No way am I gonna get shot over some stupid painting. I gave it to Victor. It's just been hanging here outside the men's room for five years, anyway."

Hanging in plain sight, amongst the grass skirts and Polynesian posters. Brilliant. Anyone who noticed it in the dim space would assume it was a cheap copy. Anyone but me. Note to self: spend more time in dive bars.

Which reminded me of what I had just seen.

"So, Toby, that's an interesting sculpture you have back there. Next to the Women's."

"You like it? I didn't even want it really. Looks gay to me. Couple local boys came in—clients of Stafford, here, actually—trying to sell it. Turned 'em down the first time they came around, but then they came back a few days later and said they'd hock it for scrap metal if I didn't buy it, I was their last chance. Seemed like a shame. Somebody made it and everything."

A real art lover.

I looked at Michael. "Don't you need the bathroom? You might check it out."

He gave me an odd look, but went down the short hall. A moment later he returned, stunned.

"That sculpture is the College Club's *Resting Hermes*. It was stolen from outside the club last week."

The bartender held up his hands, the picture of innocence. "Hey, I've got a receipt and everything."

And he did. He brought it out to show us: $300 to Alan

Dizikes and Skip Goldberg. The receipt was complete with their home address and phone number. Doh! I had an idea for a new TV show: *America's Stupidest Criminals.*

"I swear," said Toby. "I had no way of knowin' it was stolen."

"You don't watch the news?" I asked, eying the TV with the local news blaring over the bar. "Anybody else sell you anything a little, you know, fishy? I'm not police, just looking to get people their stuff back."

"Only thing new in here lately is that stuffed moose head, there, that's a favorite." It already had a red lace bra hanging off one antler. "Hey, you think I could get my money back, what I paid out for the sculpture? I don't really even want it."

"I'll bet the College Club will compensate you. Because you held on to it, it wasn't melted down. They'll be grateful. There might even be a reward in it for you. I'll put in a good word."

I felt a little surge of optimism. At last one thing had gone right. It wasn't a Gauguin, and it didn't cast much light on the mystery of Anton's assault, but *Resting Hermes* was a venerable piece of art that had been saved from destruction. I turned back to Stafford. "So where did Yeltsin take the real Gauguin?"

"We didn't exactly trade Day-Timers."

"You have no idea what his plans were?"

"He said something about a big party tonight. That's his dead-line, I guess. Quite literally. He was gonna bring it back to the club, all triumphant, or else he was a dead man," Stafford said.

"He thought they'd kill him?"

"That's what the man said. He said the guy who absconded with the fake from the club, the fake he thought was real, well that guy ended up dead. Elijah Odibajian, of all people."

"I heard about *that* one on the news—they found him in a bathtub or something?" Toby put in. "They said maybe foul play, but then they didn't follow up. How come they never follow up? They just tell you what happened and then go on to the next story, and meanwhile you gotta try to figure it out yourself."

"As a wise friend of mine once said," I told him, "the world is a strange and frightening place."

20

Edouard Manet said: "Anything containing the spark of humanity, containing the spirit of the age, is interesting." To this I would only add that "interesting" does not always equal "good." Still, I would much prefer to be interested and unhappy than the opposite.

—*Georges LeFleur, "Craquelure"*

"WHAT NOW? Presuming Victor Yeltsin brought the Gauguin back to the Fleming Mansion, how are we supposed to find it?" I mused as I turned the key in the ignition. My truck made its now-familiar, scary clunking noise. I should cash that check from Jarrah before he changed his mind.

"Good question," Michael said. "That place is pretty secure, thanks to their security staff and your boyfriend's alarm systems."

"He's not my boyfriend. He's married."

A rare silence from Michael. I felt tears prickle at the back of my eyes. How could Frank be married? Much more importantly, how could he not have told me?

I pulled away from the curb and headed for the freeway.

"Anyway, don't distract me," I said. "Is there any way we could get in the mansion for this party tonight, try to intercept Victor? Maybe I should call Annette Crawford."

"Oh, yeah, that's brilliant. Bring in the cops. They're trying to 'talk' to me about paintings supposedly stolen from the F-U, and you want to try to convince them to rescue a Gauguin from the club—the Gauguin the club thought was theirs in the first place, by the way. You might want to mention that Elijah Odibajian was killed for hawking the fake one, while you're at it. They'll really believe that."

"I already told Annette Crawford a lot of it. Anyway, you keep switching sides. I thought you were all pro-police."

251

"That's back when I thought they might help keep you alive."

"And now?"

"I honestly don't think they can help on this one. There's no way the F-U boys will let the Gauguin be found, if they know the police are looking for it. If we really want to save it, we have to get in there ourselves."

Michael may be a cynical thief and liar, but he has a true respect for art.

As we raced toward San Francisco, I had Michael call Mary and tell her to talk Wesley into taking her to the F-U party, during which she should sneak into the wine cellar and open the door to the tunnels.

Next, Michael called Jarrah and told him we had a lead on the real Gauguin.

Jarrah was waiting for us in front of Grace Cathedral when we arrived on Nob Hill. We huddled for a moment beside the truck.

"You're saying the Gauguin is somewhere in the mansion?" Jarrah asked. "How are we supposed to locate it?"

"Find Victor and make him tell us what he did with it," I said.

"That's your plan?" He looked over at Michael, who just shrugged.

"Pretty much." At Jarrah's dubious expression, I added, "I'm kind of an improviser."

"How do you plan on getting in the building?"

"I've got that part handled. Listen, Victor values his membership in this stupid club. Can he keep that with a prison record? Jarrah, you'll have to convince Victor that you met with his ex-houseboy Kyle Jones, and that Kyle told you everything before he died. That you have enough information to convict Victor if he doesn't cooperate."

Michael's phone rang. He handed it over to me.

Mary was on the line, whispering. "Wesley wimped out, but Destiny made a phone call and helped me get in with the girls. This is awesome! You should see it!"

"I'll take your word for it. Can you open the door to the tunnels for us?"

"I'm on it. No problem. By the way, I've got this *great* harem costume. You've so got to check this out, for serious."

I led Michael and Jarrah to the sewer entrance. Using a crowbar from my truck, Michael helped haul the heavy iron top off the hole. I descended the ladder. Jarrah came after me. We stood at the bottom and looked up to the circle of light above us, with Michael looking down, backlit like an angel.

"I can't," Michael balked. "I'm sorry, I really can't."

"Michael, we need you. *I* need you."

"I'll find another way in, and meet you. I promise." He replaced the manhole cover, and was gone.

Jarrah and I flashed our lights and looked around to get a sense of the place. I led the way down the corridor towards the scary fallen-in section. It was just as well that Michael wasn't here; how did I think I was going to coax Michael past this stretch? This was like his own private hell.

I squeezed through on hands and knees, desperately trying not to think of all the icky things I might be touching or picking up on my clothing. I made it to the other side, then helped Jarrah stand as he came through.

"That was...interesting," he said, speaking in a low voice. Something about these reverberating tunnel chambers seemed to inspire whispering.

"That was the worst of it," I said. "From here on we can walk, though somewhat hunched over."

We made our way down one passage, then took a right at the T. If I recalled correctly, this opened onto the bigger tunnels, and then on to the short flight of stairs that led to the club's wine cellar.

"Almost there," I said. "Here they are—the stairs."

Jarrah didn't reply. I turned around.

He just stood there, staring at me.

Gun in hand.

"Jarrah?" I asked, looking behind me to see if he was aiming at someone else. Nope, just little old me. My heart fluttered. "What's up?"

"I'm really sorry about this," Jarrah said. "I tried to warn you off."

"You hired me to look into it!"

"Yes, at first. But then I tried to fire you. But you wouldn't quit."

"My uncle was hurt. I had to find out why, and the Gauguin was mixed up in it all."

"You had no way of really knowing that. But it's a moot point. Now I have to kill you."

"Says who? There's no need for dramatics. I'll just walk away."

"I don't think so. I mean, you say that now because of the gun." I noted beads of sweat on Jarrah's brow, and the hand holding the gun shook. "Honestly, I never thought I'd be in this position. But you have no idea how much money we're talking."

"You mean your company expense account wasn't generous enough?"

"This is beyond anything I could hope to achieve at Augusta Confederated."

"Am I supposed to care about your finances at this moment?"

He shrugged. "I'm just saying."

"Well, I for one take back all the nice things I said about New Zealanders," I grumbled. I wrenched my eyes from the sight of that gun barrel, glinting dully in the dim light of the flashlights. I had been confronted with a gun up close before, not so long ago. That time it made me sick to my stomach with fear, but this time it seemed like I was standing outside myself, looking on with detached interest. I knew I should be scared, but mostly I felt weary and disillusioned. What right did the seemingly sweet New Zealander have to pull something like this? One simply didn't expect this kind of behavior from Kiwis.

"This is why you didn't know Elijah was staying at the mansion," I said.

"What?"

"It just dawned on me. It seemed strange that my friend could find out over the Internet that Elijah had moved into the Fleming-Union, but you weren't able to locate him as a trained investigator."

Jarrah shrugged.

"And then you said Anton left you a voicemail message, but he never leaves voicemail messages." How could I have been so stupid? "Are you the one who poisoned him?"

"Of course not, I'm the one who saved him. Cathy Yeltsin did it. It was so pointless, she was just angry because she thought

Anton had double-crossed them with regard to the Gauguin. I've never hurt anybody."

"Why start now?" I asked. "I hear it gets real easy. Easier each time, and pretty soon you're nothing but a killing machine."

"That's a *terrible* thing to say," Jarrah said, in a surprised, hurt tone as though I had hurled insults about his mother.

"It's the truth," I said. "Happens all the time. You could do one of us maybe, but by the time you kill Michael, too, that makes you a serial killer."

I read doubt in his eyes. He started swallowing convulsively, looking at the door that led to the wine cellar. Jarrah Preston was no fool, but he was under a whole heck of a lot of stress. You don't go from being an upstanding international insurance guy to a cold-blooded killer without passing through stages of serious self-doubt. I hoped.

"I mean, do Kiwis even kill people?" I pressed on. "Do you know how to use that gun, for example?

"How hard could it be? You just squeeze. American children kill each other all the time by accident."

Words to warm a mother's heart.

"Okay, so enough talk," said Jarrah. "Do whatever you need to before I...you know."

"What do you mean?"

"Say the Lord's Prayer, or whatever works for you."

"You mean that 'Shadow of the Valley of Death' thing?" I asked. "I'm not sure I remember all the words. Isn't that a heck of a thing, given the situation?"

Jarrah gave me a nervous little smile.

"Say it with me?" I asked.

"All right."

"Our father, who art in..." we recited together.

My mind was racing. I was reasonably sure I could jump fast enough, and that Jarrah would be a bad enough shot, that I might well survive. But then what? What if he regrouped while I was still sprawled in the sewer, and shot again? And again? He was right, at this distance even a child could manage it. Gun control was seeming like a really good idea at the moment.

"...hallowed be thy name, thy..."

There was no other choice. As I was screwing up my courage to jump, I saw a pale visage poke around the bend in the tunnel behind us, barely discernible in the reflected light from our flashlights. Frank! And behind him...the two homeless men, known to me only as Harvard and Jumpsuit. When this was over, I pledged to myself, I was going to find out their names, and rent them a damned apartment. Who needed a new truck, after all?

Luckily Preston had his back to them. He still looked nervously to the door where he expected Michael to appear momentarily. In any case, he was probably too intent on the direction of his soul to take note of what was happening in the dark tunnel behind him.

"...kingdom come, thy will be done..."

Frank seemed to catch on that things were not going According to Plan.

"Okay, now this second part I never remember," I said in a desperate bid to keep Jarrah from turning around and noticing Frank, who was creeping down the damp rat rail, clutching his own gun. "Is it 'forgive those who trespass against us,' or 'who sin against us'—that would be you in this instance, Jarrah, by the way—or 'those who are indebted to us'?"

"It doesn't *matter*," said Jarrah. His eyes were getting a little wild. "You—"

Frank held the muzzle of his gun to Jarrah's head. "Don't move."

Jarrah moved. In fact, he jumped about three feet in the air, then spun around to run. Frank leapt onto Jarrah's shoulders, knocking the gun out of Jarrah's hand; the weapon skittered along the rat rail without discharging.

The two men struggled briefly. They were well-matched physically, but Frank had the element of surprise and with a right clip followed by a knee to the stomach, soon overpowered Preston, who splashed into several inches of stagnant runoff in the bottom of the sewer.

I scooped up the gun. The safety was still on. I clicked it off, pointed it at Jarrah, and held it with a steadiness that surprised me.

"Jarrah!" I yelled. "I've got the gun, and I'm an American, damn it. Just give me a reason, any reason, to go all Dirty Harry on your ass."

He stayed down.

Harvard passed Frank a length of rope, which Frank used to tie Preston, tightly, to an iron pipe protruding from the sewer wall.

"Dirty Harry?" Frank said, his lip curling up slightly.

"People still get that reference, don't they?" I was a little out of touch, media-wise. "You know, 'make my day' and all that?"

"Yes, I believe they do get that reference, Dirty Harriette."

"We'll stay with him," said Harvard.

"Stay with 'im," echoed Jumpsuit with a firm nod.

"Thanks guys," I said. "A million thanks. We'll be back for you."

We left them our flashlights and ran up the stairs toward the wine cellar.

"Why don't you let me have the gun?" Frank said.

I swung the muzzle toward him. "Don't even get me *started* on you."

The door was open and swung in with a push. We snuck up the stone stairs and entered a back hallway. Muffled laughter and voices drew us down the hall. Through the open doors we could see the party in full swing.

By gosh if the painting of the evening wasn't *The Dance of the Bee in the Harem*, by Vincenzo Marinelli. Oriental rugs had been laid out at odd angles, a few young men played stringed instruments, and half-naked women in belly-dancing costumes lolled about, drinking wine or dancing before the appreciative audience.

I had to give the F-U boys credit: I applauded their obvious efforts. This was prostitution at its finest. I mean, how many people would think of such a thing? It took some real creativity, research, and knowledge. And there was Mary, doing her utmost in her harem costume, dancing with the other women. I spied Wesley sitting to the side in the audience, slack-jawed, glasses fogged up again. Between the visit to the Power Play, his new gay friend Bryan, and now this, I imagined good old Wes would never be quite the same.

Still, I hoped Mary wasn't planning on joining the after-party.

I paused, wondering where to start, when I saw Michael at the top of the main stairs, gesturing for us to come up.

Luckily the security guard was avidly taking in the scene through the open double doors off the foyer, and his gaze did not waver.

At the top of the stairs we could hear the muffled sounds of a man's voice, and then a woman's.

Michael eased the door open. The couple didn't notice us at first, but it appeared for all the world as though they were having their own private art re-creation. Both dressed in togas, the woman was feeding the man grapes rolled in sugar. They looked like purple frosted jewels.

"*Good Lord*," Balthazar said when he spotted us. He tried to sit up, but his efforts were hampered by a scantily clad Catrina Yeltsin draped over his chest.

"Hold it right there," I said. Among other things, I really did not want to see more of Balthazar than was strictly necessary. I still had Jarrah's gun, and I was still channeling a young, macho Clint Eastwood. "But don't let me dissuade you from your meal. Dig in, by all means. Has your girlfriend mentioned how proficient she is with arsenic?"

"What are you talking about?"

"Are you feeling woozy at all lately, Balthazar? Headaches, stomach problems...? Because Cathy seems adept at finding the killing combination. First Elijah—did you know he would eventually be poisoned by the wallpaper? The paper you kept damp and moldy from the leak in the roof? That's one way to get rid of a business liability."

Odibajian looked horrified. His gaze went first to Cathy, than back to me.

"He was ill, but surely no one hastened his..." Balthazar trailed off, nonplussed.

"And then Anton, of course. That was an easy one, just mixing the acid in with the powdered pigment you got from the fireworks distributor. Are you moving on to Balthazar now, Cathy? Are those grapes rolled in plain sugar, or do they include some special secret ingredient?"

Cathy just laughed.

"This is utterly insane." Odibajian finally found his tongue. "To what are you referring?"

"Did Cathy here forget to mention she's a chem grad from

UC Berkeley? Surely you and she worked up the plan for Elijah together?"

"What plan?" put in Balthazar. "Cathy is a good woman. She convinced me to show my brother sympathy, for the sake of the family. I let him stay here."

"In a room full of arsine gas released from the wallpaper. Are you saying you weren't the one who set him up to look like a painting, in retribution for his spiriting the Gauguin out of the club?"

"He was dead anyway. Of natural causes. I had to set an example for the others."

"We'll wait until the medical examiner runs a couple of easy tests to see what he died of, exactly. But then you realized the Gauguin had been a forgery all the time, and that Victor must have been holding out on you. He brought it back, you know. Victor must be around here somewhere. You'll never guess where the painting's been: hanging in a dive bar, just as open as you please."

"Balthazar, sweetie," said Cathy with a smile, "don't mind her, she's talking crazy."

Odibajian just shook his head in disbelief.

"Cathy, Bal-Balthazar," Victor stammered as he crashed through the door, his own gun trained on his wife and Odibajian. He dropped the Gauguin, all his concentration on the tableau in front of his eyes. "How could you?"

"Victor, sweetie!"

"You've never...I mean, without me..." Victor wore the countenance of a man betrayed. As Mary had explained to me on the way to the Power Play, even swingers had rules and limits. More than most people, even. Apparently Cathy wasn't supposed to go off on her own. "You...*whore.*"

"Victor! That's enough!" bellowed Balthazar.

"Sweetie!"

The three started yelling. Frank took my arm and started backing us out of the room. Michael followed, grabbing the Gauguin on the way out the door.

Behind us we heard more shouting, and then the sound of gunfire.

"A little help in here," Frank yelled. Two Fleming-Union

security guards finally wrested their eyes from the living art exhibit and realized they were hearing gunshots. They hurried toward the door.

Frank, Michael, and I ran the opposite way.

———

Michael disappeared before the cops showed up, though he gave me the Gauguin to turn over to the authories. Ambulances arrived on the heels of the patrol cars, but we weren't given any information as to the fate of Catrina, Balthazar, or Victor. I led a pair of police officers down to the sewer, where they took Jarrah into custody. I gave Harvard and Jumpsuit money to get a room for the night—though given their high spirits I thought they might be planning a night of celebration instead. I made arrangements to meet them in Huntington Park the next day; somehow I was going to think of a way to pay them back.

Frank and I gave our statements to Annette and other officials for what felt like hours. But we hadn't spoken a single word to each other since being in the tunnel.

It was a cold night. The air carried the briny, damp scent of a foggy San Francisco evening. In the bay a foghorn sounded its mournful cry. I put the key in the truck door.

"Annie," Frank said, standing close behind me.

"Swear to God, Frank, if I still had that gun in my hand..."

"We need to talk."

I swung around to face him. "We *needed* to talk before we spent the night together."

"You're absolutely right. I apologize. I'm scum. But I'm scum that is very nearly divorced. And I'm scum that loves you. That's got to count for something."

I swallowed, hard. "Scum that *loves* me?"

He gave a mirthless laugh. "You think I go through this sort of thing for just anyone? In case it escapes your notice, I go out of my way to support you as best I can. Even to the point of having to rescue you in tunnels and sabotage my own professional reputation. You know putting yourself in danger drives me insane, but I've been biting my tongue, trying not to tell you what to do. And right now I'm trying not to say I told you so."

"Told me what?"

"Not to get involved with Odibajian."

He had me there.

"Why don't you come back to my place with me, you can take a shower, we'll order a pizza—with anchovies, if you insist— and you can ask me all the questions you want about Ingrid and anything else you want to know."

"I...uh...I'm not sure. I don't know what to think right now, Frank. Between Anton and you and Michael..."

"What about Michael?"

"I don't know how...I mean, the man is my business partner after all, and you're sort of his brother-in-law, and—"

"And he's in love with you. Are *you* in love with *him*?"

"I don't...I mean I think I'm..." I took a deep breath. "I think I'm in love with you. But I do love him."

"I suppose it's too much to hope that this is a sisterly sort of love?"

I gave him a grudging smile. "All I want to do right now is go back to my studio and paint something. I have to think, or maybe *not* think for a while."

"Fine, if that's what you need. I'm putting a man on you, though."

"I thought that was exactly what you didn't want."

"Funny. I'm going to have Thomas trail you, and please, I beg of you, don't try to lose him. He's there for your own good until this thing settles down completely. We still don't know exactly where Odibajian stands in all of this."

"Presuming he's still alive."

Frank nodded. "Presuming Victor's got terrible aim."

"Hey, I know something you can do for me, by way of apology. Those two homeless guys, the ones who led you into the tunnels..."

"The ones who saved your life."

I nodded. "We have to do something for them. Find them a place to live, a rehab program, job training maybe?"

"I'm already on it. I made a few phone calls while we were waiting."

"Thanks." I turned to open the door of my truck.

"And Annie? Call me."

"I will."

21

I WAS HOPING for some solitude to get my head straight, but my business partner was waiting for me at the studio, a bottle of fine cabernet in hand. When solitude is impossible, wine is a good alternative. I took a glass gratefully.

"I was thinking," Michael began. "Maybe I should drop out of sight for a time."

"Oh no you don't, not again. Besides, I don't think this whole stolen-paintings thing is resolved. If you leave they'll pin it on you for sure."

"That's the point."

I looked at him for a full ten seconds. "Why would you want them to do that?"

He took a long pull on his wine and looked around the studio. "Those paintings won't ever be found. Either that, or Odibajian or McAdams or whoever else 'disappeared' them will simply put them back quietly without bothering to inform the police. In the meantime, somebody's going to take the fall."

"Okay, I'm following you so far. I'm just not getting the whole 'blame me' angle."

"They'll never be able to catch me and even if they did, somehow, they don't have a case. No fingerprints, no footage, no anything."

"Since you're actually innocent."

"Precisely."

"Okay...but how does this work to our advantage?"

"If I don't take the fall, Frank's going to get smeared. They can't prove anything against him, either, but as the guy who designed the security system, even if he doesn't get accused of out-and-out theft his name's going to be associated with failure. Meanwhile, they'll probably accuse you of the theft. The Fleming-Union's bigger than just Balthazar Odibajian, you know. Even if he's dead, someone else will pick up the mantle." Michael got up and moved to the window, looking out.

"I figure it will go something like this: these two are lovers, Frank designs the alarm and tells Annie how to disarm the thing, she gets a job there with his recommendation, all the boys are out of town, no one else had access, she disarms the alarm and snatches the paintings, and by the way did we mention her grandfather is a renowned international art criminal and she herself was once brought up on forgery charges?"

"Yeah, that scenario had occurred to me, too. Not in such stark terms, but still."

"It's a tough world out there."

"I guess I'm slow, but the part I'm *still* not getting, partner, is how your disappearing would help matters."

"They put the blame on me: here's an international art thief better than any security system, no one could possibly defend themselves from—"

"Yeah, yeah. You've got super-thief skills. Go on. What then?"

Pause. Another drink of wine.

"Then I do what I do best. I lead them on a merry chase for a while, 'til they get tired and drop it."

"Where will you go?"

"Maybe Vienna. I hear they have a whole new therapy for claustrophobia. I think I need to get that handled."

"And then?"

He gave a very French sort of shrug, sticking out his chin slightly and raising his eyebrows.

"No. Freaking. *Way.*"

"No?"

"That's the worst idea I've ever heard! Are you *listening* to yourself? What are you talking about, going on the lam for something you didn't do?"

"I don't see a lot of other options. You and Frank—"

"What are you, being *noble* all of a sudden?"

"I've been noble before."

"Have not."

"Have, too. I happen to have a very wide noble streak."

"Do not."

"Do, too."

"This is stupid. It's insane. There's got to be another way. I don't want to hear another word, you hear me? I just have to find those paintings—"

"And somehow prove that the brethren took them to set up the crime."

"Right, and that, too. And then everything will be fine."

He fixed me with his gaze. "You tracked down the Gauguin, figured out how Elijah died, and fingered the people responsible for assaulting your uncle and murdering Kyle Jones. You found *Hermes*. You even helped expose the Fleming-Union's past so they'll cough up some money for Cameron House. All of which was done at great personal risk to your health. I think you've done enough."

"So all I have to do now is find those other paintings."

"Forget the goddamned paintings!"

I was taken aback. Michael never yelled.

"I'm sorry, but for *Christ's sake*, Annie, drop it. You'll never find them. If the brethren are smart, and they are, they destroyed them already, anyway. None of those boys is going to offer a confession; they understood the message from Elijah's death tableau loud and clear, and none of them has a death wish." He shrugged again. "Anyway, I'm not really cut out for this kind of life."

"What kind of life?"

"Working in an office everyday, meeting with my parole officer, reporting to the FBI. I'm more a self-employed, footloose and fancy-free, party-of-one kind of guy."

The dawning realization: he wanted to leave. He wanted to leave *me*.

He came over to me, pulled me to him, and kissed me. Instantly I forgot what we were talking about. Michael was like crack: he made me lose track of everything, and only made me want more.

When he finally lifted his head, we were both breathing hard.

"Maybe you should come with me," he said.

"Yeah, right."

"I'm serious, Annie. Haven't you ever just wanted to embrace the lifestyle, enjoy yourself, free of restraint...?"

I swallowed hard. The temptation was always there. I shook my head. "I really hate jail. And I barely survive police interrogations. Somehow I don't think I'm up for a prison sentence."

"It won't come to that. You have my personal guarantee."

"You can't make that kind of promise. You'll be on the lam from the FBI, unless I miss my guess. If I go AWOL, why would I do it with someone who's already a wanted man?"

He fixed me with his intense green gaze for a long moment.

"Is all of this because of me and Frank?" I asked. "Because I'm not even sure—"

"I really don't want to think about you and Frank, if it's all the same to you."

"Promise me you won't do anything stupid, Michael," I said. "This is just talk, right? You'll be here at the office tomorrow, right? Promise me."

He kissed me again.

"Promise. See you tomorrow."

And he was gone.

Annie's Guide to Antiquing with Craquelure:

Porcelain-like cracks that instantly "age" painted surfaces and decoupage

Supplies and Equipment:
Oil-based "antiquing" varnish, or regular artists' oil varnish
Water-based gum arabic
Antiquing oil glaze (⅓ mineral spirits, ⅓ linseed oil or oil painting medium, ⅓ paint), tinted with artists' oil colors
Soft varnish brushes
Glaze brush
Rags

Craquelure is the French word for the network of fine cracks often found on the surface of old oil paintings. The cracks result from the layers of paint and varnish drying and shrinking in uneven patterns for decades, eventually pulling away from each other. Over time, the cracks fill with dirt and dust, creating the distinctive "antiqued" look of Old Master paintings.

To mimic this crackle, we apply an oil-based varnish that dries slowly, and top it with a water-based finish that dries quickly. As the two drying times react, the top layer pulls away from itself to form delicate cracks. The result is a beautiful effect that instantly ages and unifies painted surfaces—try it over paintings, painted furniture, cabinets, decoupage, even entire walls!

1. Make sure the painted surface is *completely* dry. This surface may be of any paint type. Apply varnish as evenly as possible, using an appropriate brush, and making sure to check from all sides to be sure that you see the glint of wet varnish all over. It's easy to accidentally miss a spot.

2. When the varnish is dry enough to pass the back of your knuckle over it without sticking, lightly apply the gum arabic over the varnish.

3. Leave in a warm area for cracking to develop as drying occurs; to speed the process and increase the number of cracks, try applying heat with a hair dryer. Allow the surface to harden for at least an hour after cracking occurs.

4. Apply an antiquing glaze, using thinned artists' oil paints. Typical colors include raw or burnt umber for a dark "dirty" look; raw sienna for a golden sheen; or a whitish-gray to stand out over dark backgrounds. Apply the color with a brush or rag and then rub it into the cracks with a rag, using a circular motion. Wipe excess glaze from the surface with a rag, or leave a light glaze for a unifying tint. Color will remain in the cracks, highlighting them. *Always* use an oil-based glaze for this stage, as a water-based glaze will re-activate the gum arabic and destroy the cracks. (Forgers sometimes mix fine dust from a vacuum cleaner bag with linseed oil, and rub this in rather than a paint glaze. That way if the material is tested, it will mimic the kind of environmental dirt that fills the cracks of real oil paintings over the course of time.)

5. When thoroughly dry, top the surface with an oil-based varnish to protect it.

Tip: Remember, this is art, not science! This process is temperamental and dependent upon room temperature, humidity, and varnish thickness. As a rule of thumb, the thicker the oil-based varnish, the bigger and more spaced-out the cracks; the thinner, the more delicate the *craquelure*. Other than controlling this aspect of the process, there is very little you can do to affect the overall outcome of the cracks, other than to apply heat. But if you look at true antique oil paintings, you'll see that the *craquelure* patterns vary over different colors of paint and portions of the picture. Just sit back and let it do its thing!

ABOUT THE AUTHORS

Hailey Lind is the pseudonym of two sisters, one a historian and the other an artist.

Carolyn J. Lawes (left) is an associate professor at Old Dominion University in Norfolk, Virginia, where she specializes in nineteenth-century U.S. history, with a particular interest in women's history.

Julie Goodson-Lawes (right) is a writer, muralist, and portrait painter who has run her own faux-finishing and design business in the San Francisco Bay Area for more than a decade. She also writes two other mystery series under the name Juliet Blackwell.

The sisters take advantage of free cell phone minutes on weekends and the magic of e-mail to write the Art Lover's Mysteries as a team. *Feint of Art* was nominated for an Agatha Award in 2007.

Hailey Lind welcomes visitors and e-mail at www.haileylind.com and www.artloversmysteries.blogspot.com.

MORE MYSTERIES
FROM PERSEVERANCE PRESS
🎭 *For the New Golden Age* 🎭

JON L. BREEN
Eye of God
ISBN 978-1-880284-89-6

TAFFY CANNON
ROXANNE PRESCOTT SERIES
Guns and Roses
*Agatha and Macavity Award
nominee, Best Novel*
ISBN 978-1-880284-34-6

Blood Matters
ISBN 978-1-880284-86-5

Open Season on Lawyers
ISBN 978-1-880284-51-3

Paradise Lost
ISBN 978-1-880284-80-3

LAURA CRUM
GAIL MCCARTHY SERIES
Moonblind
ISBN 978-1-880284-90-2

Chasing Cans
ISBN 978-1-880284-94-0

Going, Gone
ISBN 978-1-880284-98-8

JEANNE M. DAMS
HILDA JOHANSSON SERIES
Crimson Snow
ISBN 978-1-880284-79-7

Indigo Christmas
ISBN 978-1-880284-95-7

JANET DAWSON
JERI HOWARD SERIES
Bit Player *(forthcoming)*
ISBN 978-1-56474-494-4

KATHY LYNN EMERSON
LADY APPLETON SERIES
**Face Down Below
the Banqueting House**
ISBN 978-1-880284-71-1

**Face Down Beside
St. Anne's Well**
ISBN 978-1-880284-82-7

Face Down O'er the Border
ISBN 978-1-880284-91-9

ELAINE FLINN
MOLLY DOYLE SERIES
Deadly Vintage
ISBN 978-1-880284-87-2

HAL GLATZER
KATY GREEN SERIES
Too Dead To Swing
ISBN 978-1-880284-53-7

A Fugue in Hell's Kitchen
ISBN 978-1-880284-70-4

The Last Full Measure
ISBN 978-1-880284-84-1

WENDY HORNSBY
MAGGIE MACGOWEN SERIES
In the Guise of Mercy
ISBN 978-1-56474-482-1

The Paramour's Daughter
ISBN 978-1-56474-496-8

DIANA KILLIAN
POETIC DEATH SERIES
Docketful of Poesy
ISBN 978-1-880284-97-1

JANET LAPIERRE
PORT SILVA SERIES
Baby Mine
ISBN 978-1-880284-32-2

Keepers
*Shamus Award nominee,
Best Paperback Original*
ISBN 978-1-880284-44-5

Death Duties
ISBN 978-1-880284-74-2

Family Business
ISBN 978-1-880284-85-8

Run a Crooked Mile
ISBN 978-1-880284-88-9

HAILEY LIND
ART LOVER'S SERIES
Arsenic and Old Paint
ISBN 978-1-56474-490-6